Riders of the Suwannee

Riders of the Suwannee

A Cracker Western

Lee Gramling

Pineapple Press
Palm Beach, Florida

Pineapple Press

An imprint of Globe Pequot, the trade division of
The Rowman & Littlefield Publishing Group, Inc.
4501 Forbes Blvd., Ste. 200
Lanham, MD 20706
www.rowman.com

Distributed by NATIONAL BOOK NETWORK

British Library Cataloguing in Publication Information Available

Library of Congress Cataloging-in-Publication Data available

ISBN 978-1-6833-4302-8 (paper : alk. paper)
ISBN 978-1-6833-4328-8 (electronic)

♾️™ The paper used in this publication meets the minimum requirements
of American National Standard for Information Sciences—Permanence
of Paper for Printed Library Materials, ANSI/NISO Z39.48-1992.

For Joe and Margaret, who know the language

Contents

Riders of the Suwannee 9

Historical Notes 287

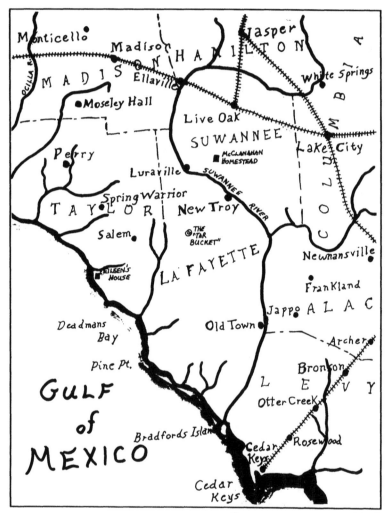

Suwannee country, 1875

1 🌿

I WASN'T HUNTIN' NO TROUBLE when I come back east acrost the Mississippi that time in '75. But sometimes what a man is looking for and what he finds can turn out to be entirely different things.

I'd crossed the Suwannee River the night before, for no other reason than I wanted to see what was over there. Didn't need to be in no particular hurry about gettin' to where I was going. Not like I had kinfolks waitin' for me. Not no more, anyways.

A few miles up from the crossing to New Troy, followin' that sand road down the northeast bank of the river, I spotted this place back on the bluff in amongst a stand of pines and hickories. Half dozen horses was tied out front, and I figured it might be a establishment which catered to the drinkin' man. Been kind of a dry trip so far, and I thought this might be a good time to give my ole roan horse a little rest.

I'd a pretty good idea what to expect if this was like most of them "blind tigers" you'd find up on the Suwannee hereabouts. Just a two-by-twice shack with a sawdust floor and one brand of whiskey, more'n likely home-growed and guaranteed to take the paint off a church steeple or the ticks off a hound dog. Good for the snakebite too, some said. Providin' you could stand to swallow enough of it before you met up with the snake.

But some of them places kept a free lunch set out too. And lately I'd been goin' without eatin' for so long that my stomach was beginnin' to think my throat might be cut.

I rode up the bluff and into the trees a little ways before stepping down from the leather. Noticed a couple gents watching me from a bench outside the building as I dismounted, but I didn't pay it much mind. I been looked at before.

Part of it's my size, I reckon. I stand a few inches over six feet and weigh maybe two-fifty or two-sixty even when I ain't been eating awful regular. And right then I imagine I come across a mite rougher than usual. Maybe four or five months since I'd had my hair cut, and a week or two since I'd seen a razor. Hadn't had no new clothes in a lot longer'n that.

I watched them two gents while I tied my horse to a scrub oak. Then I slid my Winchester out of the boot and wiped the dust off real careful before startin' across the sandy yard to the door. It wouldn't seem right somehow, goin' into a new place and meetin' new folks, without taking my best friend there along with me.

Them two gents stood up when I come near, not sayin' nothing but lookin' me over real cautious-like. Both wore pistols, one with his hitched up on the left side, butt forward for a cross draw, and the other with his holster right in front where it'd be close to hand. It was the kind of thing a man paid attention to in a country where all manner of disagreements might be settled by Judge Colt and a jury of six.

Me, I favored the Western style. My Dragoon Colt was slung low on my right hip and tied down with rawhide thongs. Which I imagine give them boys something to think about. You didn't see too many tied-down guns in those days, even west of the Mississippi.

But I reckon they decided pretty quick that whatever I was, I wasn't no kind of a lawman. And as they stepped back to let me pass I had the feeling maybe that mattered to 'em just a little more than it would to your average never-sweat who took to sittin' outside saloons in the middle of the day.

I lifted the latch on the front door, opened it, and stood there for a minute to let my eyes get accustomed to the shadows. Weren't much to see: a short bar at the far end made out of planks laid across two barrels, a couple rough tables in between, and nothin' else but sawdust an' pine needles over a dirt floor.

There was three other men in the room, not countin' the bartender. Two of 'em was sittin' at a table against the right wall; the third was leanin' on his elbows with his back to the bar. All four was looking at me without much welcome in their eyes. And all four was wearin' guns — even the bartender. I started to get the idea maybe strange riders didn't stop into this place back up in the woods too awful regular.

I noticed there wasn't no free lunch neither.

Now, a sensible man might have considered the odds and pulled his freight right about then. But nobody who knew Tate Barkley ever gave me much credit for good sense. I just reached up and give my hat-brim a little tug with my left hand, an' then I strode across the room and bellied up to the bar.

"Whiskey," I said, layin' my rifle up on the planks so's my hand could rest easy on the action.

The bartender, a big bald-headed gent with garters on his sleeves, hesitated a moment. Then he reached back and got out a bottle and a glass.

I filled the glass, tossed off a drink, and poured another, using only my left hand. Kept everbody in sight while I was doing it, kind of casual-like. It didn't take no Harvard scholar to see these folks was some kind of on edge. The atmosphere in that room wasn't exactly what I'd call sociable a-tall.

I figured to have me another drink just to say I'd done it, an' then leave out of there quiet-like before anything had a chance to get started. Man finds enough trouble in this life without going out of his way to look for it.

But then sometimes trouble has a way of findin' him. And nobody ever accused Tate Barkley of not bein' ready to meet it halfway when it did, or maybe just a mite better.

This time trouble showed itself in the form of a skinny blond-headed kid with a big .44 strapped to his hip, and a mouth to match. Didn't look like much as trouble goes when he first stood up from that table by the wall. But he had ambition, and he worked at it.

"Stranger in these parts," he said, startin' to kind of swagger across the room towards me. He didn't say it like he was asking, so I didn't say nothin' by way of a reply.

He stopped a few feet away and looked me up and down real slow, with a kind of a lopsided grin on his face. "Ain't much to look at, is it, Bay?" He spoke over his shoulder to the man still at the table. "What kind of critter you reckon this is, anyhow?"

I poured myself another drink, still saying nothing.

"Shaggy old varmint, way too big for a skunk or a possum. Hey, Bay." The kid's eyes took on a sort of a glittering mean look. "You don't s'pose this is one a' them western buffaloes I seen pictures of in *Harper's* magazine?" He sniffed the air real loud, then wrinkled up his nose. "Phew! I reckon it's got to be one a' them sour-smellin' critters. Seein' as how it don't *act* dead, an' it's way too big to be a skunk!"

13

I downed my drink.

"Reckon," I said real quiet-like, not lookin' at him, "that bein' a range buffalo's still a mite better'n bein' some other kinds of critters. Like a little egg-suckin' cur-dog what just crawled out from under somebody's back porch."

I knew he'd try it. Knew he fancied himself with that Colt, and was just itchin' for a chance to use it. I seen him crouch real sudden out of the corner of my eye, and his hand started to drop.

But before that kid's gun cleared leather the back of my own hand caught him square across the face. It's a right big hand, and a hard one. The kid staggered back acrost a table, knocked over a couple chairs, and fell sprawling to the floor. From the way his nose gushed blood, I had a idea it might be broke.

Well, you'd of thought the war was ready to start all over again at that moment. Them other three men reached for their guns at the same time.

Only they was a mite slow. That big Dragoon was already in my fist with the hammer eared back before any of 'em thought enough about it to look up an' see what it was they was facing.

"You go right on ahead," I said, "if you feel lucky." I allowed it was my turn to smile. "One or two of y'all might get some lead into me, but I expect I'll have enough dogs to lay at my feet when they bury me hereabouts."

It was a Mexican stand-off and they knew it. Three

on one give 'em a chance, but I held the aces. Somebody in their crowd was goin' to die, and nobody much wanted to find out who it would turn out to be.

I glanced at the kid layin' there on the floor at my feet, but he wasn't even thinkin' about gettin' ready to get up. Then I reached out an' picked up my rifle with my left hand, layin' the barrel over towards the front door where them two gents outside was maybe thinkin' about whether to come in and join the party. They must of decided against it finally, because the door stayed shut.

After a minute the bartender lifted his hands away from his gun real slow and laid 'em up on the bar where I could see 'em. "You've played hell," he said. "That's Big Bill Caton's nephew you knocked down, and this is Big Bill's place. He runs everthing in this neck of the woods. Nobody crosses him."

"Caton?" I glanced at him. "Used to know some Catons back before the war. Hog and chicken thieves, mostly. Never knew any of 'em was man enough to steal a full-growed milk cow."

"Big Bill's the he-coon in these parts," the bartender said grimly. "He'll kill you on sight, if his men don't get to you first. There's upwards of three dozen of 'em ridin' this Big Bend country hereabouts, and every one's salty as a piney woods rooter. It don't matter whether you try to hide or not, your life ain't worth the change from a plugged nickel right now."

The other gents was standin' real still with their hands out from their sides, but I could see what was in their minds if I give 'em half a chance. Me, I was easin' over towards the side door when I spoke again:

"I didn't come here huntin' trouble," I said, "and after I'm gone I'd just soon forget I ever seen this place." I was standin' next to the door now.

"But if you-all are bound and determined to come lookin' for it, I'll try and see can I find enough trouble to go around." I turned to the bartender. "You tell Bill Caton it was Tate Barkley said that. He may recall the name."

Soon as I'd finished speakin' I was outside, makin' for the trees a dozen yards away. A bullet clipped a limb off to my right and I let fly with my old Dragoon back under my arm. She roared once and a pine shutter split clean in two. Whilst they was all busy cussin' and dis-cussin' that, I got myself up into the brush out of sight from the cabin.

I knew they'd be after my horse first thing, and I might of left it an' got clean off into the woods. But I liked that roan. He was mean and ugly like me, but with plenty of sand and spit whenever the chips was down. I never give a thought to leavin' him behind for the likes of these.

I Injuned up through the trees till I could see the roan's back, and he was still standin' right there where I'd left him. That could only mean one thing under the circumstances: them gents had their eye on him, just waitin' and hopin' I'd step up into a cross-fire.

My mam didn't have much book-learning, but she didn't raise no foolish children. I backed off from that place, movin' careful but wasting no time, and worked my way around till I could see where my horse stood and the clearing with the cabin off to one side as well. Then I hunkered down in a palmetto brake and watched for a bit until I'd located the men layin' in ambush.

They was two of 'em, and most likely a third was still inside the cabin a-waitin' his chance. I could hear the other three somewheres across the way, stompin' through the brush an' yelpin' at each other like a pack of no-count hound dogs.

Just then ole roan decided to pick up his head an' look over his shoulder, right square into my eyes. Weren't no more time for considerin'. My watchers would be noticing that look the same as me.

So I picked up my Winchester and dusted that clump of scrub where I'd seen one of the men, firing three times as fast as I could work the lever. When I heard him grunt an' cuss I turned towards the cabin to put a couple more through the door and window.

The third man was takin' a bead on me with his Colt when I swung back in his direction, but he was a mite anxious and his first shot went wide. He didn't get a second. I put a bullet through the first button over his belt buckle, and then followed it up with another just for luck. Then I started after my horse.

I'd tied the reins in a slip-knot out of habit, and it didn't take no time a-tall to yank 'em free an' put one foot in the stirrup. I dusted out of that place ridin' the side of my horse Injun-fashion, headin' back up into the piney woods away from the river.

There was some more cussin' behind me and a couple shots ripped through the leaves over my head, but in another second I was back amongst the trees and out of sight of the cabin. When I finally slowed the roan down so's I could climb into the saddle, I took a good long listen but couldn't hear nothing close by.

I knew those boys'd be along though, an' from what the bartender said I could expect they might have some friends for company before the day got much older. In spite of my talk about Bill Caton and his brothers, I remembered the family well enough to know that they'd be right hard men by now, not exactly the type to waste a lot of thought on turnin' the other cheek.

I never been counted no wallflower when fightin' time come around, but I didn't figure to be no complete damn fool about it neither. Any way you looked at it, the Catons and three dozen like 'em spelt trouble with a capital T. Seemed like the best thing for me to do in a case like this was to let ole roan do what he enjoyed best. Which was run.

He was a Western mustang an' bigger than most Florida horses. Maybe not so agile back up in the brush as some of them cow ponies, but you give him room to get about an' he'd purely run the legs off a jackrabbit. Had plenty of bottom, too. Go all day an' all night on a couple handfuls of wire grass, an' then turn an' look at you scornful-like whenever you finally got down to rest your ownself.

What I'm sayin', me and that roan understood one another. And when I turned his head to the north this time he knew exactly what to do. Weren't the first time for neither one of us, tell you the truth. Seems like we'd both spent a sight more time up on the outlaw trail than we had chasin' any cows out of the Texas or Florida scrub.

Ole roan took to the trail like he was born to it, and after a bit I let my thoughts go back to when I'd knowed that Caton family as a youngster. They'd been a mean, no-account bunch even then.

There was six boys at one time, together with their pa who was said to be on the dodge from somewheres up north when he first come into this country. But Tarley and the old man got theirselves crosswise with some swampers up to the Okeefenokee back around '59, and they was never heard from again. Not too long after that Jimmy-boy drowned when a horse he'd stole throwed him off into the ditch.

I'd of figured the others for the end of a rope by now. But it seemed like they'd managed to survive and even maybe come up in the world a mite, if you could call it that.

It surely weren't just exactly the sort of homecoming I'd had in mind when I set my sights on returnin' to this Florida country. I'd been in the western lands for a good ten years by now, and this was my first trip back since leavin' for the war in the spring of '63.

Seems like after Petersburg and Appomattox I'd felt the need to look over some fresh territory, someplace that wasn't burned out or starved out for a change, or churned up by marchin' armies. So I headed west. Had a idea what would happen to the losers of a war that cost both sides like this one, and I just made up my mind to stay gone until the carpetbaggers an' the scalawags got all through with their RE-constructing, before comin' back to see what they'd left, if anything.

I punched cows out in Texas for awhile, rode the grub-line some. Even tried my hand at prospecting onct in Colorado. Hired my gun here an' there too, for this an' that. Most of it was legal, or close to it. But them days a man couldn't be too particular if he wanted to keep his belly button from slappin' up against the front side of his backbone.

Still, I'd always kept some right warm thoughts about this scrub and swampland where I growed up, all the while I was ridin' that high, dry country out west. Always figured to come back someday, maybe even put down some roots. Everbody likes to have a place they call home, and for me I reckon this was it.

But now if Bill Caton was runnin' things hereabouts, the place had changed a sight more than I cared to think on. Kind of put a whole different color on all the pictures I'd had in mind whilst livin' out in them western lands. And I weren't too sure I liked the new look.

Anyways, I got me a idea Mr. Stephen Foster didn't never know the Catons, when he wrote that song about the Old Folks at Home.

2

Me and the roan was headin' north now at a pretty good clip, and I figured once we'd put some distance behind us I'd turn west, get back across the river, and then make my way south towards the coast where there was a fair piece of wilderness an' a man could sort of get lost till things had a chance to quiet down some. I'd hunted and fished all over that country as a boy, and I knew it better than most.

Considerin' the odds against me, I could see that layin' low was the smart thing to do, and I aimed to do it. But it grated in my craw all the same. Bein' on the dodge ain't no fun anytime, yet it seems a whole lot worse somehow whenever you can't show your face near the place you'd thought of as home.

Not that I had any people hereabouts, leastways not above ground. Mam died of the cholera back in '58, an' pap run afoul of some raiders a year or so after I'd left for the war. My brother Luke's a travelin' man like me. Ain't seen him for a passel of years.

Still, I'd the notion to go back one last time an' pay my respects to the folks like. Then I reckoned I'd give some thought to what to do with that little piece of hammock land back up in the swamp we'd owned. I was the oldest, so by rights it was mine now.

I never done no farmin' since I'd left home. And settlin' down weren't much more than a dream I'd had time to time, which looked a whole heap farther away now than it had a couple hours ago. Prob'ly I'd just sell out, share the money with Luke if I could find him, and keep on ridin'. That is if I could find somebody with cash money who wanted a few acres of scrub an' live oaks with a couple graves on it.

After we'd left the riverbank we was out amongst the rolling fields and pine woods of the Big Bend, where that horse of mine was able to lay down some tracks. I was cuttin' cross-country, avoidin' roads an' settlements as much as I could. My idea was to cross the river somewheres south of Ellaville where the bluffs was low and ole roan wouldn't have to spend too much time gettin' into and out of the water.

It had been a hair before noon when I first stopped into that blind tiger, so there was a-plenty of daylight left. That was good for me because I wanted to put some distance behind me before I slept. But it was good for whoever might be on my back trail now too. The sandy ground and pine needles wouldn't leave many tracks, but the chance of bein' seen by a rancher or a farmer somewheres along the line was a thing I couldn't hope to stay shut of entirely.

North Florida was a mite more settled back then than say Arizona or the Indian Nation. Not that it was what you'd call crowded, but still you couldn't travel too far without seein' the smoke of a homestead or a plantation house. And more'n likely somebody was out plowin' a field or pickin' cotton or tobacco in between. There was folks who'd be almighty curious about a big shaggy rider with a Texas outfit, runnin' hell-for-leather through the brakes and the back trails hereabouts.

It couldn't be helped though, for I surely wasn't goin' to get myself out of that country by stoppin' along the road to pass the time of day. I just had to hope most people wouldn't be so curious as to come investigatin', or to talk it up amongst strangers they might see. I figured my chances was pretty good thataway. This was still frontier country, and folks was used to keepin' their own counsel. A man's business was his own, long as he didn't go botherin' others. Live and let live was the order of the day.

After a few hours I turned in amongst a clump of trees on a low hill to give ole roan a blow an' look over the countryside a bit. There was a small sinkhole there that couldn't be seen until you was right up on it, with good cover and a spring where we could have ourselves a drink. I'd taken care in approaching the place, and once the grass outside had a chance to straighten out, we'd be as well hid here as anywhere I might have found.

I picketed the roan near the runoff from the spring and climbed up to where I could just see over the rim of that sink. Ever place I looked was low rolling hills, with occasional stands of pines and hardwoods here an' there. Just a little movin' about would let me have a pretty good view in all directions. Hunkerin' down behind some brush, I took out the makings, rolled myself a smoke, and studied my back trail.

It struck me right about then that I wasn't as used to readin' the sign of this Florida country as I'd once been. A man gets accustomed to the land he's ridin' in, and I'd been out amongst the western prairies and deserts for a right smart spell. I was in the habit of seein' maybe ten or twenty miles of open country instead of only one or two, and to usin' dust clouds an' tracks on the ground to tell me when other folks was about.

Dust there might be sometimes, from a sand road or a plowed field. But you couldn't count on it in this wet country, and you couldn't see it very far off in any case. Tracks only lasted from rain to rain, which might be weeks or months where I just come from, but maybe only a few days or a few hours hereabouts.

I was going to have to be almighty careful until I got the feel of this land again. A man in the wilderness learns to use all his senses, but the ones he uses most can change with the territory. In the forest he has to count on his ears more than his eyes, and he has to pay close attention to the way the birds and the critters act around him if he wants to know somethin' out of the ordinary is going on.

All the while I was thinkin' about this, I was studyin' the far tree line and the hills around me, trying to make out any sign of riders who might be out an' about, especially those who might be huntin' me. I reckon what with all that thinkin' and studyin', I sort of forgot to remember to pay real close attention to what was near at hand.

So it like to give me the gallopin' fantods when all of a sudden I heard this voice right almost at my elbow:

"Hey, mister, are you a Texas man? Are you one-a them real honest-to-Pete cow punchers, or maybe even a gun-fighter like Wyatt Earp or Doc Halliday an' Bill Hickock?"

Well, I ain't never yet shot nothing that I didn't know what it was, an' I reckon that was a plumb good idea this time. When I looked over and saw this tow-headed kid I was just about a half a secont from pulling iron.

I took a deep breath and moved my hand away from my Colt real careful, then reached up to tug my hat-brim down so's he couldn't see how much he'd startled me. Leanin' back against a tree trunk as casual as I could manage, I glanced at him out of the corner of my eye.

He was a well set-up youngster, barefoot and wearin' short pants buttoned below the knees. Maybe eight or nine years old, close as I could figure. Never was much hand at guessin' kids' ages though. Had these pale blue eyes, just steady as a rock. Never took 'em off of me for a instant.

"What makes you suppose that?" I asked. "What makes you think I might be a Western man?"

"Well, your boots for one thing." He spoke right up, not even a little bit shy. "Folks 'round here wear brogans mostly, even those with ridin' jobs. An' the saddle on your horse there, that's a Texas saddle, some bigger'n the ones we most generally see in these parts." He paused for a second, then pointed. "Your gun's different, too. Looks like one-a them big forty-four Colts like the Rangers used to carry. An' you wear it tied down the way I heard them Western gun-fighters do."

That was a right knowing kid for his age. He didn't miss much. I took out the makings and started to build myself another smoke.

"I reckon," I said after a moment, "that I might be somethin' like that there. Anyways, I been to Texas. An' I been known to punch a cow or two, here an' about."

The kid nodded, his eyes big. "I bet you've been in some gunfights too. I seen the way your hand dropped to your pistol when I spoke up. You was all ready to draw it an' drill me through the brisket if I made a false move."

Well, it ain't generally a part of my nature to lie to kids, but right then I tried. I didn't want him to guess how right he was, because I didn't want him to start thinkin' too hard about why a total stranger would be so all-fired ready to shoot in the first place.

"Naw," I said with a shrug. "Naw, I was just slappin'

at a ole bull ant." I brushed at my pants leg with my left hand a couple times. "That's all it was."

He didn't say nothing, but I'd the idea I hadn't done much to change his mind. At last he just sort of shrugged an' said, "Well, I reckon I should-a give you some better warnin' before comin' up on you all of a sudden like that." Then he sat down next to me.

"How you know so much about the West?" I asked. "You ever spend any time out there?"

"No, but I've read plenty about it in them dime novels. Read ever one I can get my hands on." He paused. "Ma says I shouldn't ought to believe everthing that's in those books, though."

"Your ma's a smart woman," I replied. "I read one of them books my ownself, one time." I'd of been embarrassed for him to know how long it took me to do that. Readin' sign on the ground was always a sight easier for me than readin' words on a page.

"Didn't appear to me," I went on, "that the man who wrote that book I read knew too awful much about what he was writin' about. Matter of fact, I sort of suspicioned that writer hadn't never even been to the western lands." I glanced down at the kid and changed the subject. "You live around here?"

"Not far. Just over the next rise a couple miles." He seemed to be studying the ground between his feet. "That is, sis an' me's livin' there right now. Our home place is over near the coast. But we're stayin' with Aunt Mae an' Uncle Everett for a spell till Ma gets some things straightened out back home. She said she'd send for us soon as she's able."

The way he said that raised a question in my mind, an' I decided I might's well go ahead and ask it: "Your pa's there with her, is he?"

"No. Nobody's with her but old Joseph the hired man. An' he's gettin' on up in years some." I thought I detected a hint of worry in the youngster's voice. "Don't know how much help he'll be for much longer."

He paused then, and after a moment said kind of quiet-like, "Pa's dead. Back in the hurricane of '73. He was captain of a schooner sailin' out in the Gulf. Never did come home afterwards."

There wasn't much I could say to that, so I just nodded, gazin' out across the meadow towards the distant tree line. The boy had some cares sure enough, but it weren't too unusual in these hard times followin' the war. He seemed like a tough lad though, able to shoulder 'em if given half the chance.

When you come down to it, that's just about what it takes to be a man. I couldn't help wonderin' that his Ma didn't see that. Was I her, I'd want him with me to help carry the load like, and sort of grow into the job.

Well, it weren't none of my business, and I'd troubles of my own. I crushed out my cigarette with the toe of my boot and started to get up. It was way past the time I'd ought to be climbin' back up on the hurricane deck of ole roan an' makin' tracks for the far places.

But when I glanced over at the kid sittin' there, all of a sudden I had me a idea.

He was a bright youngster, no doubt about it. Likely the kind who kept his eyes open and his ear to the ground, so to speak. Nobody hears as much as kids anyways, 'specially whenever their folks think they ain't supposed to be listenin'.

It struck me that I was a man in need of information about things hereabouts, an' this kid prob'ly had just what I needed. I took out my Bowie knife, kind of like it was my plan all along, and sat back down again. Then I picked up a stick an' started in to whittlin'.

"Yep," I said after a moment. "I seen a sight of country out west. Texas, Arizony, Colorado, even Wyoming and the Montana Territory." I looked over at him. "Knowed a few of them gun-fighters like you're talkin' about too, though I was never one to put myself in a class with the likes of them." I paused. "Reckon I ain't in such a big hurry that I couldn't tell you a couple stories. That is, if you're interested."

Well, you'd of thought his face was goin' to split wide open from the way he was grinnin'. "You bet I am, mister! I never met no real Western man before. I'd give up my good Case knife to hear what it's really like out there!"

"Man needs his knife," I said, "so you keep yours. But you could do somethin' else for me if you was of the mind. You could sort of fill me in on what-all's doin' hereabouts. I'm new to this country y'see, and a travelin' man needs to find out the lay of the land if he wants to stay shut of trouble." I looked over at him. "Like f'r instance, I heerd somethin' just today about a bunch in these parts called the Catons. You know about them?"

Right at first I thought he weren't goin' to say nothing, not for all the Western stories I could tell in a month of Sundays. Yet from the way his face tightened up I could see he knew a-plenty.

Well, I just waited a bit, and at last he sort of glanced around and moved over closer to me. When he spoke his voice wasn't much over a whisper.

"I reckon everbody here knows the Catons. They been in this country since before I was born. Ma says they started out with a group of deserters an' Union raiders during the war, but later the ones who believed in some kind of a cause went on an' joined up for the fightin'. What was left, she says, wasn't nothin' but a pack of no-count thieves and murderers. That's when Bill Caton took over.

"There's upwards of thirty or forty of 'em now, maybe more. Got 'em a big camp down in the swamp 'tween here and the Gulf, though you'll see 'em most anywheres, even in the towns. Nobody wants to make trouble 'cause they know there's always more where those come from. My Uncle Everett says Big Bill Caton's got a hand in every crooked business in this part of the state. He says it's only a matter of time till he's got enough money to go into politics an' start doing his stealin' legal-like."

"Seems to me," I said after a moment, "that there'd ought to be some folks around who wouldn't cotton to that sort of thing. Most men in this country got guns and know how to use 'em. Why don't they get together and invite those boys to look for some new territory?"

The kid shrugged. "I don't know about that. Uncle says he'll fight if they try to run him off his land or start messin' with the womenfolks. But he don't seem to pay too much mind when a hog or a couple chickens turn up missin' ever now an' again. Reckon it's the same with most people. They'd rather fight shy of trouble an' hope it's somebody else gets stole from the next time."

I nodded. I'd run across that kind of thinking a time or two, though I can't say it ever made much sense to me. When the cockroaches start nosin' around my bread basket, I don't wait to see how many crumbs they mean to leave behind for me. I just start in to squashin' bugs.

But I'd no stake in this fight, for all that I was brought up only a hop and a skip from here. I was just a drifter, an' likely to remain so. And I'll admit I was gettin' the urge to drift pretty bad about now. The longer I stayed in this place the easier it was goin' to be for trouble to find me when it come a-lookin'.

But a bargain's a bargain, and so I settled back an' took the time to spin out a couple good yarns for the kid, keepin' a close watch all around the whole time. Part of what I told him was even true.

Finally I stood up and sheathed my knife. "I'd like to stay here a-jawin', boy, but I got me some miles to cover before I spread my blankets for the night." I held out a hand. "Name's Tate Barkley. You ever get out Arizona way, you look me up." I grinned. "But be careful who you go mentionin' my name to out there. Most folks have heard it an' some'll take it friendly enough, but there's a few others who might not."

He got to his feet and took my hand in a firm grip. "My name's Jamie . . . James, I mean. James McClanahan. I'm proud to make your acquaintance, Mr. Barkley."

"Proud to know you too . . . James." I caught up the reins on ole roan, and stepped up into the saddle.

"You know," I said, leanin' down kind of confidential-like, "it might just be for the best if you didn't say nothin' to your uncle about our meetin' out here. Wouldn't want you to lie about it o' course, but there's no need volunteerin' anything that might start talk about strangers in the neighborhood."

He glanced up at me. "You on the dodge, Mister Barkley?"

I smiled. "Not from the law in these parts," I said, "but there's some others I'd just as soon keep guessin' about my whereabouts. Reckon you might know who I mean. I just figure the fewer folks that hear about me, the fewer who'd have a reason to tell somebody else." I put a hand on his shoulder. "Deal?"

"Deal." He grinned, and I lifted my hand in farewell. Just before I climbed out of that hollow I looked back. He was still standin' right where I'd left him, watchin' after me.

3 🌿

THE SUN WAS DOWN below the treetops when we swum the Suwannee and turned our tracks back toward the south and west. There was a hour or two of daylight left, and that was just about long enough to get myself into the northern edge of the San Pedro lowlands before findin' a place to camp for the night.

I located a small dry hammock and staked the roan out back in the trees after we'd both had a drink from a fast-flowing creek not too far away. Then, layin' my bedroll down on a soft patch of grass, I wrapped in a blanket against the skeeters and stretched out, countin' on my horse to stand sentry for me. There wasn't no use to build a fire, even if I hadn't wanted to avoid the attention of folks in the vicinity. I'd fixed the last of my coffee that mornin', and used up all the biscuits and bacon I'd brought along a day or two before that.

I was just about as tired as I knew how to be, but before droppin' off to sleep I found my thoughts going back to Jamie and what he'd said about his ma out there on that place near the coast. Didn't make much sense to me that she'd send her kids off right when there was a passel of work to do. You'd of thought she could use all the willin' hands she could get in a situation like that.

Unless there was some other reason she didn't want 'em around, of course. Some reason which most likely had to do with trouble shapin' up on the horizon. If that was the case though, I had to wonder why she didn't just up an' leave out of there her own self.

Well, it was surely none of my affair, and I told myself that a time or two while I laid there lookin' up at the limbs overhead. But it made me kind of curious all the same, to know what sort of a woman it was who'd try and make it out there in the wilderness alone, without a husband or even her kids to help. Stubborn as a mule, more'n likely. But she'd need grit and bottom too, if she was going to have much of a chance for herself.

Those were right needful qualities when you thought about it, in a man, a horse, or a woman.

❖   ❖   ❖

It started into rainin' about a hour before daylight, and I mean *rainin'* — a regular old gully-washin' frog strangler. Come up out of nowheres so fast that I woke up swallowin' water before I even knew it was goin' to be cloudy.

I'd had my slicker over me when I laid down, but by the time I could twist around and get my arms into it I was soaked to the skin. Had to squeeze water out of my blankets before I could roll 'em up, an' my boots was so full of it that I hung 'em upside down from the saddle horn and made up my mind to ride out of there barefooted.

Even if I'd been able to start a fire, there weren't nothing to cook, not even coffee. A cigarette wouldn't of stayed lit if I'd wanted to take the time to roll one. An' that downpour didn't show no signs of lettin' up anytime in the near future.

You can bet I wasn't in no real good mood by the time I'd finally got ole roan saddled up an' started out of that place. He felt about the same way toward it I did. Started dancin' and blowin' as soon as I put my foot up in the stirrup. But we had us a couple words and he finally decided maybe right then weren't just the best time to try makin' me any madder than I already was.

The sun was high up in the sky by the time I finally got a chance to see it. We'd been makin' pretty good time under the circumstances, changin' off between a trot and a fast walk most of the way. I was following some old half growed-up Injun trails through the swamp, an' there weren't no faster way to travel in that country even without the rain. Too much chance of losin' the trail or steppin' into a deep hole under what looked like only a few inches of water.

When we finally come to a place where the ground

was halfway dry I got down and stripped the saddle from the roan's back, hangin' the blanket up in some branches to let it air out a bit. I did the same with my own gear and stuffed some Spanish moss in my boots to help 'em dry faster. Then I cleaned my pistol and rifle as best I could, takin' each of the bullets out and wipin' 'em off real careful-like before re-loading. That old pistol had been converted from cap and ball some years earlier, which made the job of re-loading a mite easier.

Finally I pulled some more Spanish moss out of the trees and started to give the roan a rubdown. He was liking it fine, but he remembered that mornin' and decided he didn't intend for me to forget about it none too soon neither. Took a bit of fancy footwork to stay clear of his teeth and hooves whilst I was tryin' to treat him decent for the first time in a couple days. But he almost forgave me when I cut the top out of a palm and shared the cabbage with him. Found a few wild plums and blackberries back in the brush too, which seemed to help.

I stayed in that place a couple of hours, lettin' my clothes an' blankets air out and takin' life easy, while the roan cropped grass an' leaves a few feet away. Figured I had plenty of time to make it to the old home place before dark anyhow, even travelin' the back trails and avoidin' settlements, of which there weren't too many in this neck of the woods in the first place.

When I finally roused myself to pack my gear and saddle up, the roan was ready. He stepped out like he was anxious to see some new country and didn't want to waste around no more about doin' it. That suited my mood too. I reckon we was both feelin' some better than we had been a few hours earlier.

❖   ❖   ❖

It was late afternoon by the time we pulled up in that patch of high hammock west of old Fort Buckeye. Right at first I just sat my horse lookin' the place over, sort of lettin' the memories come back to me. The double-pen log cabin was still there, though the roof was mostly gone by now. But the pole barn was leanin' way over to one side, an' the corral was all growed up to weeds. Weren't much left of the fields of corn and cane and sweet potatoes Pa an' me had worked so hard at cultivatin', neither.

Florida's a right thoughtless land thataways. Nothin' much a man works to build lasts very long unless he keeps on a-workin' at it. Seems like the country's most comfortable the way it's always been, and if you'll let it, it'll just go right on back to bein' forest and swampland as soon as ever it's able.

I climbed down from the saddle finally, and walked up the little rise back of the house. The graves was there, an' the two cypress markers, weathered some but with the carving still readable. I just stood lookin' down at 'em for a few minutes. Felt like I'd ought to say something, but couldn't quite seem to think of what it should be. After a little bit I put my hat on again and turned away.

Then I walked all around what used to be the yard, sort of takin' stock of what was left, which weren't much, and rememberin' how it used to be. I'd made up my mind already that I wasn't goin' to stay the night here. Never been one to believe in haints an' such, but there was a feeling comin' over me that I didn't much care for right then, call it whatever you will.

Maybe it was the time of the day, with it gettin' on towards evening and the feelin' you sometimes get in the woods, of the trees and the shadows all closin' in around you. Maybe it was just that I'd finally realized this weren't my home no more and it hadn't been for a long time. Seems like home ain't so much a place, as it is the folks who live in that place.

Anyhow, I was anxious to be away from there at least for the time being, and when I walked back to ole roan it seemed like he felt the same way I did. I saw his head was part-ways up and his ears was pricked like he was startin' to hear them ghosts that I was trying to keep from imaginin'.

It was only after I'd gathered the reins an' put my hand up on the pommel that it struck me.

Ole roan weren't just exactly the sort to let hisself get spooked by anything that wasn't there. Never mind me, if that mustang thought there was something out there in the shadows, you could just bet the hacienda it weren't no figment of his imagination. It might be a painter or a wildcat, or maybe even a gator crawled up out of the swamp. Or it might be somethin' else. But it surely weren't no haint.

My hand dropped down to the butt of the Winchester

in my saddle boot whilst I did some quick thinkin' and some slow listenin'. The house was maybe twenty-five yards away on my left, and I'd just walked all around behind it without seein' or hearin' anything out of the ordinary. The fields out back was still open enough so that I didn't believe anything short of a Injun could of got close thataway without me knowin' about it.

Out in front was a grove of huge old live oaks, with scarcely anything at all growin' underneath 'em. Their trunks was big enough to hide several men apiece, but I'd been lookin' in that direction from time to time an' the ground thereabouts was covered with leaves that'd rustle at the slightest move anybody made.

Most likely whatever it was was somewheres in the woods behind me or to my right. It was growed up thick in there except for the grass-covered road leadin' to and from the homestead, but there was places a careful man or a stalkin' critter might move about without makin' too much noise. And the evening breeze was from that direction, which would partly explain how ole roan might come to know about a visitor before I did.

I thought about all this a lot faster than it takes to tell it, an' it weren't no more than a couple seconds before I'd made up my mind what to do. First I bent down like I was checkin' on the cinch, but without takin' my hand off'n the stock of that Winchester. Then I jerked the rifle free and just kept right on going under the horse's belly, turnin' and comin' up again with the barrel resting across my saddle bow.

There was still enough light to see most things pretty good, but I didn't spot nothin' right off. I let my eyes roam back and forth over that thicket, knowing the chances was better of seein' something move out of the corners of my eyes than if I was lookin' at it straight on. Tell you the truth, I wasn't so worried about cats an' gators as I was about some of them two-legged varmints like I'd met the day before. Seemed to be more of them around the countryside, and they'd surely bear a sight more watchin'.

But after a bit I decided it must be some kind of forest critter, for I'd seen and heard nothin' at all since I'd turned around. Ole roan was still alert, but he didn't argue none when I gathered the reins again and started to turn him so's that I could step up into the saddle.

And then all of a sudden three men was standin' there at the edge of the woods. Two of 'em had pistols and the third carried a old muzzle-loading shotgun. A minute later a fourth man come around a bend in the road on horseback. I recognized the rider as one of them I'd seen at that blind tiger back on the Suwannee River.

"Hold it up right there, mister. We got you dead to rights." The man on the horse was talkin', and he was looking mighty pleased with himself. "Wasn't many around here who'd remember this old Barkley place any more, but when I heard your name I just naturally got a notion it might be here that you was a-headin'."

One of the others looked kind of funny when he heard my name mentioned, and he turned toward the rider. "Barkley, you say?" He glanced back at me and I thought I saw something like recognition in his eyes. "Not *Tate* Barkley? From out in the Tonto basin?"

"I been there," I said.

Fact is, I was a known man all over that part of the country. An' what was known about me didn't always set too well with some who figured using a gun was a easy way to make a living.

"You know this man?" the rider asked, glancing over his shoulder at his compadre.

"Hell, yes, I know him. I saw him take three men in a fight down to Prescott a couple years ago. It was . . ."

Well, they was having a real nice conversation and it sounded pretty flatterin', but it weren't doing a whole lot to get me out of this situation. I'd a idea they meant to kill me pretty quick right after they got finished talkin'.

So I put a bullet into the gut of the man who was holdin' the shotgun. Then I singed the rump of the mounted man's horse to sort of distract the others, an' whilst they was all trying to get out of the way of the hooves and get set for a shot, I mounted up and took off out of there.

I heard a crash of pistols a few seconds later, and felt a blow in my side, low down. One of 'em had managed to hit me, though the fading light an' the moving horse prob'ly meant it was more luck than marksmanship. Not that that made me feel any better about it.

I managed to stay in the saddle and keep movin' whilst I worked to plug the holes with pieces of cloth torn from my shirt. The bullet had gone clean through me about a inch above my gun-belt. I just hoped it hadn't hit nothing vital while it was on its way through.

At least, I told myself, there weren't much chance of a pursuit tonight. It was already too dark for tracking, and the only man with a horse between his legs was prob'ly wishin' it was somewheres else right at the moment.

I was headin' southwest towards the Gulf, with no more plan that minute than to put some distance between myself and those fellows behind me. There was a piece of a moon up, an' we could see our way pretty good. Ole roan could, that is. Me, I was startin' to look at things through a kind of a red fog.

I was losin' some blood, though I couldn't be sure how much. My pants leg was wet with it, and I could feel it startin' to drain down into my boot.

What I needed pretty quick was to find some place to hole up whilst I tried to take care of things and get myself on the mend. But where I was ridin' I couldn't see nothing but marshland an' wet prairie on both sides. I knew what was behind me, so the only way to go was straight ahead.

Finally we come to a sort of a road leadin' off towards the coast, and I turned the roan down that. The shock from the bullet had worn off by this time and that hole in my side was hurtin' something fierce. I was sort of fadin' in and out, closin' my eyes and noddin' my head for longer and longer spells.

I let ole roan have his head. With no more idea of where I was goin' than I had, I expected he could figure out how to get there just about as good as me.

It must of been sometime after midnight when we come into this open place with salt marshes all around, and I could see the moon shinin' away out over the waters of the Gulf. We surely weren't about to go much further in that direction. So I forced myself to sit up some and take stock, tryin' to figure out which way we'd ought to head from here.

Right about then I saw the house.

It was settin' up on some pilings a short ways from the Gulf, alongside a little creek that led into the big water. There wasn't no lights at this hour and I'd no way of tellin' whether anybody was to home, much less whether they'd be friendly if they was. But I reckoned to chance it, 'cause I was purely used up and this were the best lookin' place I'd seen all night. The only place, in fact.

Ole roan was already startin' to walk that way, so I just let him keep on with what he was doin'. He stopped next to a wooden gate leadin' into the sand yard around the house. The gate an' the fence both seemed to be made out of some sort of driftwood or pieces from wrecked ships.

I kind of half-slid, half-fell to the ground and then had to put my hand on the gate post to keep from goin' down on my knees. When I tried to call out, all that come from my throat was a sort of a rasping croak.

I stood there a minute, shook my head to clear it,

then straightened up a mite an' tried to peer into the open windows of the house. But I couldn't see nothin' inside there but darkness. After droppin' my right hand to take the thong off my six-shooter, I went ahead an' pushed the gate open with my left.

The hinges was rusty and the gate creaked some when it swung aside. But it wasn't that creak which got my attention so much as what I heard right afterwards.

There ain't no sound in this world that's quite the same as the sound of the two hammers on a double-barreled steel shotgun clicking back into the cocked position.

Right about then I found my voice. "Don't shoot. I've been hurt and I need a place to stop for a bit, that's all. I'm friendly."

"I expect you'll stay that way, too." The voice came from one of the pilings underneath the house, but in the darkness I couldn't tell which one. "If you don't take your hand away from that pistol," it went on, "you're going to be the friendliest corpse in the graveyard."

"All right. Just watch it with that scatter-gun." I raised up both hands and slowly held them out from my body. "Don't you go doing nothin' we'll both be sorry about in the morning."

"I'm watching. And don't you worry. If you give me a reason to shoot, I won't feel the least bit sorry about it in the morning."

Suddenly I felt my legs start to go soft underneath me. I went down on my knees, tried to catch myself, but couldn't manage it. I rolled on over in the sand, layin' there starin' up at the stars. And just before they faded into blackness I thought about that voice in the dark.

Funny thing about it was, it was the voice of a woman.

4 🌿

NEXT TIME I OPENED MY EYES it was daylight. I was layin' on a bed in a high-ceilinged room with windows in two of the walls. There was white curtains in the windows, movin' back and forth a little from the breeze off the Gulf, and I could hear the sound of gulls an' pelicans outside. Somewhere nearby water was lapping at the pilings of a dock or a pier.

I felt weaker than a fresh-borned baby possum, and was near 'bout as helpless it seemed like. When I tried swingin' my feet over the edge of the bed I suddenly got all sick inside and had to give it up. For a while I just laid there, starin' up at the ceiling and sort of takin' stock.

My side was bandaged, and it appeared like somebody had done a right knowin' job of it. I'd been undressed too. I could see my clothes laying on a chair acrost the room, all folded up proper-like with my boots settin' on the floor underneath. My gun belt was nowhere in sight.

After a while I just sort of drifted off to sleep again.

Next thing I knew it was growing on to twilight and this old colored fellow was standin' over the bed starin' down at me.

He was kind of stoop-shouldered, with curly white hair and a creased mahogany face that looked old enough to have wore out two or three bodies. There weren't nothing wore out about that Colt six-shooter he had stuck in his waistband though, and when I glanced up I seen a pair of measurin' blue eyes that suggested to me this here weren't exactly the sort of gentleman who'd be packin' that hardware just for show.

The blue eyes struck me a mite strange, but I'd seen 'em a time or two amongst Negroes here an' there, and Injuns too. Just goes to show that us humans is all more alike than not I reckon. It surely weren't something you'd ever ask another man about, no more'n I'd take it friendly if somebody was to ask where I'd got my own high cheekbones from.

He saw me lookin' at him and raised up his white eyebrows, watching me for a long minute without sayin' nothing. Then he took a step closer and set the tray he was carrying down on the table by the bed.

"Evenin'," he said at last. "You feel up to feedin' yo'self this evenin', or do you want some he'p with it?"

I considered that. "Reckon I'll give the eatin' a try," I said, "if you'll lend a hand with the settin' up. I ain't too certain I can manage that part by myself just yet."

After fixin' the pillows the old man reached over and lifted me up till I was settin' straight so's he could put the tray on my lap. He was a sight stronger than he'd looked, 'cause I'm a big man and yet he handled me with no more trouble than if he'd been takin' a couple sacks of potatoes out of a wagon.

The broth was a sort of a fish chowder, and it was some kind of good. I cleaned the bowl an' sopped up what was left with a piece of cornbread before I finally give out and laid my head back against the pillows. All the while the old man just stood there watchin' me. It weren't until he'd took up the tray again that he said anything more:

"We don't see too many strangers in this neck of the woods. Leastways not so terrible many what come a-callin' in the middle o' the night with bullet holes in 'em." He gave me a hard look. "Was you stayin' hereabouts, or was you just passin' through?"

"Hadn't quite made my mind up on that," I said, smiling a little. "Sorta took to this country when I first seen it. But this here gettin' shot can make a fellow right thoughtful. I reckon I better study on it a mite longer."

"Uh huh." He looked at me for another minute before steppin' to the door and opening it. "You study on it." His back was turned now, and it was almost like he was talkin' to himself. "But 'f I was you I wouldn't take too great a time about doin' it. Ain't much room hereabouts for folks what straddles fences, 'thout they come down on one side or t'other perty quick."

The door closed behind him, and I laid there tryin' to figure out what he'd meant by that last remark. But somehow I couldn't seem to keep my mind on it, an' next thing I knew it was morning.

❖   ❖   ❖

When my eyes opened this time I was feelin' some better than I had earlier. The sun was streamin' in the window acrost the room, and there was a cool breeze off the Gulf. I took a couple deep breaths and stretched kind of careful-like so's not to pull my wound open, then I moved the covers to one side and swung my legs over to the floor.

I made it this time, but I was still weak as a kitten. Sat on the edge of that bed for a long while, just studyin' on things. What I had in mind to do was to get across the room to that chair where my pants was layin'. 'T weren't no way proper for a man to be in a house full of strangers an' wearing nothin' but his underdrawers. 'Specially a house with a lady in it.

'Course I hadn't seen no lady yet. But I recalled that voice in the dark, the one behind the shotgun. And if that hadn't been a woman's voice I was some sicker than I'd imagined at the time.

It prob'ly weren't no more than a dozen feet to that chair, but right about then I surely didn't feel in the mood to hurry. The sickness was startin' to come over me again, and a dozen feet looked awful far all of a sudden.

But finally I made up my mind the only way I'd ever get my pants on was to be about doin' it. So I took a deep breath and stood up. Right about then the door opened and instead of that colored fellow I'd talked to the night before, there was a woman standin' there.

What I mean, there was a *woman* standin' in that doorway. She weren't too tall an' she weren't too short, an' though she was dressed ever bit like a lady, 't wasn't no trouble at all to see that everthing about her was arranged in just the right places. She had this long red hair tied up on top of her head in a loose bun, and these great big hazel-colored eyes that looked right at you without no pretending nor foolishness about 'em a-tall.

Her eyes got even bigger for a secont there, when she saw I was up and about. Stood in that doorway for a good long minute, like she was maybe thinkin' about where she'd left that scatter gun of hers. But then she seemed to reach a decision and took a step into the room, watching me careful-like all the while.

Well, I won't pretend that I wasn't some embarrassed, standin' there in my underwear an' lookin' right straight into the eyes of the prettiest bit of femininity I'd had the pleasure to see in a good many years. But there weren't much I could do about it, 'cause there she was and there I was. So I grinned as wide as I could manage and bowed a little bit from the waist, without takin' my hand off the bedpost where I was helpin' to keep myself up.

"Good mornin', ma'am," I said. "Right fine weather

we seem to be having this mornin', don't you think? I had in mind to take me a little stroll on the waterfront to catch a bit of the bracin' sea air." I started in to bow again. "Don't suppose you'd be interested in joining me . . . ?"

Well, I shouldn't have tried that second bow, 'cause I let go the bedpost and started to go over on my face without no way of stoppin' myself. I'd have broke my nose again for sure on that hardwood floor if she hadn't stepped up and caught me before I went down. She held me up by pushin' me against the side of the bed, whilst I managed to get a arm around her waist for support.

In the process that hole in my side started to pull open and the pain just nearly brought tears into my eyes. But I looked down at her and grinned again. "You reckon I might take this to mean you accept my offer? I'd consider it a genuine pleasure, even though I do find your manner just a mite forward."

Her eyes didn't look quite so awful pretty for a second there. She give me a push and took a couple of steps backwards. I sat down hard on the edge of the bed.

"You'll keep your hands to yourself, Mr. — whatever your name is. And when you're well enough to go walking outside you'll do it alone. If you stay here that long. I still haven't made up my mind whether to keep you or throw you to the fishes." She gave her head a sort of a toss — right fetching, I thought. "It might be a good idea if you were a little more mindful of your manners until I've decided!"

My side was painin' me from the rough treatment,

but there weren't no way I was goin' to let her see it. I just eased myself back onto the pillows real careful-like, and started to pull the covers up over me again. She was watching me the whole time, but I noticed she didn't act scared even one little bit.

I managed another smile. "The name's Barkley, ma'am. Tate Barkley." She didn't say anything to that, so after a moment I asked: "And who is it I have the honor to thank for their kind hospitality in taking me in?"

She sort of half shrugged then, and met my eyes. "My name's Eileen McClanahan. I own this place."

McClanahan. Seemed to me like that was the same name as that kid I'd met up-country a day or so ago. The one whose ma was so bent on stickin' it out in the wilderness without no help from family, neighbors or anybody else.

"I'm mighty grateful for your help, Miz McClanahan," I said seriously. "I hope I won't be troublin' you too much longer."

"It's little enough trouble." Her voice softened just a tiny bit. "And you surely needed someone's help the night we found you." I'd thought her manner seemed almost kindly right then, but it turned back cold again awful quick. "I'd do as much for any hurt animal, two-legged or four-legged." She stepped to the door and looked back.

"You'd best take it easy, Mr. Barkley. That's a nasty wound and it could pull open again if you try doing too much too soon." Seemed like there was a hint of a smile

52

in her eyes, though her lips didn't show no sign of it. "You stay put in that bed for the time being. It will be a good deal more comfortable for the both of us."

Then she closed the door behind her and I was left with only the memory of her eyes and all that red hair. Eileen McClanahan. She surely didn't fit my picture of a widder-woman, though on thinkin' about it I'd no doubt that she was Jamie's ma. They favored each other a mite, and there couldn't be two such stubborn women in all of Lafayette and Taylor Counties put together.

I considered the matter, layin' there on the bed with my arms behind my neck. Nothin' to do with me an' her, you understand. That was just bold talk on my part. Whatever else she was, Eileen McClanahan shaped up to be a lady. And I didn't have too much experience with a woman of that sort, nor any expectations that you could talk about.

But there was something else naggin' at the edges of my mind. Something in her manner and that of her hired man Joseph, which spoke to me of trouble. Shootin' trouble maybe, 'cause neither one of them folks ever seemed to let theirselves get too far from a gun no matter what the time of day or night. And it just happened that shootin' trouble was something I did have a small amount of experience with.

It was only a hunch though, and maybe not a real good one at that. I needed more time, and a mite more information, before I could get a rope around that idea. But from what the lady said, I wasn't too awful sure how much more time I was going to have to spend around these parts.

❖   ❖   ❖

Turned out I didn't make it out of the house that morning, nor the next morning neither. Matter of fact, considering that as I found out later I'd been laying in that bed there for several days before I opened my eyes the first time, it was almost the better part of a week until I was up to stirrin' about much at all. Longest time I could remember layin' around doin' nothing since I was knee-high to a short rooster.

Yet I reckon I mended quick enough under the circumstances. One of the advantages, I guess you'd call it, of livin' a hard life in some right hard places time to time. Before too long I was able to take a few of those walks alongside the water like I'd said, breathing in the salt air and startin' to feel a bit like my old self again.

I did most of my walkin' alone though, and that's a fact.

Ain't been too much for workin' with my hands since I left home. But onct I was up and about I reckoned I might as well do what I could to help, fixin' up here an' there, tendin' to the livestock and such. That McClanahan place was a right nice layout, with a kitchen garden, a milk cow, some chickens, and a bunch of hogs and steers back up in the woods. Had a small boat too, with all that it needed to take a bait of food from the sea.

Since I grew up with boats and traps and nets and such, like any Florida youngster, and since we'd done a mite of farming too, I reckon I was handy enough. Seems like there's always something needs mendin' or patchin' around a place like that. I managed to keep myself busy.

But after a couple weeks I was startin' to give some serious thought to movin' on. Ole roan was gettin' fat and sassy, unaccustomed as he was to the easy life and the corn he was bein' fed most ever day now. I was afraid if we didn't leave out of there pretty soon he'd start in to thinking he was some kind of a thoroughbred that was just too good to be seen travelin' with the likes of me.

Trouble was, we didn't have much place to go right then. Wherever I showed myself hereabouts there was like to be some considerable shootin' and feudin' if those Caton boys heard I was in the neighborhood.

Yet still it weren't in my thoughts to leave this Florida country right away. I didn't mean to let no renegade swamp rats run me out of no place I'd rode into of my own accord. Not until I decided I was plumb good and ready to leave.

I'll admit I was some curious too, about what it was that kept frettin' Eileen McClanahan and that hired man Joseph of hers. They was the most watchful folks I'd ever seen outside of Apache country. She never went anywhere without that scatter gun, nor Joseph without his Colt Peacemaker.

And it seemed like one of 'em was always awake no matter what the hour of day or night. I was up and about for several days before they let me have my own guns back, and it appeared to me they'd give some almighty careful thought to it before they did.

'Course the Catons was in the country, but I found it hard to believe even they'd take a chance on botherin' a decent woman in that time and place. Best way I knew to get your neck stretched without benefit of a trial in the West or the old South. I'd known outlaws to shoot one of their own kind like a dog for even suggesting such a thing.

I finally decided to put off leavin' for a day or so, just to try an' get to the bottom of things a mite. It hadn't been in me to pry up until then, 'specially since they hadn't said nothin' to me about it. But it was plain enough they was in some kind of trouble. I figured I owed 'em for pullin' me out of a bad spot, and trouble was a thing I knew a little bit about. If there was any way I could repay the debt before I left out of here, I'd a mind to do it.

It was after I'd gone to bed for the night when I'd finally made up my mind about all this. So the first chance I got to talk to Eileen — reckon I'd kind of started thinkin' of her that way, though I was careful never to call her anything but ma'am or Miz McClanahan to her face — was after breakfast the next morning. She was in her garden pulling out some weeds, about fifty yards away across the road, and after a bit I just ambled over there casual-like, as if I weren't going no place particular.

When I got to the split-rail fence I leaned on it without goin' inside, just watchin'. She was pretty easy to watch 'most any time, and especially right then with the morning sun catchin' highlights in her hair underneath that little straw bonnet she was wearing. After a bit she glanced up at me, but went right back to working without sayin' nothing.

"You need some help with that?" I asked.

"No thank you." She smiled me a quick smile, and went on with what she was doin'.

Well, I'd meant to sneak up on the subject kind of offhand-like, but I reckon I hadn't spent enough time figurin' out how to do that. Speakin' plain was the natural way with me. And though it had brought me a mite of trouble time to time, it did tend to save a good bit on misunderstanding. So I just plunged ahead and said my piece:

"Ma'am, I can't help noticin' that you folks look to be shapin' up for some kind of trouble." She stopped pullin' weeds and glanced up at me, quick an' sharp. "Ain't none of my business," I went on before she could interrupt, "and you sure don't have to tell me nothin' you ain't of a mind to tell. But I'm a man who's seen a bit of trouble myself off an' on. No stranger to it, you might say . . ."

She was looking at me funny now, and from her expression I couldn't quite figure what was in her mind. Might of been anger. But then it might of been somethin' else too.

"I just wanted to let you know that I'm grateful for all you done, and if you need any help with this matter that's concernin' you . . ." I finished up kind of lame, because I didn't want to come right out and offer my gun to folks who mightn't want any part of it. "Well, I reckon I'd be pleased to do whatever was needful."

She got up slow, brushing a strand of hair away from her face, and then looked at me out of those hazel eyes for a long moment before saying anything.

"I thank you, Mr. Barkley. It's very kind of you to offer. But I see no need to involve you in something that is none of your affair." She hesitated just a little before going on. "In any case, I hope there will be no trouble. If it does come, Joseph and I will manage well enough by ourselves."

"As you say, ma'am. Just thought I'd make the offer." I paused. "I figure I'm pretty much on the mend now, and I've been eatin' of your vittles long enough. Reckon it's about time for me to ride." I held out a hand to her. "Thanks again for everything."

She took my hand and held it a short moment before letting go. "Think nothing of it, Mr. Barkley. And if you're in the neighborhood again, please feel free to call."

I turned and walked back across the road to the house, picking up my rifle and saddlebags from the porch where I'd left them. Then I went into the stable where the roan was waitin'. He tossed his head as I threw the saddle up on him, and blew himself up like a bullfrog when I reached underneath to take hold of the cinch.

"Don't you fret none about it, boy," I said, punching him a good lick to let the air out. "If that lady says she can manage, I reckon she can manage. Likely a sight better without the likes of us than with us."

I was pulling the cinch tight when I heard the creak of saddles and harness from the road out front. Sort of eased over beside the door of the stable, stayin' back in the shadows more out of habit than anything else. Then I took a look outside.

What I saw was four riders pulled up next to the fenced-in garden plot across the road. Eileen McClanahan was standin' up facing 'em, and she didn't look none too pleased about the meetin'.

5 🌿

I RECOGNIZED ONE OF THE RIDERS as the blond-headed kid I'd had words with back at that blind tiger on the Suwannee River. Another was the fellow who'd been with him then, the one he called Bay. Couldn't recall ever seeing the other two, but there weren't much doubt about who they was all ridin' for.

I wasn't close enough to make out the words they was sayin', but when the kid spoke and the lady replied, I could tell that he didn't take real kindly to her answer. Seemed to me like it might not of been just exactly the answer he'd been lookin' for.

Eileen's scatter-gun was leanin' up against the fence, 'bout as close to the riders as it was to her. Suddenly I saw the kid reach down and take it up, breaking it open and shucking the shells before you could say Jack Robinson. Then he threw the gun back down in the dirt at her feet. He said something to one of the other riders, a big redhead with a greasy beard and a Texas rig.

Red shook out a rope and tossed it over one of the fence posts. When he looped it a couple times around his saddle horn and started to back his horse, I made up my mind to have a word with those boys. But danged if old Joseph didn't beat me to it. One moment the porch was empty and the next that old man was standin' up on the steps with a Colt in his fist and cold steel in his eyes. His deep voice rang like a bell in the clear morning air.

"You gent'mens best stop what you doin' an' leave out-a heah now, 'fore I forgets me there's a lady present. I don't mean to tell you more than onct: You ain't welcome here. You ain't ever goin' to be welcome on this place, so don't you be comin' round it any more."

The kid's hand was startin' to drop even while his head was turning toward the sound of Joseph's voice. But his pal Bay managed to side-step his horse up against him and spoil his play.

"Save it, kid," he said. "It's a cold deck. That old man ain't fooling. And he's pointin' that six-shooter right square at your brisket."

Red had drawn up and turned in the saddle, his face gettin' all flushed and splotchy as he realized who it was that was talking. Now he pushed his hat back with his left hand and spat onto the ground.

"A damned nigger!" he said with feeling. "A God-

61

damned sassy nigger with a shootin' iron! I'll be damned if I ain't got a mind to . . ."

Well, he might of had the mind, but just then he surely didn't have much else going for him. His right hand was still holdin' onto the rope, and his horse was turned backside toward the house where Joseph was standing. I ain't never seen a man more out of position for a shootin' scrape.

"I done told you," Joseph was saying, his voice cold and dangerous, "that there's a lady present. You mind your tongue. What you say about me can be settled in God's good time. But I won't have you takin' His name in vain here in front of Miz Eileen."

The hammer on his Colt eared back and the muzzle swung towards Red. "Now you 'pologize to the lady."

"I'll be damned if I will! I'll see you both in . . ."

Red's voice broke off in a shout of pain and rage; there was blood spurting from where his left ear had been. The old man stood like a statue, seeming like he'd never moved an eyebrow. But a wisp of smoke was curling up from the gun in his fist.

"I told you once," he said quietly. "Now I'll tell you again. You 'pologize to the lady, an' you say it like you meant it. Then you and your friends ride out of here before somebody gets hurt serious."

The kid was fit to be tied. He side stepped his horse and glared at his companions.

"Bay, you goin' to let him get away with that? One old man agin the four of us? Come on, let's take him!"

Seemed like maybe I'd ought to make my presence known, though I weren't real sure that old man needed any help from me. I seen some shootin' in my day, but that just now was 'bout as pretty as any I ever come acrost.

I called out from the stable. "You take another look at your hole card, kid. It's four on two, with one of your four not feelin' so sprightly as he was a couple minutes ago. Could be he'd just soon apologize like the man says, and save his hide for hangin'."

I was back out of the light where they couldn't see me, and the position of the stable was such that they was pretty well boxed. I wouldn't of cared for the chances if I'd been in their shoes, and after lookin' the situation over it seemed like even that hot-headed kid had enough sense to agree with me this time.

Oh, he was mad all right. Mad enough to chew up nails and spit out bullets. But I could see him thinkin', and one of the things he was thinkin' was how nice it might be to wake up tomorrow mornin' and see another sunrise. After a second he laid both his hands up on his pommel real careful-like and spoke to the redheaded man.

"All right, Red. You do what he says. Apologize to the lady."

Red had dropped his rope and was holding both hands to his head. The blood was oozing between his fingers. "Damn it, kid . . ."

"Red." This was Bay speakin', and he sounded like

a man who was just nearly at the end of his patience. "Red, if you don't apologize to that lady this second, I swear I'm going to shoot you my own self!"

Red glanced at Bay and didn't care much for what he saw. After a long moment he turned to Eileen and nodded, still holding his head in his hands. "I'm sorry, ma'am, for my language in front of you." He glanced at Joseph, then lowered his right hand to take up the reins. "But that's the only thing I'm sorry for!"

He slapped spurs to his horse and lit off down the road toward the forest like there was a fire underneath him. As the others turned to follow, the kid drew rein deliberately and met Eileen's eyes.

"I thank you for your hospitality, ma'am," he said, grinnin' that lopsided grin of his. "I'll come callin' again real soon." He touched his hat, then started after his companions.

I watched 'em down the road a piece and out of sight. Then I holstered my ole Dragoon and took up my Winchester, walking across the yard to the porch where Eileen and Joseph were standing.

The old man was thumbing a cartridge into the empty chamber of his pistol. "Just no-counts and white trash," he said with a shake of his head. "Ain't nothin' like the old days. I seen the time nary one of those low-lifes would make a pimple on a tough man's neck!"

Well I just looked at him, wondering where he'd been and what kind of trouble he'd seen to make him say something like that. He finished loading, spun the chamber, and shoved the Colt back into his trousers. For a long moment neither one of us spoke. Then he looked up at me and our eyes met.

"We was about to set down for some coffee and biscuits, Mr. Barkley. You care to join us? Or do you need to be leavin' right this second?"

"I reckon I could be convinced to wait a little bit," I said, "for a couple more of Miz McClanahan's biscuits and syrup." We both smiled, and I followed the hired man into the kitchen. Eileen was already there, putting coffee on as we entered.

When we sat down at the kitchen table, both Joseph and me took up chairs where we could watch out the windows on the landward side. Eileen glanced at us with a knowing look, but she didn't say nothing.

I'd a feeling there was a reason Joseph had asked me in just now, like maybe he wanted to talk about some things hadn't none of us mentioned before. Such as Eileen and the Catons. But it weren't my place to bring it up, so I just waited, enjoying the smell of coffee and last night's biscuits warming. After a bit Eileen brought cups and set a pitcher of cane syrup on the table, and when the coffee was ready and the biscuits was hot she brought them too. Then she sat down to join us.

I've knowed some who'd think it strange to be sittin' down to table with a colored hired man, but that's how we usually took our meals at Eileen's, an' I never paid it much mind. Only colored folks I'd knowed growin' up was poor farmers like ourselves, and I reckon I never seen all that much difference between us.

The other kind of thinkin' was for them as felt they had to show the world how important they was by makin' others feel unimportant. Seemed to be a lot of that here in the East, both north and south. In the western lands a man was judged by what he did. If his word was good and he'd stand hitched in a fight, his past was his own business. And so was the color of his skin.

Still, I had to admit that old Joseph weren't exactly typical for this time and place. I was some curious about that, and like I've said, I ain't never been much hand at beatin' round the bush. Besides, I figured we needed something to open up the conversation or I might be sittin' here all day.

So after a bit I just up and out with her. "Meanin' no offense," I said, "but your words out there didn't sound much like the words of a former slave. Nor the shootin' neither. Seems I might ought to have heard about you somewheres in my travels. It's hard for a man who handles a gun like you do to keep hisself from bein' talked about."

He looked at me out of those cold blue eyes for a moment. Then he smiled and leaned back in his chair. "I reckon you ain't near old enough, Mistah Barkley. There ain't too many 'round any more knows aught of old Joseph's past." '

He poured himself another cup of coffee. "I wasn't rightly born a slave, you see. Florida was a Spanish colony back then, and though some folks of color was slaves, there was plenty more that wasn't. My people farmed, fit Injuns, traded with 'em when we wasn't fightin'. Pretty much like everbody else in those days.

"'Course that all changed when the men from Tennessee and Georgia started comin' down here regular. 'Bout then a person of color who wasn't a slave was apt to become one awful quick. We seen the writin' on the wall an' moved south to join some kinfolks round Tampa Bay, though in the long run it didn't do us no good a-tall.

"Eighteen an' twenty-one it was, when them Coweta Creeks come a-raidin' down out of Georgia. They burnt our place along with the others, then kilt my pa an' my brother Jim when they tried to make a stand. Ma an' the twins was took prisoner a couple days later, tryin' to reach a water well at another settlement. That left me an' Joshua, with him only fourteen at the time, and me twelve.

"Well, somehow we managed to 'scape all them wild Injuns at last, but there weren't nothing left for us then. Not one stick on top of another. So we lit out and hid around the country for a time, finally made our way up towards the Natchez Trace. I stayed on there for several years." He smiled without humor. "Reckon you might say I served my apprenticeship up there on the Trace."

Joseph didn't need to explain that last part to me, 'cause I knew the Trace and I knew the kind of men it bred back before the war. If that was his "apprenticeship," t'weren't no wonder a-tall that he'd struck me as a right hard man, and a dangerous one.

"After a bit," he went on, "I made my way downriver and shipped out to sea. Saw a piece of the world before finally meetin' up with Cap'n McClanahan down Jamaica way. Sailed with him then for a dozen years all told, 'round the Gulf and the Caribbean. A finer sea captain and a better man I've never known."

The way he said that made me glance over at Eileen, almost in spite of myself. She was watchin' Joseph and not lookin' at me. But I saw a kind of fierce pride come over her face when her husband's name was mentioned. And though her eyes stayed dry, it seemed like maybe she was having just a little bit of trouble keepin' 'em that way.

The old man shrugged and continued. "After while we both sort of decided I was gettin' on a bit, and I might be more he'pful ashore. Cap'n had him a new bride by then, an' it just seemed the natural thing to stay on here and sort of look after her."

He drained his coffee. "I reckon it turned out for the best, seein' as he never made it back from that last voyage." The old man paused and stared at the empty cup for a long moment before settin' it back on its saucer.

"I am pleased it's been given me to be around to he'p out when the lady needed me," he said finally. "But when it comes down to that, I'd a-not been ashamed to go down to Davy Jones along with the Cap'n neither. And that's a fact."

He paused, and I glanced over again at Eileen McClanahan. She was sittin' up straight as a post, her face pale but with a little smile playing about her lips. Some wives might of gone all weepy when the talk turned to a husband so recently lost at sea. But there was steel in that woman. Pride in her man, surely. And a sorrow that seemed like it might be too deep for words. But no tears. Not a one.

For a while I sat lookin' out the window at the road and the salt flats, and the forest beyond. Then I turned to face them both.

"What now?" I asked.

Eileen met my eyes for the first time since we'd sat down at the table.

"We stay here," she said. "We stay here, and we build, and we maintain. Just as he meant for us to do. And when James is grown, and Mary, they'll have a home place they can look on with pride, whether they choose to stay on here or not. A place that will remind them of their father, and his dreams for all of us."

"What about the Catons?" I asked. "They got any stake in this?" Eileen gave me a hard look, and I shrugged. "Couldn't help noticin' that those gents this morning seemed to take more'n a casual interest in you and your place." I paused. "'Specially the kid."

Joseph took hold of the coffee pot and refilled my cup, then his own.

"This here crick," he said, setting the pot down and gesturing out the window, "leads up through the salt flats into those deep woods. A shallow-draft vessel can make it up there a far piece when the tide's full. Right handy for those that trades in midnight imports, if you know what I mean." He glanced at me slyly.

"On'y trouble is," — the old man took a swallow of coffee — "this here house sits right square at the mouth of it."

Now that made a kind of sense to me. Smugglin's always been a important part of Florida's economy, with a couple thousand miles of coastline and more rivers an' inlets than you can shake a stick at. Most natives took to it as a kind of a sideline, but there was some big money to be made with the right kind of organization. And from what I knew about him, Big Bill Caton was more'n likely to have a finger in that particular pie.

"Uh-huh," I said. "I can see where that might be a caution to folks what does their business mostly after the sun goes down." I glanced at both of 'em. "'Course, if it's only you folks here, and you was just to go sort of deaf and blind whenever visitors was around . . ."

"Might work," Joseph said, "if they trusted us, which they don't. But the trouble of it is, Cap'n McClanahan was a well-known man on this coast, and a well-liked one. Now that he's gone, there's several hundred sailors an' fishermen like to look in on his widow whenever they're in the neighborhood, just to see how she's makin' out, like."

I glanced at Eileen, and thought I saw a bit of a smile start to show through the serious expression on her face. She knew as well as I did that a good-looking widow, and one who could cook on top of it, was the kind of temptation most men in this world would find it mighty hard to fight shy of.

"Upshot is," the hired man continued, "we've boats puttin' in here 'most ever couple weeks. Even if the Catons could count on us to keep quiet, somebody else'd be sure to notice somethin' sooner or later. And you know how folks is. They talk."

I nodded. That explained a lot. For if Big Bill had the kind of sweet setup here it sounded like, he surely wouldn't want all kinds of strangers nosin' into his private affairs. 'Specially not if he planned to keep the tight rein on this country he'd seemed to put his mind to.

"I can see that," I said. "But wouldn't there be some talk too if anything was to happen to you-all, or you was to just up an' disappear one day?"

"Not so much as you might think," Joseph answered. "Oh, there'd be some might wonder. But most folks'd just figure keepin' this place up was too much for a old man and a woman alone, and that we'd moved on to more civilized parts. There's already some as says we's crazy to stay here like we doin'."

I studied my coffee cup for a bit, 'cause that very thought had crossed my own mind a time or two. At last I looked up and saw Eileen watchin' me.

"What about that kid out there?" I asked. "He seemed to have more than smugglin' on his mind when he come here this morning."

Her jaw set and her eyes flashed pure fire. But it

lasted only a second, and then she shuddered and shook her head as if somebody'd stepped on her grave. When she spoke, her voice was quiet and full of contempt.

"Riley Caton is a killer and an outlaw. For some reason, he also imagines himself to be a ladies' man."

"Riley? I grew up knowin' them Caton boys, but I surely don't recall one named Riley."

"He's some kind of a cousin from up Thomasville way," Joseph said. "Meaner'n a snake an' twict as deadly. Somethin' wrong in his head, so folks say. We'd of had us some killin' for sure this mornin', if it hadn't been for his brother Bay."

"Sounds to me like you got a whole passel of unpleasant folks for neighbors," I said. "And ever one of 'em is interested in seein' you off this place, for one reason or another." I looked at Eileen again. "You sure it's worth stayin' on here?"

"Worth it or not, Mr. Barkley, we're staying." Her voice had got real chilly all of a sudden. "And I don't expect that it's any of your business whether we do or not!"

"Yes, ma'am." I pushed myself back from the table and got up. "You're right about that. It ain't none of my business a-tall." I put on my hat. "I reckon I'll be goin' on my way now, if it's all the same to you. Thanks again for your help. You've been mighty kind, under the circumstances."

"Good day, Mr. Barkley. Have a pleasant ride." She picked up some dishes and turned away, leaving me standing there by the door. I stepped outside.

Joseph followed me onto the porch. "She's a proud woman," he said, speaking low so that Eileen wouldn't overhear. "A good woman, but proud. And stubborn. Like to kill her to ask anybody for he'p." He looked me in the eye.

"Now if it was me, I wouldn't turn down the he'p if it was offered right this minute. That's a mean bunch of men over there, and I ain't hardly so spry as I used to be." He paused and shook his head. "But you'd best do what you said, and ride. She's the boss here, and I'm just the hired he'p." He offered me his hand, and I took it. "You ride careful, Mr. Barkley. You hear?"

Just as I was startin' to turn away, something in Joseph's manner changed. He stopped lookin' at me and cocked his head to one side, listening. Then he stepped up to the porch rail and squinted off towards the distant tree line. After a moment he glanced back.

"You might's well wait around a few minutes longer," he said, "after all. Leastways till we find out what it is this time." When I looked at him, he jerked his head toward the road. "Rider comin'."

6 🌿

THE TALL, THIN GENT who drew rein at the gate a couple minutes later had streaks of dust and sweat all down his face and shirt. And I could see that his horse had been rode hard. It seemed like Joseph knew him, for he stepped off the porch and walked out in the front yard before the man even had a chance to dismount. They exchanged a couple words, and when they come to the house the old Negro was lookin' mighty grim.

He motioned me to follow 'em into the kitchen and spoke under his breath. "Bad news," he said. "Worst ever I can recall since Cap'n McClanahan was reported missin' at sea." He acted like he might of told me more, but all of a sudden Eileen was there, just come in from the front part of the house.

"Wilt! Wilt Brady! What brings you down here to the coast?" She turned to get coffee and a clean cup while the tall man sat hisself down at the table with a grateful sigh. "How are Ev and Mae getting on? And the children? Seems like a year since I've seen them, though of course it's been only a couple of months. I wish . . ."

She turned back and started to pour the coffee. Then she saw the look in her visitor's eyes. Her hand trembled for just a instant and her voice sort of trailed off. After a moment she finished filling the cup. "What is it, Wilt?" she said. "What's happened?"

Brady took a sip of coffee before answering. Then he shook his head.

"It's bad news, Eileen. Real bad. Ev and Mae are dead. Murdered."

There was a long silence in the room after he'd said that. Nobody spoke. Nobody moved. It was like ever one of us had been turned into stone. Then after what seemed like a age, Eileen stepped over to the stove and put the coffee pot down, standing with her back to us for another long moment.

When she finally turned around she came over to the table and sat in the chair across from the tall man. Her voice was steady but real quiet as she asked, "What happened, Wilt?"

"Nobody knows. None of the neighbors seen a thing. Ole Lijah Banks found their bodies yestiddy morning. Shot and stabbed, both of 'em. Seems like they was robbed, too. Nary a clue as to who might of done it. Some drifter, more'n likely."

"And . . ." There was another long pause whilst Eileen drew herself up to meet the newcomer's eyes. ". . . the children? James and Mary?"

"Nary sign of 'em. Like they done disappeared off the face of the earth. From all we could tell, they wasn't to home at the time of the killin's. But where they got to afterwards is anybody's guess. Folks was organizin' to look for 'em when I left, but I figured you'd ought to know right away. So I saddled up and rode straight here."

Eileen laid her hands over his where he held the cup. "I'm grateful, Wilt. I'm very grateful." After a second she shook her head like she was waking from a long sleep, and then she pushed herself up from the table. In another minute she was movin' 'round the kitchen, stirrin' up the fire in the stove and gettin' a frying pan down from the cupboard.

"Forgive me, Wilt. I've completely forgotten my manners. You must be half-starved and exhausted after riding all night. I'll fix you a good breakfast, and then you must get some sleep. I've just finished making up the guest room and you're welcome to stay as long as you like. Joseph will see to your needs tomorrow." She'd found a slab of bacon and was cutting thick slices into the pan. When the meat begun to sizzle, she spoke over her shoulder to her hired hand.

"Joseph, I'll need Maggie saddled right away. I'll be busy here for a little while, so you pack some food — enough for several days — and have it ready when I finish." She glanced at the old Negro. "And put a couple of dozen extra shotgun shells in my saddlebags too, will you?"

Joseph started for the door. "Yes'm," he said. "You want I should saddle up ole Becky, too?"

"No. With the Catons around and wanting us off this place so badly, I don't dare leave it abandoned. You'll have to stay here and — if need be — defend it from them as best you can."

The old man turned and stared at her. His mouth opened and closed a couple times like a fish gulping in the air. Then he shut it and drew himself up to his full height in the doorway, folding his arms acrost his chest.

"No, ma'am," he said with a firm shake of his head. "No'm, I ain't goin' to let you do it. I ain't denied you a single thing since the Cap'n died, but this time I got to put my foot down. You ain't goin' up into that country alone, not with no Catons and who knows what other kinds of trash ridin' the night from one end of this land to the other." He shook his head again. "Ma'am, it ain't safe nor proper. And I won't allow it."

Eileen was turning the bacon, not looking at him. "Joseph, I appreciate your concern, and if we had any other choice I would certainly do as you ask. But my son and daughter need me, and I am going to them. We can't both leave here without risking this place being burned to the ground while we're gone, and you know it. So I must go and you must stay. It's as simple as that." She turned to look at him.

"Now, I'd appreciate your help. But if I must saddle Maggie myself and get my own things together I'll do it. And I'll ride out of here when I'm ready, with or without your assistance. As for stopping me . . ." Her hands were on her hips, the long-handled fork still in her right hand. "I'd just like to know how you propose to do it!"

Well, old Joseph seemed like he couldn't think of much else to say then, and I surely didn't blame him. Lookin' at that redheaded woman standing there with her back up and that fork in her hand, I'd sooner tackle two sacks of wildcats than try to keep her from doin' anything a-tall that she'd got her mind set on doin'.

Yet I didn't like the idea of her traveling alone through this country no better'n Joseph did. From what I'd seen so far, them Caton boys wasn't too much in the way of bein' respecters of womankind. An' then there was them kids out there, that Jamie which I'd met on the road, and a little girl-child. . . .

"Look here, ma'am." The words sort of popped out of my mouth before I could put a stop to 'em. And they wasn't even true. "I was already of a mind to ride into that Big Bend country my ownself. Matter of fact, that's where I was headin' when I saddled up this mornin'. So if you wouldn't mind the comp'ny, I reckon I could sort of ride along and see that you got to where you was goin' okay."

She turned on me sudden-like, and appeared as if she was about to spit fire for a moment there. But then she seemed to think better of it and just stood real still, watching me out of them big hazel eyes. "That is," I finished, some quieter than before, "if you was of a mind to have the company."

She considered for a moment. And then she shook her head.

"I thank you, Mr. Barkley. But this is none of your affair. I prefer not to involve others in my troubles, and I believe I'm quite capable of managing on my own. After all, I'll only be on the road for a day and a night before I'm back among friends. I'm a light sleeper and a good shot, so there's no need for you to put yourself out. I think it would be better if you just went your way, while I go mine."

"All right, ma'am," I answered. But I got to admit I was gettin' my dander up a mite now. There ain't nothing worse than offerin' to get yourself shot over something that don't concern you, unless it's gettin' turned down when you're fool enough to offer it in the first place.

"But like I said, Miz McClanahan, my way'll take me north anyhow. Wouldn't be too surprised if we was to run into each other somewheres along the road, just accidental-like."

She smiled, and I couldn't be sure if it was a friendly smile or not. "If I were you, Mr. Barkley, I'd be very careful about coming upon me unawares. I'm afraid I'm a little on edge right now, and I wouldn't want to shoot anybody . . . accidental-like."

Well, that's how we left it, and I rode out of there almost as soon as we'd finished talking — prob'ly a hour or so before Eileen could be gettin' under way. I knew the route she'd likely take, and it was in my mind to circle back an' sort of trail her along until she got to where she was goin'. But a fellow could get plumb lost in that palmetto and scrub country near the coast if he went too far from a road or a trail. So I had to wait until we reached some higher ground before I could make my move.

Turned out it started gettin' dark before the woods opened up enough for me to leave the trail, and though I'd been ridin' slow and easy, there still weren't no sign of the lady behind me. I finally had to decide whether to camp for the night, or head on back and try to meet up with her.

I give a bit of thought to her warnin' me about not comin' upon her unawares. And then I thought about the high-toned way she'd looked at me when she said, "I believe I'm quite capable of managing on my own." And then I drew rein and made camp.

I figured a night alone in the Florida wilderness might do Eileen McClanahan a whole heap of good.

❖   ❖   ❖

'Course I didn't get a awful lot of sleep that night, what with the skeeters and the other critters. And what with wakin' up ever few minutes to listen into the night air, tryin' to hear anything that might be happenin' behind me to a woman alone.

Finally, a couple hours before dawn I rolled out of my blankets for good. I'd made up my mind by then that I was goin' to have to backtrack myself and go see what was delaying the lady. Had to do it for myself, you understand. Not for her. For aught I knew she was just dilly-dallying along the way — though I didn't really suppose that, not with her kids missin' and all. But one way or the other I had to find out, for my own danged peace of mind.

If it had been my first choice in the matter, I wouldn't even be where I was. When I'd saddled up the roan yesterday morning that was the furthest thing from my thoughts. There was too many Catons out an' about on these roads for my health and peace of mind. And ever one of those boys was lookin' to nail my hide to a tree or a fence post.

What I'd meant to do was ease on over to the north an' west a mite, find myself a nice hidey-hole back up in the thicket, and settle down to meditate on the wonders of nature for a while. I figured after a couple weeks the Catons might simmer down a bit and stop actin' so much like a nest of stirred-up yellow jackets. Maybe they wouldn't completely forget all the trouble I'd caused 'em, but leastways by then they might have some other things to think about.

Maybe I could avoid 'em long enough to visit the courthouse in Perry anyhow, and check on that title to my family estate. When I'd done that I weren't too sure what I was going to do next. Find some rich Yankee speculator more'n likely, and just sell out.

But then I had to open my big mouth in front of Eileen McClanahan, tellin' stories and offerin' to protect her when she hadn't even asked for it. And so here I was, trying my dangdest not to make a liar out of myself, an' not get shot dead into the bargain.

By the time it was coming on to daylight, I'd made it back four or five miles, ridin' careful so as not to lose the trail in the dark. And tryin' real hard too not to spook that lady wherever she might be camped out with her shotgun. There was a fine white mist over everthing, shuttin' out the rest of the world except right where the roan and me was riding. It was a eerie feeling, though I'd known plenty such mornings as a boy. Even the birds and crickets seemed less noisy somehow, like they was having their first cup of coffee before startin' the day's serenade.

Speakin' of coffee, I sure wished I'd had me some right about then. I'd left out of that place on the coast so fast I'd brought nothin' at all with me but what I'd rode in with, which was only my guns and the clothes on my back. Old Joseph would have fixed me up sure enough, but with all the excitement yesterday mornin', and with my own itchin' to be gone before Eileen left — so's it wouldn't look like I was waitin' for her — I plumb forgot about it entirely.

The more I thought about that cup of coffee I was wantin', the more I could just about taste it. I'd got right used to Eileen's coffee and biscuits ever mornin', along with whatever side meat was handy, some grits an' butter, and all the fixin's. Spoiled. That was what I'd been gettin'. Plumb spoiled.

If'n I didn't know better, I'd swear I could smell that coffee and bacon cookin' right this second. Then it struck me: that *was* what I'd been smellin', for maybe the last twenty minutes or so off and on. Somebody was cooking breakfast, and not too far away from where I was at the moment.

I reached over and put my hand on the roan's neck, lettin' him know I'd take it kindly if he'd hold off on makin' any unnecessary noises for the next little while. Then I slid my Winchester out of the boot real careful, and let myself down to the ground.

I eased along the road a dozen feet or so, and thought I saw the glow of a fire about twenty yards off to my left. Another few steps and I was sure. Hunkerin' down behind a pine tree, I watched and waited. There was no sound but the occasional scrape of a pan on the coals. The smell of that coffee and bacon was strong and good.

After another few minutes of listening, I called out. "Hello the fire. What's the chances for a bite of breakfast?"

There was a long pause, and I considered taking a chance and cocking my Winchester. Then a woman's voice answered:

"I'd say they're pretty good, Mr. Barkley. You can come on in if you like."

She was sittin' by the fire in a little clearing, a fry pan and coffee pot in front of her, and her shotgun no more'n a foot away within easy reach. She handed me a empty cup as soon as I squatted down beside her.

"The bacon will be done in a few minutes. And I've a couple of sweet potatoes heating in the coals. The coffee is ready now, I think."

I took up the pot and filled my cup and hers, while she rustled around in her saddlebags and got out a couple of blue enameled plates.

"I wasn't expecting company so early in the morning," she said, "but it never hurts to have a little extra on hand, just in case." When I looked at her up close, I could see she had a dark bruise over her left eye. She saw me starin' at it, and shrugged.

"Maggie was scared by a moccasin a few miles back. She never has cared much for snakes, and I'm afraid I lost control of her. The next thing I knew I was lying on the ground with a knot on my head." She smiled. "The moccasin, I'm happy to say, was no longer around."

Eileen blew gently across her cup to cool it. "The worst thing about the whole experience was that in the process of being thrown, my stirrup-leather broke clean in two. As you may or may not know, Mr. Barkley, it is very difficult to ride a side-saddle without a stirrup." She tasted the coffee. "I don't suppose you have a piece of leather, or a rope, that we might use to make repairs?"

"I reckon." She was looking at me kind of strange, half smiling and half serious, in a way that didn't make me feel too comfortable a-tall. "I think I got a little piece of rope in my saddlebag that might do the trick."

"That will be a big help. I've already lost more time than I intended to." She took a sip of coffee and looked at me over her cup. "You must have been delayed yourself somehow, to have gotten no farther than this since yesterday. I would have expected you to be north of the Suwannee by now."

I didn't answer till after I'd scalded my mouth on a swallow of coffee. An' then I took my time, meeting her eyes deliberately.

"Reckon I was lookin' for you," I said finally. "In spite of what was said back there, I don't cotton to the idea of a woman traveling alone through this here country, not with them Catons and who knows what other kinds of no-counts skulkin' about — maybe even that fellow who murdered your kinfolks. I meant to keep a eye on you, whether you wanted me to or not."

She turned to start forking bacon out of the pan, then paused and glanced back over her shoulder at me.

"And what about you, Mr. Barkley? Am I really any safer with you than I would be with them? I believe you said at one time that you'd been an outlaw yourself."

I swore real quiet under my breath. I never met any woman who was so hell-bent and determined to rile folks up and push 'em away, just because they was tryin' to help her out a little bit.

"Ma'am," I said, settin' my coffee cup down and shoving my hat back on my head, "I been in my share of fights an' shootin' scrapes, that's true. And I been on the wrong side of the law a time or two whilst I was about it. If you think that makes me a outlaw then I guess that's what I am." I paused.

"But I'll have you know my folks did try to raise me right. Just some of it took maybe, and some of it didn't." Eileen's back was to me now, so I couldn't see the expression on her face — or guess at what she might be thinkin'. And right at that moment, I didn't much care.

I could feel myself startin' to get mad, so I got up and took a couple steps away from the fire to sort of let my thoughts cool down a mite. The roan looked up from where he was picketed to a nearby scrub oak. Then he shook his head and went back to cropping grass. I turned back.

"I'll tell you one thing, though. I ain't no mis-treater of women, and I ain't no murderer, and I ain't no man what takes advantage of folks in trouble when they need a helpin' hand. That ain't even a little bitty part of the kind of man I am."

I took off my hat and slapped my britches with it. "Hell!" Eileen turned to look at me. "If that's what you thought, why in the blue blazes did you keep me in your house, and feed me, and nurse me back to health in the first place?"

She didn't say nothing to that, and we both looked at each other for a long moment. Then she turned back to the fire and started pullin' sweet potatoes out of the coals with her fingers.

"You'd better come and eat your breakfast, Mr. Barkley. It's a long ride to Luraville, and my brother-in-law's place is still some several miles beyond that."

7

WE TOOK OUR NOONIN' in a little clearing in the woods on the north bank of the Suwannee, between New Troy and Luraville where we wasn't so likely to be spotted by Caton riders or them who might have commerce with 'em. I'd managed to convince Eileen that we'd best keep out of sight an' off the main roads as much as possible, just so's not to tempt any extra trouble which might come huntin' for us.

After I'd unsaddled the horses and turned 'em loose to roll a bit, we made a lunch of cold biscuits and ham, sittin' in the sun to dry out from our swim across the river. A little fire would of been nice too, but there wasn't no sense takin' a chance of some passerby smellin' the smoke. Anyways, it was a clear day and plenty warm.

Whilst we was restin' I tried to get Eileen to talk to me a little about what she had in mind to do once we'd reached that homestead of her kinfolks. Turned out about like I'd expected. She didn't have no more idea of a plan than a blind cow in a cornfield.

"We'll just have to search the countryside, Mr. Barkley, and talk to everyone we meet. Those children can't have gotten far on foot, and perhaps one of the neighbors has seen them. If not, then we'll just keep looking until we come across some sign of them."

"Uh-huh." I took a sprig of grass and put it between my teeth, leaning back on my elbows on the warm ground. "That might work, but then again it might not. At least not soon enough. There's little sloughs an' thickets an' sinkholes all through that country, if I mind me right. Couple small young-uns could get theirselves lost back up in one of those, maybe hurt or somethin', an' not get found till after they'd starved to death — or worse."

She turned on me, her eyes flashing. "I suppose you have a better idea!"

"Well . . ." I watched a hawk circlin' lazy overhead for several seconds. "I done me a mite of trackin' time to time, and I've always found the place to start is in the minds of the men — or young-uns, in this case — that you're followin' after. Best thing to do is take a little time at the beginnin' to consider what they might be tryin' to get to, or away from. And how they'd be most apt to go about doin' it." I glanced at her.

"'Course, when we get there we might find out the kids was just scared by what happened, or maybe they didn't even know about it at first. And then they'd prob'ly turn up at one of the neighbors' houses sooner or later, so we won't need to go huntin' for 'em after all. But if they still ain't come to light after two days, I'd be wantin' to ask myself a couple questions."

Eileen was watching me real careful now. "What questions?" she said.

"Well for one thing, I'd want to know why that was. I mean, bein' out all night in the wilderness can't be too pleasant for two kids alone, an' one of 'em a girl child. It'd seem to me like they'd be apt to head straight for the closest farmhouse in hopes of gettin' a warm meal, a place to sleep, and some way of sendin' word to you about what-all had happened. If they didn't do it, then there must of been some powerful reason why." I paused.

"Might be one of 'em got hurt." I didn't look at her. "Maybe even both. Could be they wasn't able to make it to a neighbor's house. In that case we'll just have to do like you said, and scour over the countryside from one end to the other hopin' to pick up some sign before it's too late."

Eileen's eyes had got real big when I said that, but she kept quiet whilst I continued.

"But what if that ain't what happened?" I asked, speakin' more to myself now than to her. "What if there was another reason why they didn't want to be found?

89

Now that's the sort of question sets a fellow to ponderin'.

"Was it me," I went on, glancing at her, "I'd guess that last thing was what's kept 'em from showin' theirselves so far — if they haven't. Your Jamie strikes me as a right canny youngster. Not hardly the type to get hisself into any fix that a thinkin' man could manage to avoid."

I'd turned my back for just a second there as I picked another sprig of grass to chew on. Then something in Eileen's voice caught me real funny, bringin' me to realize what I'd forgot to mention to her in all this time I'd known her.

"Why do you say that, Mr. Barkley? You sound almost as if you know my son James."

Well, 'tweren't no reason to keep it a secret, so I told her about my meetin' up with the kid whilst I was ridin' out of this Big Bend country the first time. She smiled a little when I mentioned the part about them dime novels, and my tellin' stories about the Western lands.

"That's a real fine boy," I said at last. "From what I've heard of your Captain McClanahan, the line surely did breed true. Boy like that'll grow to manhood just about as soon as you'll let him." I glanced at her from under my hat brim. "Was it me, I reckon I'd go ahead and start lettin' him. 'Tain't like you couldn't use the help an' all."

Eileen looked at me real hard for a moment. Then she got up and started gathering things back into her saddlebags.

"Once again, Mr. Barkley, I find you are giving me

advice about things which are none of your affair. It is an annoying habit that I wish you would try to refrain from in the future."

Well, there we was again. I was either bein' too nosy, or she was bein' too stand-offish, and it was right hard to cipher out which was the worst. I reckoned the best thing to do was just try an' keep a close rein on my tongue from now on. So when I'd saddled up, we rode out of that place without another word.

❖   ❖   ❖

The McClanahan homestead was made up of a two-story double-chimneyed farmhouse, unpainted since the war, and with a half-dozen board-and-batten outbuildings. Looked to be a right respectable outfit, considerin' the times.

There was several men standin' in the yard as we rode up, and Eileen greeted each one of 'em by name. Then this gent in a suit and a boiled collar come over and reached up a hand whilst we stopped at a hitchin' post near the front steps. Eileen took his hand.

"Mrs. McClanahan," he said, "I'm so sorry about what has happened here. It's a terrible thing. Terrible! We've a citizens' committee riding through the country right now, looking for the killers and for any sign of those two children. If there is anything more that I might do to help you in your time of need, you have only to say the word."

"Thank you, Mr. Tinsley. I'm very grateful. No doubt everything is being done that can be. I want only to refresh myself briefly, and then I will join the search for

James and Mary. I would hate to think of them spending another night out-of-doors."

"Join the search? Why, Mrs. McClanahan, there's no need for that. You mustn't think of it. You're among friends now." He looked over at me with the kind of expression some folks get when they bite into a sour orange. "We'll take good care of you. And I'm sure one of our people will locate the youngsters before nightfall."

"Thank you again, Mr. Tinsley." Eileen flashed him a quick smile. "But I'm quite determined. I don't think I could stand just to sit around idly wringing my hands while my children are out there lost and alone."

As Tinsley helped her to the ground, a big over-stuffed woman come out the door and down the steps. She grabbed Eileen and held her to her bosom so hard and so long, that I thought for a moment there she was goin' to plumb suffocate that gal. But at last she let go and stepped back, and after they'd exchanged a couple words Eileen turned around to introduce me.

"Mama Curry, this is Mr. Barkley. He has been kind enough to accompany me from the coast. Mama Curry is the wife of our Methodist minister," she said to me, "and a very old and dear friend."

"Pleased to meet you, ma'am." I touched my hat.

Eileen hesitated a moment, and her eyes seemed to twinkle just a little bit. "Mr. Barkley has been a house guest of ours for the past several weeks," she said innocently. "He was traveling through our neighborhood it seems, and found the sea air and secluded location of our place quite beneficial to his health."

The big woman smiled and bobbed her head. "You're welcome, Mr. Barkley. If you don't see something you need right away, you just ask. Now Eileen, come on inside and set yourself down this minute. I've some lemonade made, and there's fried chicken and other fixin's in case you haven't eaten. When you've had a chance to rest up a bit, we'll have us a good long talk."

"Thank you, Mama Curry. Some lemonade would be very pleasant after the day's heat." Eileen untied her bonnet and started up the steps with the older woman. "But if it's all the same to you, I would just as soon have our talk now. Since James and Mary have not yet been located, there are things to be discussed and plans to be made. I want to join the search for my children as quickly as possible."

"Why, honey, don't you give a thought to that. The menfolks are scouring the whole country right this minute. I'm sure before much longer . . ."

The rest of their conversation was lost to me as they stepped up on the porch and went inside the farmhouse. But I could imagine what was bein' said, and I smiled a bit to myself as I took hold of the reins and led the horses toward the log and plank lean-to which served as a stable. Mama Curry could talk herself blue in the face if she wanted to, but it wouldn't make no difference. None at all. Once that McClanahan woman'd got her mind made up, you might just as well look for tree frogs in a gator hole as try and change it for her.

I unsaddled the roan and Eileen's mare, then rubbed 'em down real good with a piece of old Kroker sack that I found back up in the stable. When I'd forked over some hay and fed 'em a mite of corn by hand, both animals seemed pleased enough with the accommodations.

There was two other horses inside there, and I give one of 'em a good long study before headin' back to the house. It had the look of a western mustang about it, like you'd see out in Texas or Arizona. And that was a curious thing, considerin' how far away I was from those places now.

When I'd walked back outside thinkin' to see if maybe I could locate a pot of coffee somewheres near about, I suddenly pulled up short. A gent was leanin' against a split rail fence some dozen yards away, watchin' me from underneath his hat brim with what I took to be more'n just a casual interest. I'd the feeling he'd been standin' there for quite a spell.

Now, when you've been the places I been and seen the things I seen, you learn pretty quick that there's only one or two reasons why a fellow's liable to be lookin' at you in that particular way. I'd no enemies in this part of the country that I knew about, 'cept the Catons, and this fellow didn't appear to be just exactly their kind of rider. That left some sort of lawman as the other possibility. But I surely couldn't recall anything I'd done back in Arizona that was so serious somebody'd want to chase me all the way to Florida over it.

I'd never took the rawhide thong off my pistol since

ridin' in here, and right now I was carryin' my Winchester in my left hand. Reckon I was gettin' plumb careless and forgetful in my old age. For about a half a second I wondered how fast I'd be able to get my rifle into action if I was to grab hold of it with both hands. Then I forgot the idea. There was somethin' in this gent's manner which told me it wouldn't be near fast enough.

At last I raised up my right hand real careful an' pushed my hat back off my forehead. "Howdy," I said, smiling.

The stranger nodded, then cocked his head to one side. "Don't I know you from someplace?"

"Could be," I replied. "I been there."

"My name's Tom Bristoe. From Comanche County, Texas."

"Uh-huh." I studied him for a moment. "Sort of thought you had the look. Tate Barkley here. You huntin' me?"

"Nope. Reckon I've seen you a couple times. But they was both fair shootin's." He straightened up and hooked his thumbs behind his belt. "Don't know that you ever broke any laws in Texas." Bristoe's eyes crinkled a little around the edges. "Leastways not that we've found out about yet."

"I'm pleased to hear you say that." And I meant it. "I don't want no trouble with the Rangers no time, and especially not now that I've set my mind to helpin' these folks find a couple youngsters out there in the brush."

"Heard about that. Thought I might offer to lend a

95

hand with the lookin', if folks was willing. That fellow I'm after will keep a little while longer."

I was right curious about who this gent might be, though I'd no intention of askin'. They must want him pretty bad though, to send a Ranger all the way here to Florida after him.

"Be pleased to have you with us," I said. "Speakin' for myself, anyhow. Come on, let's go see can we scare us up a pot or two of coffee."

When we got back to the house, Eileen and Mama Curry was sittin' in the kitchen talkin'. But as soon as Eileen saw me come in she got up from her chair and walked across the room to meet us.

"Mr. Barkley, could we be ready to leave again in half an hour? There's still no word of James and Mary, and I just can't sit here any longer without doing something. At least if I ride out to look myself I won't feel so completely useless." She put her hand on my arm. "Would you mind very much?"

"No, ma'am," I said, trying my best to ignore her hand where it was. "I reckon we can do that. But it would be a sight better if you didn't ride that mare of yours any more today. She ain't used to all this hard travelin', and she looks plumb played out. Do you suppose there's somebody here who might give you the loan of a horse for the afternoon?"

Eileen looked at Mama Curry, who had gotten up to join us.

"Most of the men who were here have already left,"

the large woman said, "and the others will be leaving shortly. There are no spare horses on the place." She gave Eileen a hard look and then shook her head. "But if you're bound and determined to go, I suppose you could use my buggy and my black gelding. I'll be staying here till the funeral tomorrow, so I won't need them this evening."

"Thank you, Mama Curry." Eileen turned to the other woman and smiled that smile of hers, the one that could almost make a person forget how bull-headed stubborn she was. "I'll take good care of them. And I promise we will be careful as well."

She started toward the door, but stopped when she saw Bristoe standing behind me in the shadow of the stairway. "This is Tom Bristoe," I said as he stepped forward. "He'd like to come with us, if it's all right with you. I think he'd be a good man to have along."

The Ranger straightened up and bowed real formal, like he was asking the lady for a dance. "I'm pleased to make your acquaintance, ma'am. I've a little bit of experience following a trail, and I'd like to be of help in any way I can."

Eileen studied him for a second, then nodded.

"We'll be pleased to have you join us, Mr. Bristoe. We can use all the help we can get." She turned to me. "If you wouldn't mind hitching up the buggy, Mr. Barkley, I've a few more matters to talk over with Mrs. Curry. I shall be ready to leave as soon as you're finished."

While we walked across the yard to the stable, Bristoe's eyes scanned the fields and the trees in the distance. "Lots of places for a couple kids to get lost in out there," he said. "You got any idea where we'd ought to start?"

"Uh-huh. I got one idea, anyway." We went into the stable and I explained my thinkin' about how maybe them kids had some reason they didn't want to be found, leastways not by just anybody. Then I told him how I'd happened to meet up with Jamie a few weeks back at that old sinkhole.

"You think he might of taken his sister there to hide out?"

"If I wanted me a spot where I wasn't likely to be noticed, I could do a sight worse. That sinkhole's nigh onto invisible from a hundred yards off. Sits up on a little hill in a clump of trees so small you'd swear nothin' of any size could be hidin' there. It was pure-dee luck that I ever come acrost it in the first place."

"Makes sense, all right. Most boys'll have them some kind of a private spot like that, and it's the first place they'd head for if there was trouble shapin' up."

"Onliest problem," I said, leading Mama Curry's gelding out of the stable, "is that I just come on that place one time, and from a different direction than this here. I been studyin' on that, and I think I could find it again. But we'll have to do us some ridin' off to the north an' east first, so's I can get a feel for the country an' sort of see where I was the last time."

Bristoe squinted at the sun. "Best not take too long a time doin' that, if you hope to reach that sinkhole before dark. I'd guess we only got maybe three, four hours of daylight left."

"I know it," I said. "And I surely don't mean to waste around any longer than I have to findin' that place. Eileen McClanahan'd be likely to have us out there beatin' the bushes by starlight if we don't come up on some kind of a sign before nightfall."

"That does appear to be a strong-willed woman," Bristoe agreed. He glanced at me. "Handsome, too."

"Uh-huh." I busied myself with the trace harness. "I reckon."

8 🌿

O<small>LE ROAN</small> surely weren't none too pleased when I throwed the saddle up on him again. But we'd spent us a heap of longer days on the trail before this, so I didn't pay too much mind to all his snortin' an' blowin'. I knew he could stand it at least as good as I could.

When I led him out in the yard to where Bristoe was waitin', I happened to glance over towards the corral and saw a couple gents watchin' us. One was that Tinsley fellow who'd spoke to Eileen when we first arrived. The other was a man I hadn't seen before, a little weasel-faced gent in dirty overalls and a slouch hat. They was talkin' real confidential, like they'd got some important things to say that they didn't want nobody else to know about but them. Ever now and again they'd glance over at me or Bristoe, then go on back to their talking.

I could see Tom Bristoe had noticed 'em too. He was leanin' up against the front porch rail of the house lookin' like he wasn't paying no mind, just studyin' on the way Mama Curry's gelding had of flicking at flies with his tail. But ever now and again I'd see his eyes shift under his hat brim to take in those gents, always in such a way that his head never moved from where it was.

I didn't have no chance to talk to him about it though, because just about the time I come up to where he was standin' Eileen appeared at the door. She walked down the steps real brisk and climbed into the buggy. When Tom and I mounted up I managed to turn my head just enough to where I could see the corral, but by then that weasel-faced gent was gone. Tinsley was crossin' the yard towards us at a fast walk.

"Mrs. McClanahan. Eileen. I beg you to reconsider. There's no good to be gained from your galavanting all over the countryside like this, and it might not be safe. The killer, or killers, may still be somewhere nearby. Why don't you just get down from there and come on back inside the house? If you like, I'll stay here and keep you and Mrs. Curry company." He pulled his coat aside so's we could see the little .32 revolver he had stuck down inside his waistband. "And provide protection if need be."

I thought Eileen's smile was just a tad chilly when she turned to answer him. "Thank you again for your concern, Mr. Tinsley, but I do believe I shall be perfectly safe with these gentlemen." She laid a hand on her shotgun, which was setting in the buggy next to her. "And as you can see, I am armed as well. However, if you wish to keep Mrs. Curry company until her husband returns, I'm sure she would consider it a kindness."

Without another look at him, Eileen picked up the reins and clucked to the gelding. She took off out of there at a quick trot, so that Mr. Tinsley was left standing in a cloud of dust. Bristoe and me had to touch spurs to our horses in order to catch up.

Once we were out of sight of the farmhouse she slowed the buggy down to a fast walk, and I took over the lead so's I could start to head us up country to where I'd crossed the Big Bend that last time. We rode along without talking for several minutes before Eileen looked over at me and Bristoe.

"Mr. Tinsley keeps a general store not far from here," she said, as if maybe she felt she'd ought to do some explaining about how we'd left the house back there. "And he imagines himself to be one of the leading citizens of the community. Actually, I suppose he is in a way. He is certainly successful enough, although he's only been in the neighborhood a few years." She smiled. "But I'm afraid I can't help finding his manner rather irritating at times, especially when he is trying to take charge of other people's affairs."

I didn't reply to that, but I'd a mind to agree with the lady this once. There was something about that

Tinsley fellow which sort of got under your skin just from his attitude and the way he looked at you. Leave alone him saying anything to you.

We followed some farm roads north for a few miles, then east, then north again after a bit. Finally we turned back to the west. We was right close to my earlier route now, and before long I thought I was beginning to recognize a landmark or two. It was fairly open country thereabouts, with fields and grazing pasture separated by only a few stands of pines and hardwoods.

At last I spotted a big old oak tree up on a hill that I'd noticed the first time. I recognized it right off because of its odd shape and the fact that it stood up there all by itself, without no other trees around it. Slowing my horse to drop back beside the buggy, I spoke to Bristoe and the lady, telling 'em what I'd seen.

From here I'd a pretty good idea of how to find that sinkhole, and maybe with a little luck, the kids. We'd still a few miles to go yet though, traveling west and a mite south. Since we'd been ridin' in a big circle around the McClanahan place, I figured the sink-hole itself weren't prob'ly no more'n three, four miles from the house as the crow flies.

After a few minutes we come up through some scattered trees over a little rise, and I was about to start down the other side when Tom Bristoe trotted his horse forward and pulled up alongside of me. When I saw him draw rein I did the same, and Eileen brought her buggy to a stop a few yards in back of us. Bristoe was pointin' off in the distance to where a thick stand of pines stood up tall against the horizon.

The sun was pretty low down by then, and I had to squint my eyes up real tight to see what he was pointin' at. Finally I managed to make out a group of riders movin' in and amongst the pine trees. I watched 'em for several seconds without sayin' nothing. Then I glanced at Bristoe.

"How many you figure?" I asked.

"Hard to say with all them trees and the sun like it is. Eight or ten at least. Maybe a dozen."

"That's about what I figured. You reckon it's some of them neighbor folks lookin' for the kids?"

"Might be. They seem to be lookin' for something all right." He shook his head. "But talkin' to them people back yonder I didn't figure they was able to muster much more'n a dozen all told. More'n likely those would be traveling in twos or threes so's to cover more country." Bristoe hesitated. "'Course then maybe they've all gathered up there because they found somethin' back in those woods."

"Uh-huh." I reached back and slipped the thong off my Dragoon Colt. "Maybe. But I don't feel so awful sure of it that I'd want to ride down there right this second and ask 'em. Way things is in this country, I get a real uncomfortable feelin' anytime I see that many men together in one place." I shifted around in the saddle so's I could speak to Eileen.

"Might be a good idea," I said, "if we was to turn

around and head back over that rise before we call attention to ourselves here. Don't want to be in too big a hurry about it, just sorta slow an' easy like we was out for a Sunday picnic. But let's do it now."

I took hold of the gelding's harness and helped Eileen turn the buggy. Then I let her and Bristoe lead off whilst I held back to take one last look at the men across the way. Near as I could tell they hadn't seen us, or leastwise didn't think nothin' particular about it if they did. There was folks travelin' here an' about all the time, so there'd be no reason to pay too much mind to us unless that bunch happened to be lookin' for somebody special — like Eileen an' me. If they was, maybe the buggy and the extra rider would of throwed 'em off the scent.

I rode back and started leading us in a wide circle around them woods where we'd seen the men, meanin' to come on back to our original route only after we'd put a good piece of distance behind us. We'd gone maybe half a mile when Bristoe pulled up next to me.

"'Peared you might-a thought you knowed them men back yonder," he said in a low voice, so's Eileen couldn't overhear. "Trouble?"

"Likely. If they're the men I suspect they were." I jerked my head over my shoulder. "Eileen — Miz McClanahan — an' me have had our troubles with 'em before."

"Who'd you reckon they was?"

I looked at him. "You hear anything about Big Bill Caton an' his gang since you been in this country?"

Bristoe nodded. "I have. Matter of fact, I been to their camp and made talk with 'em a time or two." I must of looked at him awful funny, because he sort of shrugged before takin' out the makin's and startin' to roll himself a smoke.

"I told you I was huntin' a man. Needed to be sure he hadn't hooked up with that bunch, and I also wanted to find out if maybe they'd seen anybody hereabouts who might be on the dodge." He licked the paper and stuck the butt in his mouth, then grinned. "Onliest one they could think of when I asked 'em about it sounded a awful lot like you."

"Well," I said, starting to get my dander up a mite, "I reckon that's just fine. Outlaws an' gun artists killin' and thievin' all over this country, scarin' decent folks half out of their wits, and a Texas Ranger can't think of nothing better to do than smoke peace pipe an' make pow-wow with 'em!"

Tom Bristoe cupped his hand around his cigarette and lit it. "Look here, Barkley," he said calmly. "We got all the outlaws and renegades that we can use back in Texas already. We surely don't have to cross the border into other states lookin' for more. I'm out of my jurisdiction here anyway, and if I got a man to find it's only because he's one of ours and we want him back." He took a deep drag on his cigarette. "Now, I got no particular liking for the Catons an' their kind, but it appears to me that they're Florida's outlaws, and Florida's problem."

The Ranger squinted at me through the cigarette smoke. "They just ain't none of my affair one way or the other."

Well, it weren't no use arguing with him, so I let the matter drop and concentrated on finding my way back to that sinkhole. After a bit we come out of some trees into a open place, and I saw the hill I was lookin' for not half a mile in front of us.

"There she is," I said, drawing rein whilst Eileen and Tom come out of the woods behind me. I lifted up my hand to point. "Back in there amongst that little piece of dog fennel and hardwood scrub is the place where I met your boy Jamie at. The sinkhole's hid behind them trees an' bushes there."

Bristoe studied the hill for several minutes, then shook his head. "You sure were right about that place," he said. "If you hadn't told me it was there, I'd of never known there was a sinkhole within ten miles of where we are."

The sun was dipping behind the trees now, and there wasn't prob'ly no more'n a half hour of daylight left. If we was going to have any hope of findin' them kids before night set in, we was going to have to be about doing it. I spoke to the roan and he started up the hill at a quick trot.

Ten seconds later something buzzed by my ear and I heard the crack of a rifle away off on my right. Didn't have no time to think. I just kicked a leg free and fell to the ground on the roan's left side, leavin' him to keep on runnin' up the hill. My pistol was in my hand when I hit the ground, and I rolled over three times, coming to rest facin' the direction of the shot with the barrel layin' acrost my left forearm.

Instinct was all it was that got me into a shootin' position. But when I let fly a couple blasts with that big Dragoon somebody up in the grass started getting right nervous. I caught a flash of movement as the rifleman started to pull back, and I nailed him dead center with my third shot.

There was other guns firing now, some from the direction I was facing, some from behind me. I couldn't tell for sure if I was the only one bein' shot at, but I knew I was one of 'em. When dirt started kicking up little fountains around me, I rolled over again, four or five times till I'd got myself down into a little gully where I was part-way hid from my attackers.

Whilst I was layin' there on my back shoving cartridges into the empty chambers of my pistol, I heard this wild Rebel yell an' looked up to see seven riders coming up the slope towards me. One of 'em was holding his Winchester in one hand and sightin' down the barrel like he meant to ventilate me from here into next Tuesday. I spoilt his fun by puttin' a hole though the Bull Durham tag that was hangin' out from his left shirt pocket.

As I watched him roll off his horse tail over teakettle, I caught a glimpse of Tom Bristoe. He was standin' there by his own mount calm as you please, and squeezing off shots like he was in the middle of a parade ground. 'Bout the time I looked at him he cut down on another rider, and then I heard the boom of Eileen's shotgun. A third man's head exploded into bloody pulp as he fell to the ground almost at my feet.

The other riders were abreast of me then, and I was just about a frog's whisker more than half angry about this situation. I grabbed holt of the nearest man, jerked him off his horse, and threw him to the ground, crushin' in his skull with two blows from the barrel of my Dragoon.

Bristoe got another as he tried to turn his mount to come help his comrade, and a minute after that there weren't nobody in sight. I stayed on the ground for a good long count of twenty, kneeling down amongst the bodies and keeping a sharp lookout for anyone else who might be wantin' to try his luck from the cover of the trees.

But it seemed like we'd run 'em off, at least for the time bein'. The whole battle hadn't lasted no more'n a couple of minutes.

'Bout the time I figured it was safe to drop my guard and reload, ole roan come sidlin' down the slope with a baleful look in his eye, like I'd led him into this whole mess a-purpose just so's I could watch him run when the shootin' got started.

After I'd caught him up, I walked back over to the trees to where Eileen and Bristoe was waitin'.

"You folks all right?" I asked, glancing from one to the other of 'em.

Tom Bristoe spun the fresh reloaded cylinder of his Colt and dropped it into his holster. "I reckon," he said. He turned to Eileen. "You weren't hurt, were you ma'am?"

She didn't answer. Just sat real still where she was on the buggy seat, with her shotgun across her lap. Her eyes was starin' out over the field where the bodies of the bad men lay.

Bristoe and me took a step closer just to make sure that she was okay, and then she seemed to come to herself all of a sudden. Like maybe she'd been dreaming or something.

"Yes," she said. "Yes, I'm fine, only . . ." She hesitated. "Only . . . I've never killed a man before." She shuddered and clutched at the little shawl she was wearing, then shook her head as if to clear it. After a second she turned to me. "They meant to kill us, didn't they?"

"Yes'm. I reckon that's just exactly what they meant to do."

"They meant to kill all of us." When she repeated that, it struck me of a sudden what she was saying. Them men hadn't been out to get only me an' Bristoe. They'd been shootin' at Eileen as well.

"I recognized a couple of them riders," the Ranger said grimly. "They was at that Caton camp back south of here, the time I went down there to see 'em."

My back was to him as I gathered up the reins and climbed into the saddle. "Mite friendlier the last time, was they?" I asked dryly. I started the roan up the hill as I spoke, bringin' him into a trot before Bristoe had any chance to answer.

When I'd got up into the trees and scrub around that

sinkhole, I dismounted and stood there for a little bit, just listening and lettin' my eyes adjust to the deep shadows of the place. The sun was almost gone by now, and it was pretty near black as night underneath them leaves an' branches.

I couldn't hear nothin' nearby but a few frogs and crickets, and ever onct in awhile a chuck-will's-widow called out from somewheres in the fields around. It was 'most as quiet at that moment as a Florida evening's ever likely to get. After awhile I knelt down, still holdin' onto the reins, an' called out real low:

"Jamie? Jamie boy, you there?"

No answer.

"Jamie, this is Tate Barkley. You remember me? We spent a afternoon together a few weeks back, talkin' about cowboys and Arizony an' all that."

Still nothing. But I'd a feelin'. Couldn't explain why, but something just told me I was in the right place. I spoke again.

"Jamie, I reckon it'd be okay to show yourself now. I got your ma with me." I paused. Was there a little rustlin' in the brush back there on my left? I couldn't be sure. ". . . an' I brought along a honest-to-Pete Texas Ranger too, just for extra protection."

"No foolin'? A Texas Ranger?" The voice come from the darkness behind a clump of blackjack an' scrub oak a dozen yards away.

"No foolin', boy. He'll be along with your ma any minute now."

111

"I'll wait till they get here, Mr. Barkley, if it's all the same to you." The voice had moved. It was almost straight out in front of me now, and farther away. "Meanin' no offense sir, but I don't hardly know you. And there's a awful lot of men seems to want to lay hands on me an' sis here in the worst way."

I shook my head and let my breath out real slow. This not wantin' to take help from a body must run in the McClanahan family right down from oldest to youngest. Not that I blamed the kid, though. He was just bein' cautious. An' smart. Likely live to a ripe old age doin' that, if he was to keep it up.

"All right, boy. You just hold your horses, and I'll go see what's keepin' 'em." I stood up and turned around. Just then I heard Eileen's voice.

"Mr. Barkley, are you there? Have you found anything?"

"Yes to both questions, ma'am. I'm right here. And I've found a couple young folks who 'low as how they'd be right pleased to see you."

"James! Mary!"

In another second she was standing next to me, an' the kids was runnin' out of the woods into her arms. It was too dark to see much of anything by then, but I'd the feelin' if I could have, I just might of noticed a tear or two in Eileen McClanahan's eyes for the first time since I'd met her.

9

I LET 'EM HOLD ON to each other for a minute or so, but then I figured I might better say somethin' about our situation here.

"Meanin' no offense, ma'am, but I think it'd be a good idea if we was to make some tracks out of this place just soon as we're able. There's still likely to be some mighty mean men around here somewheres, and I surely wouldn't want to come up on any of them unexpected-like in the dark. 'Specially not with these kids along."

"Yes of course, Mr. Barkley. You're absolutely right." She got up from where she'd been kneeling and took each child by the hand. "Come on, children. There's a buggy waiting, and in another hour you can have some supper and spend the night in a nice warm bed."

There was a bit of a moon peepin' over the trees when we come out of the woods, an' Tom Bristoe was there waitin', already in the saddle. I could tell by his manner that he was about more'n half ready to leave this place his ownself. He was watchful as a cat, keepin' his eyes on the far treeline and his ears pricked for any sound that might suggest more trouble a-comin'.

Like me, he knew we'd been uncommon lucky in that last attack. And neither one of us felt much like pushin' our luck no further than necessary this evening.

There wasn't a lot said whilst I got Eileen an' the kids situated in the buggy. But when I'd mounted up and we was startin' to move out, Bristoe brought his horse up close to mine.

"I went lookin' for that rifleman who fired the shots at you back yonder," he said in a low voice. "He must of not been quite dead, because somehow he crawled off or was dragged off into the woods before I got there." The Ranger paused. "Left his rifle behind, and a deal of blood. And he left something else that might interest you."

He reached back of his saddle and took out a dark object which he handed to me. It was a raggedy old slouch hat. "You recognize that?"

I studied it for a moment. "Looks a mite like the hat that wiry gent was wearin' this afternoon. The one we seen talkin' to Mr. Tinsley."

Bristoe nodded. "That was my thinking. Can't be certain, of course. But I ain't seen another quite like it since I come into this country."

I glanced at him and handed the hat back. "Sort of makes a man curious to know what them two could of been talkin' about, now don't it? And how they'd come to be acquainted in the first place."

"Uh-huh." The Ranger give his own hat brim a tug and dropped back to ride drag, leaving me alone with my thoughts.

And I had a few things to think on. Like why would a fine, upstanding citizen like that Mr. Tinsley be conversin' with a man what rode for the Catons? And why only a couple hours later them riders was all out in force, beatin' the bushes — for who? Was they lookin' for the two kids like Jamie had suggested, and come on us by accident? Or was they lookin' for us three from the git-go?

Maybe it was both. And when that last thought started rattlin' around in my brain-cage, I had to set back and ask myself another why.

There weren't so many reasons for tryin' to kill folks a-purpose like that as a fellow might think at first look. One was revenge, of course. And that would explain their wantin' me. Another was wishin' after something the other person had — which might be a cause for makin' Eileen a target. Bristoe could of just happened to be in the wrong place at the wrong time.

But the kids? None o' that had nothing to do with them that I could see. Nor was a couple half-growed younguns likely to be anybody the Catons needed to be feared of, which was another popular reason for bush-whack killin's.

Unless . . .

Now that was a idea. What if them kids seen something they wasn't supposed to see, whilst their aunt and uncle was bein' murdered? What if they seen the killers theirselves, and could point the finger right at the men who done it? Thing like that would be right embarrassin' to somebody who wanted to keep their deeds a secret, or to blame 'em on somebody else.

Folks in these parts was in a fair way to bein' riled up over the McClanahan killin's anyway. But so far they'd got it in their heads that it must of been some drifters or outsiders who done it, of which there was a-plenty ridin' through the country right then. Nobody'd give much thought at all to the possibility the murderers might be anybody local.

For all his thievin' and smugglin' and ridin' high and mighty through the Florida panhandle, Bill Caton was looked on as a home boy by folks hereabouts. Not somebody to be especial proud of maybe, but one of their own just the same. It'd even been suggested he might have some political ambitions once he'd made hisself a stake and things got settled down a bit.

If it had been him or his men who done such a thing — killin' a honest farmer and his wife in their own home — it'd be liable to set the whole country against him. There was plenty of trees hereabouts, and rope was cheap. I seen vigilance committees formed over a whole heap less.

I turned in the saddle, meanin' to ask a question or

two of Jamie where he rode in the buggy next to me. But wouldn't you know it? Both them kids was plumb sound asleep.

❖   ❖   ❖

It was getting right late when we finally pulled up at the McClanahan place again. But there was a light burnin' in the window, and Mama Curry was standing in the doorway before we'd even got down to the ground.

"Eileen, where in creation have you folks been? We was startin' to get plumb worried." Then she seen the kids. "Oh, thank the Lord you found 'em! Come on, come on, get 'em up here into the house. We got some grits an' greens on, and I'll start some chicken. Their beds is already turned down and waitin'." She disappeared back inside the house.

I helped Eileen out of the buggy, along with the little girl who was so tuckered she had to be carried. When I looked for Jamie, he was standin' next to Tom Bristoe's horse. The Ranger didn't see the kid until he'd dismounted and turned to lead his mustang to the stable.

"Excuse me, mister." Jamie stood his ground and spoke up bold as brass. "Is it true that you're a real for-sure Texas Ranger?"

Bristoe looked down at the kid for a long moment. Then he nodded. "I reckon it's true, son. But now that you know," — he gave me a hard glance over the kid's head — "I'd just as soon you didn't go tellin' everybody in the neighborhood about it. I'm s'posed to be here incognito. That means there ain't nobody supposed to know what

I'm doin' in Florida, or even that I'm here in the first place."

Jamie nodded and lowered his voice. "I understand sir," he said real serious-like. "I won't say another word about it."

Bristoe put a hand on the kid's shoulder. "Thanks," he said, just as serious. "Now you go on up to the house and get something to eat. I'll be along soon's I get these here horses put away."

I carried little Mary into the kitchen an' sat her down in a big chair at one end of the table. She perked up and started rubbing her eyes soon as she could smell the chicken frying, and a moment later Eileen sat next to her.

"It's all right, honey. I'm here now, and Mama Curry's here, and we're among friends." She looked up at me in a way that she hadn't never looked before, and I'll admit it made me feel some awkward. I turned my back kind of quick to find cups and pick up the coffeepot to bring it over to the table.

Jamie sat down and I sat across from him, and for a little while there none of us said much of anything. Then, 'bout the time Tom Bristoe come in from outside, Mama Curry laid a big platter of chicken on the table together with biscuits an' gravy, grits an' collards, and we all fell in to eatin'. We was some hungry, an' conversation just didn't seem to be a part of takin' care of important business like that.

But at last when the plates had been cleared and the adults had got theirselves a refill of coffee, I looked over the table at Jamie. His eyes was puffy and I knew he was plumb wore to a frazzle after all he'd been through. Yet I'd a couple questions that I wasn't sure would keep till morning, and I was of a mind to ask 'em.

"I know you're tired, son, and it's a heap past your bedtime. But I got to know what you seen a couple days ago, if anything. You know when I mean?" I glanced at Eileen, who appeared just about to get her dander up and say something. The look in my eye must of made her think better of it though, 'cause after a second she just sat back in her chair, watchin' us.

The kid was studyin' the tablecloth in front of him, and he didn't say nothing for a long moment. At last he lifted up his eyes and looked at me.

"We was out by the spring house when the riders come," he said, speaking in a low, clear voice. "It was a little before suppertime and Mary an' me had gone out to fetch a jug of buttermilk for Aunt Mae. We was just startin' back when I seen 'em. They was six or eight, maybe. I didn't stop to count 'cause something about 'em told me they might be trouble. Instead I ducked back inside real quick, takin' Mary with me, and we pulled the door to." He glanced at his mother, then lowered his eyes.

"Pretty soon we heard Aunt Mae scream, an' there was shootin' inside the house. Half-dozen shots maybe, followed after a little bit by two more. I put my hand over Mary's mouth to keep her from cryin' out, and we got back behind some shelves an' sacking to hide." He paused again.

119

"Nothing happened then for a long time. I could still hear noises out in the yard though, so we stayed put where we was. Finally the door of the spring house opened and a man was there, standin' in the light lookin' in. He must of not been able to see us, cause after a couple seconds he called back over his shoulder, 'They ain't here, Rye.'

"'You sure?' another man asked. And then he was standin' in the doorway too. 'You be real sure about that, Red. They ain't in the stable nor any of the other buildings. They got to be around here somewheres.'

"He looked in too, but we was scrunched down makin' ourselves as small as we could, so he didn't see us neither. After a minute the second man said, 'All right, come on!' He kicked the door to, like he was real mad, and they walked away. After a few minutes longer all of 'em mounted up and rode off." Jamie looked at me.

"Reckon that was all I seen, Mr. Barkley. And all I heard too, 'cept one more thing. I heard that second man talkin' right after he'd shut the door to the spring house. And I ain't likely to forget that." The kid looked over at his ma and his sister, and I watched his fist clench up on the table in front of him.

"He said, 'We got to find those kids an' kill 'em. Right now. I don't mean to quit till there ain't a McClanahan alive this side of New Orleans!'"

For a second there Jamie looked like he might be gettin' ready to cry. But he shook his head and swallowed real hard, and then I saw a look come into those blue eyes

120

that would of made me feel right fearful if I'd been the one who said that, and he'd been a man growed.

"Mr. Barkley?" The kid was looking at me now. "Will you teach me how to shoot? I mean really shoot? I done a bit of huntin' with Uncle Ev and Joseph, squirrels an' birds an' such. An' they said I wasn't too bad. You s'pose you could teach me how to handle a pistol? And a rifle like that Winchester of yours?"

I met Eileen McClanahan's eyes for a quick moment, but I couldn't even begin to guess what she was thinkin'. "I might," I said carefully, "though you'd have to ask your ma about it first. Anyways," I went on, "I reckon it'd still be quite a spell before you was ready to tackle the kind of men you're talking about. Best let some others take a hand if there's anything like that needs doin' right away."

Jamie lowered his eyes. "I reckon you're right," he said. "But I got to do something." His voice trembled just a little bit. "I ain't been much help so far. Aunt Mae an' Uncle Everett . . . An' all I could do was hide out in the spring house, an' then take to the woods when them men was gone!"

"You done fine," I said. "You had your sister to think of. And besides, whenever you find out the deck's stacked against you like that, the most important thing to do is to stay alive. So's you can bring the war to them the next time around."

I paused and looked from one to another of the folks around the table. "Now, Jamie," I said after a moment, "I got to ask you one more thing. You saw the two men who was looking for you, standin' at the door of that spring house. Did you recognize either one of 'em? Had you ever seen those men before?"

"I knew 'em, Mr. Barkley. I knew 'em both." He looked over at his ma, then back at me.

"I seen that redheaded feller ridin' with the Caton bunch a couple times, whenever they come around our house back on the coast. And the other one, the man the redhead called 'Rye'? Why, that was Riley Caton himself. The one they call the Kid."

Well, there it was. What I'd more'n half suspected all along. I met Bristoe's eyes. Then I turned to Eileen. She was looking mighty grim.

"I reckon that explains why them riders was so all-fired set on locatin' the kids," Bristoe said, "sure enough. And why they felt they'd got to try and kill us too, before we'd had any chance to talk to 'em."

"Uh-huh," I agreed. "Story like Jamie's here'll blow this country wide open. Won't be no hole deep enough for them Catons to hide in once the word gets about."

The Ranger looked at me kind of funny over his coffee cup. "If it gets about," he said quietly. "'Pears to me the only ones who've heard it so far are sittin' right around this table."

Well now, that thought had been nagging at the back corners of my brain a little bit, but I hadn't yet brought it up front to where I could look at it. Tom Bristoe's words set it out in the open so's it was starin' me square in the face.

"You're right," I said. "Those boys got it to do. And tonight would be the only time, seein' as folks'll likely start comin' round for the funeral bright an' early tomorrow." I looked over at Mama Curry. "When's your mister due back?"

"He'd a meeting down to Spring Warrior this evening, or he'd be here already. I expect he's heading back right now. But it'll likely take him all night to make the trip. That's more'n thirty mile down there."

I glanced around the table. "Just us four then, plus the kids. And maybe a half a dozen Catons, if they haven't joined up with some others of their bunch." I looked at Eileen. "Reckon we could gather up everbody an' head for one of the neighbors . . ."

She thought for a second, then shook her head. "No, Mr. Barkley. It's a tempting idea, but no." I opened my mouth to speak, but Eileen McClanahan wasn't finished talking yet.

"I've no particular desire to rouse my neighbors in the middle of the night in any case," she went on, "just so they can face a possible attack by that pack of murdering scum. Yet for the children's sake I would do it." She paused. "Except for one thing which you seem to have overlooked. Those riders know this country, and even if they did not follow us — which I think likely — they would have every reason to know where we are now.

"There is an excellent chance they are outside at this very moment, watching and waiting for just such a move."

Well, I got to admit that give me pause. And the more I thought about it, the more I suspected the lady might be right.

"No," Eileen was saying, "I believe we are as safe in this house as we would be anywhere tonight. We are concealed, they must expose themselves in order to attack, and if we are prepared they have lost the advantage of surprise." She looked from me to Tom Bristoe and shrugged. "At least that is my opinion."

Bristoe nodded. "Makes sense to me ma'am," he said. "I'll admit I don't care much for the odds as things stand, but it sure beats chancin' a ambush out there in the dark."

Eileen smiled at him. "I might be wrong, of course. In that event we will not be disturbed, and the children will get some much-needed rest." She put a arm around the little girl and looked at Jamie, who was having a deal of trouble keeping his eyes open. "They are both quite exhausted, I'm afraid."

I agreed that the way she'd laid it out for us, it sure made sense to stay put for the night. But I wasn't so keen on just sittin' back and waitin' for other folks to start the ball neither. I watched Eileen and Mama Curry leave to put the kids to bed, an' then I turned to Bristoe.

"When you reckon they'd make their move?" I asked. "If they're out there, that is, an' if we sit tight like she says."

He thought for a moment. "Hour or so before dawn, maybe. When they'd figure us all to be asleep, or leastways when anybody on guard might be beginnin' to let his eyes droop a mite."

I nodded. "That'd be my thinkin'. Right now they'll be watchful in case we decided to leave out of here. But when we don't do it they'll most likely ease on back and set theirselves to waitin'." I got up and blew out the kerosene lamp on the table, then stepped to the side of the window and looked out. Everything was still and quiet in the moonlight.

"I got first watch," I said after a little bit. "Wake you up 'round two o'clock?"

"Okay." The Ranger didn't move to stand up right away. "You got somethin' in mind?" he asked quietly.

"Mebbe." I walked over to check the bar on the door, then come back and poured myself another cup of coffee. "Best tell them ladies to put out the lights up yonder. Won't help us none to have 'em, just make it easier for other folks to see in."

10 🌴

Bristoe rose and went to the front of the house whilst I pulled a chair around to rest my feet on. Then I sat down and settled in to listening to the night sounds.

Nights in Florida don't never get to be what most folks'd think of as quiet. But with a little bit of practice you can sort of teach yourself to shut out the ordinary sounds like frogs an' crickets an' such. After you've done that, anything out of the ordinary gets to be where it'll stand out right plain in your mind.

I didn't hear nothin' special for a right long spell. Little rustlin' in the brush here an' there that might of been a possum or a covey of bobwhites, or it might not have been. Heard a panther scream onct away off in the distance, and a wildcat a couple times closer by. An' one time I heard a horse blow from a direction that didn't seem to be exactly where I remembered the stable to be.

After while I laid my Dragoon up on the table and went to cleanin' my Winchester, makin' sure the action was smooth and she was fully loaded with seventeen .44's. Then with the cocked rifle across my knees, I went to work on the Colt, runnin' a rag through the barrel and wiping off each bullet real careful-like before reloading. 'Bout the time I'd finished doin' that, it was gettin' on towards two in the morning.

I rose an' made the rounds of the windows one more time. The moon was lower, and it was clouding up a mite. Right favorable for somebody to be making their move, maybe.

I went to get Bristoe.

"Nothin' much doing," I whispered as he strapped on his Colt and followed me into the kitchen. "But I've a idea they're out there. Little things, you know?"

"Uh-huh." He took hold of the coffee pot and poured himself a cup. Like me, Tom Bristoe put stock in the little things. Kept us both alive a time or two, here an' there around the country.

"Are the women asleep?" I asked.

"Far as I can tell." He took a swallow of coffee. "Can't be too sure about that McClanahan woman. She's right watchful."

"Reckon she'll do her share too," I said, "if it comes to a fight. Don't know about that preacher's wife."

127

"Well," Bristoe said, warming his hands on his coffee cup, "she's got herself a Police Five-Shot revolver in that reticule of hers. Acted like she knew what it was for, anyways."

We listened into the night for a while without saying anything. Then I glanced over at him. "Thought I might go for a little walk, take in a bit of the night air like. You reckon you can hold the fort?"

"I reckon." He looked over his coffee cup at me. "But you sure that's what you want to do? 'Pears to me that ain't no bunch of pilgrims out there. Some of them boys looked like they been up the creek and over the mountain."

"I been there myself," I said, "time or two. And it ain't in me to let them go choosin' their own time an' place. They done started this war agin children an' women. Now I mean to bring it back to them just a little bit."

I took off my spurs and laid 'em up on the kitchen table, together with my Winchester which might only get in my way if the work was close. Then I slid my Bowie knife from its sheath and held it in my hand whilst I eased the bolt out of its bracket on the back door. After listening for a good two minutes, I slipped through the door and into the night.

There was a big old magnolia tree standing right by the porch, keepin' that whole side of the house in deep shadow. I'd checked it ahead of time, planning my route in my mind before I ever woke Bristoe. Now I crossed the porch in two quick strides, eased myself to the ground under the railing, and hunkered down beside the bole of that tree to listen and study the yard and the side buildings.

I was hopin' most of them Caton men would be tryin' to catch a couple hours of sleep about now, leaving maybe one man on watch in the meantime. I let my gaze swing across the yard, using the corners of my eyes to see any movement that there might be. But after a few minutes of lookin', I was pretty well convinced there weren't nothing in sight.

Tryin' hard to keep a rein on the devil that was ridin' me to get out there and do unto those boys before they'd any chance to do unto me, I made myself count slowly to a hundred. Then with one more quick glance all around, I crossed a small open place to the shadow of a split-rail fence and moved along it till I was kneeling next to the stable building.

I could hear the horses inside stirrin' around a bit, but no more'n usual for this time of the night. After waitin' and listenin' a while longer to be sure, I decided there wasn't no Catons inside there, nor anywheres else close by that I could tell.

Maybe Eileen McClanahan had guessed wrong about what they'd had in mind after all. And maybe I'd let her words color my own thinkin' enough so's that all those little sounds I'd thought I heard earlier weren't no more'n just some part of my imagination. But as long as I was out here anyway, it only made sense to be real sure of that before headin' back in towards the house.

I stood up and flattened myself against the log wall

of the stable so's I could take a better look around. Off on my left was the chicken pen and the hen house, which I didn't want to go near and neither did nobody else who intended to keep the world in doubt about whether they was out in the night.

To my right the closest building was the smoke-house, maybe twenty yards from where I was and with a couple wax myrtle bushes an' tall weeds in between that offered a mite of cover. I decided to have me a look over thataways.

Now, maybe there weren't no Catons within fifty miles of this place, an' maybe they was a couple dozen of 'em hidin' right behind them bushes. Since I didn't know which it was, I figured I'd look a heap more foolish stumbling into a pack of 'em in the dark than trying to keep out of sight of some folks who wasn't there. I crossed the open space between the stable and them bushes on my belly, movin' just as slow an' careful as I was able.

Right about when I'd got into the shadow of the closest wax myrtle, I heard a sort of a muffled cough no more'n eight feet away. A minute later I saw the glow of a match cupped in somebody's hand as he lit a cigarette behind the smokehouse.

"Damn it, Len!" The voice was a harsh whisper, comin' from a few yards the other side of the man with the cigarette. "Put that out! You want the whole blamed world to know where we're at?"

"Aw, hell, Luke. I'm down behind this here shed out of sight. An' besides, ain't nobody . . ."

He didn't get to finish whatever it was he was saying, 'cause my Bowie sort of interrupted his train of thought. When I slid the knife into his belly he let out a shudderin' groan that I was only able to partly cover up with my hand over his mouth. I let him slump to the ground, and took a couple quick steps back around the other side of the smokehouse. Flattening myself there against the wall, I waited till I could locate the second man from the sound of his voice.

"Len? Len, what in the . . . ?" He paused then, and I could almost see in my mind's eye the look that was coming onto his face. "Pete! Sam!" he called out, maybe not so quiet as he'd had it in his mind to do. "Jake! Look sharp! I think we got company." A minute later he'd found his dying friend. "Aw hell, Len."

I stepped from behind the smokehouse to face him, with my Dragoon in my right hand and the Bowie in my left. There was a Colt in his fist too, but he had friends out here and I didn't. Took him a second to be sure who I was. And it was a second too long.

"Evenin'," I said as I drilled him through the brisket. I took a step to my right and fired again, then kept on movin'. It was a good thing I did, 'cause two bullets cut the air a second later right where I'd been standin'. I threw a shot at the closest muzzle flash, hit the ground, and rolled till I was maybe a dozen feet away.

When I got to my knees I heard the crack of a Winchester from the house and figured Tom Bristoe must of found hisself something to shoot at. Just had to hope that Ranger could see good enough to tell who was which out here.

He fired twice, and then it got almighty quiet all of a sudden. I stayed put where I was, listening. But there weren't nothing to hear. They was layin' low same as me, knowin' like I did that in a situation like this the first one to move is often the first one to die.

The place where I was kneeling was in amongst some tall weeds and a couple little hawthorn bushes, not what you'd call proper cover a-tall. It was a mighty uncomfortable feelin' to stay there, but the slightest move I made would stir up that brush an' leaves, turnin' me into the most popular target of the night. I forced myself to sit tight.

After what seemed like a long time but was prob'ly no more'n a few minutes, I heard a horse leave out of there like it had a fire under its tail. Few minutes later there was another one. I did a little calculatin'.

They'd been five men whose names I'd heard. Two of those was dead or goin' to be. Two more'd done just now rode off into the night. That left one for sure, an' maybe a couple others but maybe not. Surely weren't no more'n that. I decided to take a chance.

"Gettin' a mite lonely out there ain't it?" I called from my hiding place. "You real sure you want to see this through to the finish?" There was a shot, but I was already moving as I spoke.

"Damn you, Barkley! I'll see you in hell!" He fired again and I let fly at the flash, but he was movin' too. I

hit the ground and rolled over a couple times, bringin'
up against the split-rail fence around the corral. Another
bullet took a chunk out of the pine next to my head,
showering me with splinters. I swore.

I fired once at where I thought he might be, then
scrambled for the cover of a log water-trough a few feet
away. Layin' there on my belly, I fought to stop my chest
from heavin'. I was down to one bullet now, an' there
weren't no room behind that trough to turn about an' get
at the cartridges in my belt loops. One way or another,
this fight weren't goin' to last a whole lot longer.

When I'd finally got my breathing under control so's
I could listen to what was around me, what I heard made
the hair on the back of my neck stand straight up on end.
A boot had struck stone no more'n five feet from where
I was. That gent was just about a step away from standin'
over me with a pistol aimed square at my head.

Leastways, that's how I'd of done it if I'd been in his
shoes.

Time like that you don't think, you just do. My
shoulder was already up against that log trough, an' I
give her a mighty heave all of a sudden, with everthing
I had behind it. Which was considerable, since us
Barkleys got a reputation for pretty much movin' whatever it is that we take aholt of.

That gent sure wasn't expecting it. He yelped like a
coon dog when the log knocked against his shinbones,
and then he sat down hard on the ground.

Somehow he'd managed to hang onto his pistol, but

the surprise was enough to let me get in the first shot, and I put it where it mattered. He was game though, and would of still ventilated me if I hadn't stepped up to kick the gun out of his hand whilst he was tryin' to bring it to bear.

When I looked down at him in the moonlight, I saw it was that same gent who'd recognized me a few weeks back, sayin' he'd seen me out to the Tonto Basin.

"You give it a try," I said, startin' to reload my Colt. "I got to hand you that."

"Go to hell." He glared at me, then went to coughing up blood.

"Fightin' a man is some different from goin' after women an' kids, ain't it?" I glanced at him. "Sort of leaves a different taste in your mouth."

He turned his head an' spit, then looked up at me again. "I'll still see you in hell, Barkley. I watched you, an' I've watched that Kid. The Kid's a heap faster."

"Maybe."

"Just wish I could be here to see him do it to you." He went to coughing again. "Just wish . . ."

I spun the cylinder and dropped the Dragoon into its holster. The man on the ground was dead.

After looking all around me real careful and listenin' for a minute or two longer, I called out. "Hello the house! This is Barkley. I'm coming in!"

Eileen was there waitin' for me, together with Bristoe and the rest. But it was her I was lookin' at mostly. Her eyes was real big when I come through that back door, and it seemed like her face was some paler than usual, though it might of been only the light from the lantern in Mama Curry's hand.

She laid her shotgun aside and took a step forward, reachin' out her hands for a second there like she was going to put 'em up on my arms. Then she stopped herself and stepped back, wrapping her hands in her apron instead.

"Mr. Barkley," she said, her voice kind of low and husky. "Thank goodness you're all right. We thought perhaps . . ." She turned away. "It was a very foolish thing to do, Mr. Barkley. But I'm happy to see that you have come through it none the worse for wear." A minute later she went back into the bedroom with her kids and closed the door.

Well, I got to admit it was a right pleasant feelin' to know that Eileen McClanahan was worried about me. And I tried not to act too smug about it as I walked past Bristoe into the kitchen for some more coffee.

❖   ❖   ❖

Daylight come slow, with a heavy overcast and little spurts of rain at the dawnin'. A hour later she settled down into a solid drizzle. Just the kind of weather for a funeral, I thought. It'd been a day like this when they buried my mam.

Bristoe an' me'd already tended to a sort of unofficial funeral, soon's it got light enough to see good. We planted them men I'd killed back up in the woods, where the graves wouldn't call particular attention to theirselves. Tom even spoke a few words over 'em, as was the proper thing to do no matter what kind of men they'd been when alive.

We spent a little while after that lookin' to see if they was any more out there, for Bristoe had the notion he'd winged one with the Winchester. But all we found was a few spots of blood on some leaves, so we figured it must of been one of them two who'd rode out after things started getting a mite too warm for 'em.

'Bout the time we'd got back to the house the first guests was beginnin' to arrive to pay their respects to Ev and Mae McClanahan. They was well-liked folks, and near 'bout everbody in the neighborhood who could make it would be comin' to their funeral. Most would leave home at first light with their families in wagons and buckboards loaded down with pies an' cakes an' fried chicken and what-all, plannin' to make a day of it.

Before Eileen could get herself too busy with the greetin' and entertainin', we took her into one of the back bedrooms to hold a quick council of war. Upshot of it was that me an' Tom Bristoe wouldn't wait for the funeral, but would leave right off to try an' round up some local law. Bristoe would head for Live Oak after the sheriff of Suwannee County, where the McClanahans' homestead was and where the murders had been done.

Since that was some fifteen miles off, and since findin' a lawman right when you needed one was always a chancy thing, I'd go ahead an' cross the river to Troy, which was county seat of Lafayette County an' a good deal closer, meanin' to speak to the sheriff there. Between us we hoped we'd be able to round up some sort of a posse an' get back to the homestead before nightfall.

Eileen would spread the word here, but without tryin' to cause too big a stir till after the funeral was over. She figured her kids'd had it rough enough already, an' she wanted to be able to hold 'em off to theirselves a bit once the fireworks got started. If anything serious happened in the meantime, like the Catons showin' up in force or something, they'd try and make it over to the Currys' house near Luraville. As a last resort if worst come to worst, they figured to head on down to Eileen's place by the coast.

I let Bristoe go on out to saddle up his horse whilst I lingered in the kitchen over one last cup of coffee. It had been a couple days since I'd got anything like a good night's sleep, and I was beginnin' to feel the lack of it. But the way things was shapin' up, it seemed like sleep would just have to wait a while longer yet.

I could hear folks gatherin' and talkin' in the front of the house, where the bodies was laid out and Eileen an' Mama Curry was greetin' the guests. Just as well that I'd got places to go about now, I figured. I wasn't hardly dressed for the occasion in the first place, an' I'd never cared too much for funerals in the second. And in the third place, this here business with the Catons had got me so up on edge that I weren't feelin' none too sociable a-tall.

I finished my coffee and went out the door toward the stable.

11 ⚡

Just when I was startin' off acrost the yard, holdin' my head down against the rain, I almost run slap into that storekeeper Tinsley comin' from where he'd tied his buggy horses to a tree out back. Neither one of us was paying too close attention and I reckon we was both some surprised to meet the other like that. But I got the idea from the way he sidestepped real quick that he might of been just a tad more surprised than me.

"Mr. Barkley," he said, catching himself up and touchin' the brim of his hat. "Leaving already?" He smiled then, and it weren't the kind of smile I cared a awful lot for.

"Leavin' for now," I answered, meetin' his eyes. "I got a errand or two to run. Be back before nightfall, more'n likely."

He cocked his head to one side and looked me up an' down for a long minute. "Strange to be leaving right before the funeral. I should think you'd want to stay and pay your respects to the deceased."

"Ain't my kinfolks," I said. "Didn't even know 'em." He was startin' to get under my skin about then. What I did or didn't do was none of his danged business. "An' like I told you, I got these errands to run."

Tinsley smiled again, real cool an' haughty-like. "We should all have respect for the dead, Mr. Barkley. It's the natural and proper thing to do. 'There but for the grace of God go we,' you know." He paused and sort of shrugged. "Of course, I suppose if they are *important* errands . . ."

Well, I reckoned I'd had me just about enough of standin' here talkin' to this self-righteous dude in the pouring rain. So I tugged my hat down a mite and said maybe a little more'n what I'd meant to say at the start.

"Important enough. I got to go talk to the sheriff over to Troy about some killin's." Then I turned my back and walked on to the stable without givin' him a chance to answer.

When I'd saddled up the roan and we left out of there, they was maybe a dozen wagons an' buggies round the house and it looked like things was in full swing. I sure didn't envy Eileen none. Seemed to me buryin' kinfolks was hard enough to do without having to entertain half the countryside while you was at it.

But maybe that's just the way I looked at things,

bein' used to livin' alone and keepin' my own affairs private, an' all.

I turned the roan's head to the southwest and brought him up to a easy trot, pulling my slicker more tight where a few drops of rain was startin' to find their way down my neck. In another couple hours I'd be in Troy, warm an' dry and tellin' the story of the McClanahan murders to the law.

After that, maybe I'd be able to find someplace out of the rain and catch myself a few hours of sleep.

❖   ❖   ❖

The town of Troy, or New Troy as it was rightly called, didn't have no sheriff's office. Didn't have no courthouse neither. Didn't even have what most folks would recognize as a main street. What it did have was just a bunch of double-pen log houses scattered across a acre or so of them rolling sand ridges throwed up by the river's flooding, where everthing was all shaded over by big pine an' live oak trees.

Had a general store too, which sort of took the place of a courthouse, meetin' hall, and all-round news exchange. If you wanted to find somebody, or find out something, that's where you went. I went in there to ask after the sheriff.

"Ain't seen him in a day or two," the storekeeper said. He considered a moment, scratching around the bald spot on top of his head. "More like three-four days, come to think on it. Got him a little place he farms some five mile south of here." The wiry little man smiled and shrugged. "More'n likely that's where you'll find him."

Well, the prospect of ridin' another hour or more in this weather didn't appeal to me much, but I reckoned there weren't no help for it. That rain had been comin' down steady all mornin', and with that plus swimmin' the river not too long since I was plumb near chilled to the bone. After thanking the storekeeper and turning to go, I had me a thought.

"You got any whiskey?" I asked, turning back. "Or any kind of spirits a-tall hereabouts?"

He looked at me real hard for a moment. Then he glanced past me toward the open door and lowered his voice. "This here's a dry county, son. I don't sell the stuff. An' George our bootlegger don't generally make his rounds till sometime after dark." He jerked his head toward a pot on the stove. "Reckon coffee's the best I can do for you."

I went over and poured myself a cup. "Thanks," I said. "It'll help to take the chill off anyways." The coffee was strong and black, and after a couple swallows I was startin' to feel a mite more relaxed. I unbuttoned my slicker and leaned against the counter.

"How much for some of that cheese an' crackers?" I asked after a minute.

"Nickel." When I'd done fished the money out of my pocket he took the cover off the cheese an' cut a thick slice. "He'p yourself to crackers out'n that box at your feet." He watched me start eatin', then said, "Got some real fine canned oysters up from the Cedar Keys. Only

141

'nother quarter."

"Thanks," I said. "Better not. If I let you talk me into any more fancy food I'm going to have to pay you on account."

"On account?"

"On account of I ain't got no more'n a couple dollars to my name. An' I been savin' that for a rainy day." I nodded toward the door and then we both grinned at the old joke.

After a minute he walked to the stove and poured a cup of coffee for himself. "You from around these parts?" he asked, taking a sip.

"Used to be. Grew up over Taylor County way. But this here's my first trip back in quite a spell." I didn't offer my name, and I reckon he couldn't help noticin' it. He studied me for a long while.

"Any kin to the Catons?" he asked at last.

"No kin." I looked over at him. "And no friend neither, if it makes a difference to you."

He glanced at the door and took another swallow of coffee. "It does," he said quietly. "There's a few folks in these parts that'd just soon be shut of their kind now an' for good." He met my eyes. "But for the time bein', we got to be sort of careful who we go mentionin' it to."

I nodded. "I hear that." There was a moment while we both listened to the rain outside. "But maybe," I went on slowly, "after I've got a chance to talk to your sheriff, there could be a little difference of opinion about things."

The storekeeper looked at me. "Sheriff Deal's a good

man," he said. "But he's a politician too. And Bill Caton's been right careful not to stir up trouble with the locals hereabouts. It'd take something pretty serious to change some people's minds about the way he's been handling things."

"Maybe," I said, "I got some right serious matters to speak about."

I decided to leave it at that, not wanting to start no loose talk that couldn't be backed up with witnesses when the time was right. After another cup of coffee and some general discussion of the weather an' such, I buttoned up my slicker and made ready to go on back out in the rain.

The storekeeper followed me to the door. "If you're still of a mind to have that drink you was talking about," he said with a sly wink, "there's a sort of a blind tiger a couple miles down south an' back off the road a bit. This fella's got him a lard-can still or two up in the woods there, and he's been known to share a drop of the corn with neighbor folks. If there's any questions about it, you just tell him I sent you."

"Thanks," I said. "I might do that."

Then he reached out and handed me something. It was a tin of them Cedar Keys oysters. "You pay me whenever you're able," he said. "On account of I got the feeling you're a man who'll do what he says he will."

I'd been riding south for less than a hour when I heard a sound of men's voices, seemin' to come from a thick stand of pine and palmetto a hundred yards or so off the road to my left. This was about where the storekeeper had told me I might find that moonshiner he'd spoke of, and I decided I might's well stop off and have me a little look-see. It was the chance for information which appealed to me right then, 'bout as much as the chance for a drink.

When I got closer the voices grew louder and I could see the glow of a fire from somewheres back in the brush. I dismounted a good fifty yards off, tying ole roan under a cedar tree where he'd have a mite of protection from the rain. Then I slipped my Winchester out of its boot and approached the voices.

"Hello the fire!" I called when I was maybe thirty yards away. "Would it be all right for a man to come in?"

"What you want here?" a deep booming voice answered. "You got business with us?"

"Man back at the store in Troy said a fellow might wet his whistle somewhere hereabouts. I thought this might be the place."

There was a moment's pause. Then the voice said, "Come on in. But come careful!"

I walked through the trees into a little clearing, and saw that the fire was burning in a large metal can under a open-sided lean-to thatched over with palmetto leaves. They was a half dozen men gathered around it, passin' a clay jug.

All of 'em looked me over pretty careful when I come in, but I just acted like I didn't notice it. After a moment a big gent in a slouch hat and a growth of black beard all round his face took the jug from one of his neighbors and handed it up to me. I put her over my shoulder and took a swallow. Then when I'd caught my breath again, I took another.

"That's some real fine whiskey," I said, handing the jug back and blinking a couple tears out of my eyes. "Warms a body right down to the bone."

"My own make," the bearded man said with pride. "An' not a bad batch if I do say so." He took a swig and passed the jug on. "If you like it, I'll take a quarter. Let you know when you've drunk that up."

Well, a quarter was a mite steep seeing as I didn't figure to be stickin' round here long enough to get my full money's worth. But I was a stranger, and that gent didn't look like the type who'd extend credit even to his friends. So I kept my mouth shut an' reached down into my jeans.

"I got that one, Zeb. Just put it down to my account."

I looked over to see who the speaker was. He hadn't been there when I'd come in. Now he was standin' across the fire from me on the far side of the lean-to, lookin' even bigger than I remembered. Our eyes met and we studied each other for a long moment.

"Howdy, Bill," I said at last. "Long time no see."

"Uh huh." Bill Caton reached for the jug and took himself a swallow. "But I been hearing things about you, boy. You done stirred up a heap of trouble in the couple weeks you been back in this country. Cost me three, four good men."

An' a few more he didn't know about, evidently. But

I couldn't see no point in bringin' that up right at the moment.

I noticed he was wearing a black broadcloth suit which made him look a good bit more respectable than I remembered from the old days. But there was still that look in Bill Caton's eyes to tell me he hadn't changed all that much inside. He'd still kill a man right quick if he saw something to be gained from it, and I figured I needed to be right careful here so's not to give him no better reason than what he already had.

"They come lookin' for it, Bill," I said quietly, "and they found it. You know I ain't never been much of a one for shyin' away from a fight."

"I know that, Barkley. Better'n most I reckon. Just wish we'd had us a chance to talk before all that got started."

Well, I don't know what I'd expected when I finally got the chance to meet up with Big Bill Caton, but this surely weren't it. I was startin' to get plumb curious to know what was on his mind. "You're talkin' now," I said, looking across the fire at him.

He jerked his head to indicate a stump back out of the way at one corner of the lean-to, so I walked over there and hunkered down whilst he come around to take a seat on the stump.

"You know, Tate," he said, speaking low so's the others couldn't hear him, "I got me a prime organization here. Prime. Liquor, gamblin', smugglin', ever way you can think to make a dollar in this country. What little law there is hereabouts I've managed to buy off, or else keep buffaloed.

"I got this Big Bend country by the tail, boy. And right now the political climate is a-changing, so I got me a few plans thataway too. You know Reconstruction's about done for. Pretty soon folks'll be lookin' for locals to take things over again. And I mean to be one of 'em." Bill Caton glanced up at them gents around the fire. Then he leaned forward on his elbows and met my eyes.

"What I need now more'n anything," he said, "is a few of the right kind of men to back me. Men who're tough enough to stand the gaff, but who can still keep their wits about 'em when they need to." He glanced over his shoulder again and lowered his voice even more.

"I got to get shut of some of that bunch been with me up till now. And I got to do it soon. One of them lame-brains is liable to up an' get me into some kind of a fix that the voters wouldn't forgive." Then he grinned at me. "Local boy like you wouldn't be such a bad choice neither, just politically speakin' that is."

He watched me awful close after he'd finished talking, but I still didn't say nothin' right away. Didn't know what to say, to tell the truth. I knowed from the git-go that I wasn't about to hook up with no Catons, no how. But the way I chose to explain that to Big Bill here could have a whole lot to do with whether I left this little clearing in the woods alive or dead.

Also, I was startin' to have me some different ideas now about who might be responsible for them McClanahan murders, an' for the attacks on us and the kids afterwards. It wasn't that Bill Caton couldn't of done it, or wouldn't of done it if he thought he had a reason. But from what he'd just said, it sounded to me like that there would be one of the last things in the world he'd want to get hisself involved in at the moment. Just wouldn't of made no sense, 'politically speakin'.'

When I looked up to meet his eyes, he was still sittin' on that stump, leanin' on his elbows studying me. After a moment I shook my head kind of regretful-like and grinned at him.

"Bill, I got to tell you that's a real tempting offer. And I'm flattered that you'd think of me. But I ain't plannin' to stay around these parts more'n another week on the outside. I just come back here to settle up on the folks' estate an' all. Then I got some mighty important business waitin' for me back Arizona-way."

Well, I was lying in my teeth right now. Or at least I was doing some pretty serious embroiderin' on the truth. But I didn't want Bill Caton to think I'd turn him down flat for no better reason than I just didn't care for him and his family. Might of been the truth, but I figured it wouldn't of been altogether healthy to say it right there an' then.

He sat looking at me for another long moment. Then he put his hands on his knees and stood up.

"All right, Tate. If you say you got to move on I'll take you at your word. We'll call a truce for a week so's you can get your business took care of, an' then you can leave.

"But Tate. . ." he looked me in the eye real hard. "You mind I said a week. If I or my boys see you after that time I'm going to figure you lied to me. Then I reckon I wouldn't have no choice a-tall but to tell ever one of 'em it'd be okay to shoot you on sight."

He grinned real wide, and then walked over to get the jug from one of the men by the fire. After taking a deep pull, he handed it to me.

"Might's well have one more for the road, Barkley. Zeb here's already got me down for a quarter on account of you. I'd like to see us get just a little bit of our money's worth back."

I thanked him, and managed to choke down one more swallow of that liquid fire. Then with a parting wave of my hand, I stepped out into the rain and walked through the woods to where I'd tied my horse.

My hand wasn't quite as steady as I'd have liked it to be when I shoved my Winchester back into the boot.

"I don't know if you realize it, boy," I said as I climbed up onto the roan. "But it was a right near thing there between me comin' back here today, and you findin' yourself with a brand new owner."

Ole roan just snorted and tossed his head, not givin' me the satisfaction of knowing which one of those he thought was the better idea. Then I turned his nose to the south and we took off out of that place at a steady distance-eatin' trot.

12 🌿

I FIGURED IT WAS A MITE PAST NOON when I rode up through some corn and tobacco fields to that log farmhouse where I was hopin' to speak to the sheriff of Lafayette County. The rain was beginnin' to let up a little bit now, and I could see a couple kids out playing in some mud puddles beside the barn. When I got close to the house a woman stood up from a table on the porch where she'd been shellin' peas and watched me as I drew rein at the front gate.

"Mrs. Deal?" I said. "Is your husband to home?"

"Who wants to know?" She was a young woman, comely enough in a unvarnished sort of way. But like many another in these parts, her eyes was some deeper than they needed to be on account of the daily cares of frontier living. I knew it weren't no accident there was a rifle leanin' up against the wall right next to the table where she'd been working.

"My name's Tate Barkley, ma'am. I need to speak with the sheriff on a official matter."

"He ain't here. Had to ride down towards Old Town yesterday morning to look into a shootin'. Expect him home tonight, maybe."

Well, if it'd been only me an' ole roan without no lady present, I might of found me some choice words to say just about then. It looked like I'd had a long, wet mornin's ride for nothing. An' that on top of a night without no sleep.

Her "tonight, maybe" meant just what it said and no more. Weren't never any way to tell what would happen when a man set out ridin' in this country. Sheriff Deal might be home this evenin', or he might be home tomorrow or the next day, or he might not come home at all. His woman knew it too. That was one of the reasons for them dark circles around her eyes.

"All right, ma'am," I said after a moment. "I'll try and see him later on. Sorry to have bothered you."

"No bother. Stop by whenever you're in the neighborhood." She didn't invite me in, and I didn't expect it. Folks in this country was hospitable but they wasn't no fools. Hospitality to strangers come a whole sight easier when there was a man about the house.

I turned the roan's head around and started to ride out. When I glanced back over my shoulder the sheriff's wife had gone back to shelling peas, her rifle no more'n six inches from her hand.

On the way back to Troy I made it a point to give that moonshiner's camp a wide berth, ridin' off in the woods for a good long distance before comin' back onto the road. I figured maybe Bill Caton's talk of truce would stand, an' maybe it wouldn't. But either way I couldn't see nothin' to be gained by meetin' up with him again real soon.

When we was a mile or so from the town, I reached down to give ole roan's neck a pat. He was bein' uncommon tolerant, considerin' the circumstances.

"I don't know about you, boy," I said, "but I'm startin' to feel plumb tuckered. What would you say to a little rest before we swim back across that river?"

It made me feel a shade guilty to be thinkin' about a nap just now, what with Eileen up at that farmhouse and enemies all over the country. But for the time being she wasn't alone, an' there was reason to hope that Tom Bristoe had had some better luck than me in rounding up a posse. If I slept for a couple hours I'd still have time to get back there before nightfall.

A little farther on I saw a old abandoned house an' barn that looked like it might be just the spot. Both buildings sat back from the road a good ways, with the yard all growed up to weeds in front and thick pine woods comin' right up to the back door. Looked like nobody hadn't lived there or even visited the place for several years.

I stayed in the saddle and studied on the situation for a few minutes, making sure there weren't nobody else around and that the place was just as deserted as it looked. Then I got down and led the roan through the woods in a wide circle until we come up to the back door of the barn. It was off the hinges, so we went on inside and made ourselves to home.

What with being careful not to trample down no grass out in front and staying shut of the house itself, I figured we was as likely not to be disturbed here as anyplace I could have found. There was even a bit of hay left inside there for the roan to eat. When I'd pulled the saddle off and rubbed him down a mite, I dug a hole in the dirt floor for my hips, spread a little of the hay on top of it, and stretched myself out to catch forty winks.

❖   ❖   ❖

I woke up with the cold barrel of a rifle pressed against my forehead and a angry voice ringing in my ears:

"Get up, damn you! Get on your feet and get out there in the light where we can see you!"

Without thinking, I reached out a hand to take hold of the Winchester that I'd put next to me before going to sleep. But it was gone. A instant later a heavy boot come crashing down, grinding my fingers into the dirt. I howled with pain.

"I said get up, you murderin' scum! Or by God I'll shoot you where you lay!"

I rolled over an' started to get up, but as soon as my head come off the ground another boot caught me square under the jaw and knocked me flat. Little spots of light was dancin' in front of my eyes now, and I was beginnin' to get mad.

I come off the ground with a roar, meanin' to tear somebody's meat house down an' I didn't much care whose. But four men grabbed me and held me while the one with the rifle laid my cheekbone open with the butt. Then he kicked me in the stomach for good measure.

"Get him out of here before I waste a bullet on his sorry carcass. A rope and a tree's all his kind is good for." As they started draggin' me towards the door I shook my head and looked around. These wasn't Catons. They appeared to be more like farmers an' townsfolk.

"What the hell is all this about?" I managed to yell as they brought me out into the light.

"It's about hangin' a murdering skunk," one of the men who held my arms said. "'S if you didn't know!"

"I ain't no murderer. I never killed no man what didn't have him a gun and a fair chance!"

"No *man*, maybe!" The gent with the rifle swung the butt into my stomach and I doubled over. "But how about a *woman*?"

I fought for breath. "A woman!" I felt a cold chill comin' over me, right down to my toes. "I never hurt no woman. Who the blazes is it that you think I murdered?"

"Mae McClanahan, and her husband Everett. Two of the finest people who ever walked this earth. And now we're going to watch you swing for it!"

When they got me outside I seen there was six of

'em in all: the man with the rifle, the four hangin' onto me, an' another gent out by the trees who was holdin' the horses. I looked around at their faces an' couldn't find a ounce of sympathy nor doubt about what they meant to do in a single one of 'em.

Didn't reckon I'd blame 'em none neither, if they thought I really done what they said. I'd of felt the same way myself about a man who murdered a woman and her husband in cold blood like that. Only trouble of it was, it weren't me who done it.

Without wasting no more words they all started manhandling me back into the woods where there was a couple of good-sized live oak trees. I saw the man with the horses tie 'em to some shrubs, and then he grabbed a rope from the saddle of one, and come along after us.

You can bet I was fightin' every step of the way, but it just wasn't doin' me no good. Only thing it did was catch me a few more blows to the body and face with that rifle butt, until I was feeling sort of groggy and weak all over.

When they'd got me under the nearest tree they threw me to the ground and a couple of them gents tied my hands behind me so tight that I couldn't hardly wiggle my fingers. They'd already got my guns an' my knife, and now they started going through my pockets to make sure I didn't have no hide-out on me anywhere. When one of 'em took the cigarette makings from my shirt, I had a thought to buy myself a few more seconds of living anyhow.

"How about a smoke?" I said. "You wouldn't deny a man a last smoke, would you?"

Well I'd a idea the gent with the rifle would of done just that, but the fellow next to me rolled one, lit it, and stuck it in my mouth. Then he put the makings in his own pocket.

"Don't see so much store-bought in these parts," he said with a grin. "Reckon you won't be needin' the rest of this anyways."

I took a couple puffs while I watched one of his friends toss the rope over a limb and begin makin' a noose. When it was ready they slapped the cigarette away an' laid the noose over my neck. Then the man with the rifle held it pointed at my belly whilst the others lifted me up to my feet.

They started a-pullin' on that rope, but like I said I'm a big man, and they was making a real rough go of gettin' me off the ground. I was chokin' and stranglin', but still not making it no easier for 'em than I had to. And at last they let me back down to the ground an' sort of took a rest whilst one of 'em walked over toward where the horses was tied. The man with the rifle spoke to me.

"I reckon it ain't no sense gettin' ourselves all tired out and wore out over the likes of you. Puttin' a horse to that rope'll prob'ly break your neck an' make the end easier on you too. Don't much matter how we do it, just as long as we stretch your neck."

Well, I'd of liked to of told him that it mattered a heap to me. But I was having a deal of trouble catchin' my breath right then, let alone talking.

The gent who'd gone after the horse took a mite longer about it than I'd of expected, which was all right with me. And when he come back he weren't alone.

"What you boys fixing to do here? Don't you know we got laws in this county?" I thought I knew that voice, and when I'd twisted around so's I could get a glimpse of the speaker I recognized the storekeeper I'd talked to earlier that morning. He had a shotgun cradled in the crook of his arm, and was standin' a little apart from the others.

"Ain't no sense wastin' time with no judge and jury here, Dan." The man with the rifle was talking. "We got us a murderer, and we got us a rope and a tree. Seems to me they'll do the job just fine."

"That ain't no proper way to do things, Ira. We've had enough of it this past ten years, and it's about time we started doin' things legal. If this man's guilty of murderin' them folks . . ." He walked around to where he could take a look at me, and it wasn't a real friendly look. ". . . I reckon we can wait a week or so to give him a fair trial, before we hang him."

"I ain't got no time for all that foolishness." The man called Ira was startin' to get a little red around the ears. "I mean to see him hang, and I mean to see him hang now!" He stepped back to face the storekeeper. "If you don't want to watch or help out, Dan, then why don't you just go on back down to the store an' count your cans an' bottles?"

The storekeeper's shotgun had lifted up a mite,

almost as if by accident. It was covering the man with the rifle now, and takin' in a couple of them other gents at the same time.

"Can't do it, Ira. You know Ned Deal made me deputy awhile back, to act in his absence. Well, he's absent now and I'm callin' the tune. I say we take this man and lock him in my storehouse until we can either arrange for a trial here, or ship him on up to Suwannee County for one."

There was a long moment while the two men stared hard at one another, with me sittin' right in the middle if any shootin' should get started between 'em. But then the man named Ira turned on his heel and stalked off towards the horses.

"All right, Dan," he said over his shoulder. "You go on ahead and do whatever you damned please!" He was still muttering to hisself as he untied his horse, climbed into the saddle and rode off through the woods.

Two of the others followed him, but the remaining three seemed agreeable enough to the storekeeper's idea. They got me on my feet and led me back to the barn. When they'd saddled the roan, they put me up on him with my hands still tied, and we started out for town.

Dan the storekeeper rode behind, his shotgun ready, until we come in amongst the houses by the river. Then he went and led us back of the store to a little building he used to keep odds an' ends in. It weren't no bigger'n six feet on a side and six feet high, built solid out of cypress logs without no windows. When we pulled up in front of it a couple of the men tipped me off my horse, bein' none too gentle about it, and Dan spoke to his companions.

"If you boys would take them couple of sacks and kegs out of there and set 'em up on the porch I'd be obliged. I'll watch this gent in the meantime." Whilst they started moving the goods out of the shed, he leaned up with his back against a tree and studied me without much pleasure.

"I reckon I had the wrong idea about you this morning, son. Guess I'd ought to have better sense than to trust any kind of strangers I meet in this country any more." He spat on the ground. "If there's one thing around here worse than that Caton bunch, I just expect you're it!"

I wanted to tell him he had the wrong man, that if he'd just talk to Jamie McClanahan and his ma, and Tom Bristoe, they'd explain the whole thing. They'd tell him it was Caton men an' that Kid Riley who done the murders, not me. And we'd ought to be gettin' after 'em right away, before they'd had a chance to do any more harm.

But that rope had crushed up against my voice box an' I still couldn't hardly speak, except to shake my head and sort of whisper: "Not . . . me. Wrong . . . man."

Dan looked at me almost pityingly then, but he kept his shotgun right steady on my chest while he did it. "You can't expect us to believe that, not with the word that come across the river this mornin'." He met my eyes.

"Don't get no wrong ideas about me savin' you from that necktie party back there. I believe in hangin' murderers same as those others do, only I believe in doin' it legal. From what I heard, there's going to be a-plenty of evidence for that when the time comes."

The men had finished moving out what supplies an' tools was in the shed, and now they took out the pieces of wood that those things had been settin' up on too. When they untied my hands and threw me into that place there weren't nothin' inside but a bare dirt floor. I only had me one quick look at it before the heavy door slammed shut and I was alone in the dark.

For a little while I just sat there rubbing my wrists to try an' get some circulation back into my hands, sort of takin' stock of my situation here. I was some bruised an' cut up from the beating I'd took, and I thought I might have a rib or two busted as well.

My neck was skinned something fierce from that rope a-pulling on it, and my wrists was pretty raw too. The hand that had been stomped on was beginnin' to swell up now, but near as I could tell it wasn't broke. Weren't nothing about me that wouldn't heal, given time.

What worried me more was the thought that some-how or another these folks seemed to have it awful powerful strong in their heads that I was the murderer of Ev and Mae McClanahan. I couldn't guess what kind of evidence they imagined they'd got for such a thing, but ole Dan the storekeeper sounded like whatever it was, it was mighty convincing to them.

And that made me even more worried about Eileen and the kids, because I could be pretty sure if they was around to tell their story wouldn't nobody be so awful certain I'd done the killings. Something must of happened to keep 'em from talking, and whatever that something was it didn't shape up to be too pleasant.

After studyin' on that for a while, I finally come to the conclusion there wasn't no way I was going to be able to unravel the mystery of what-all had happened by just sittin' here inside this log pen. That's when I begin to give some serious consideration to how I might get shut of this place. I had to admit it didn't look too promising at first glance.

I remembered the matches I'd had in my shirt pocket, and how one of them gents back there had kept 'em together with my other cigarette makings. Looked like whatever it was I chose to do would have to be done in the dark, too.

After a moment I started checkin' the door, running the fingers of my good hand over and around the edges, where I could see tiny bits of daylight peepin' through, an' then testing it by pushing my feet up against it. But that door was a single slab of cypress more'n a inch thick, and there weren't hardly no give to it a-tall. The hinges was iron and seemed to be set solid into the frame, and anyways I knew that on the other side it was being held in place by two heavy log bolts as well as a padlock.

When I stood up to start explorin' the log walls and their tops where the roof was attached, I felt a sharp pain

161

in my side that made me stop and close my eyes, just breathing shallow and easy for several long minutes. That's when I was real sure I had me some busted ribs.

After a while I managed to get my shirt off, rip it up into strips, and bind the pieces round me to hold everthing in place. It wasn't a easy job considerin' my condition, and when I'd finished I had to rest again for a spell.

At last I got myself up and started goin' over the walls, moving a mite slower and more careful this time.

Them walls was solid as could be all around, which didn't surprise me none since cypress ain't especially given to wet rot. The roof was made out of pine shingles, nailed to cypress rafters set into notches in the top row of the logs. I couldn't find no give there either to speak of, except at one corner where there was maybe a quarter inch of play in two of the shingles — not hardly enough to give me even false hope under the circumstances.

Bein' so high off the ground and with nothing to stand on, I wouldn't of had much chance of moving 'em even without a couple broke ribs.

13 🌿

WELL, THAT PRETTY MUCH LEFT THE FLOOR. When I'd got down on my knees and started feelin' 'round, I could tell the dirt here was a mixture of sand and clay, and that it'd been pounded down with the end of a log till it was smooth and near hard as rock. I might could dig myself out in time, but it wouldn't be no easy task, an' me with only one good hand.

Startin' at one corner of the door I began to feel along the bottom of the walls where they met up with the floor. There wasn't even a hairline of a opening anyplace that I could tell, an' when I'd got halfway round I decided I might's well stop and give myself a breather. It was gettin' hot in that little wood box now, and the sweat was runnin' into my eyes and down into the cuts on my face and neck. I took out my kerchief and tried to dab at them places a bit, but pretty soon the cloth was soaked through, and I had to give it up.

Reckon I don't mind admittin' that I was beginning to get just a little bit discouraged about now. I didn't much feature waitin' here till they'd got a trial together, because I'd already met six of the men who'd likely sit on the jury an' they wasn't exactly what you'd call sympathetic to my case. I didn't imagine nobody else in these parts would be neither, unless Eileen an' Jamie showed up somehow an' spoke their piece.

But they didn't know I was here, and even if I'd had a idea where they'd got to I didn't have no way of sendin' word to 'em. They might not of been believed anyhow. Jamie was just a kid, and Eileen didn't really know nothing of her ownself, not first hand.

Besides that I was a stranger here, and a feller back in Arizona once told me I'd a sort of a hangin' look about me, which weren't likely to inspire too much confidence in a jury.

Nope, it wasn't in me to chance a trial, even assuming the locals here was of a mind to wait that long. And I'd reason enough to suspect that some of 'em, like that Ira gent, might not be willin' to wait much past sundown before tryin' to offer me another suspended sentence.

I started in again to feelin' round the floor from where I'd left off last time, not expecting to find nothin' but still hoping for some small advantage. I meant to start trying to dig myself out of here anyways, soon as I'd finished makin' the rounds. It was a awful long shot, but I needed to do something to keep myself busy.

Suddenly my hand run up against a low mound, back by the far corner and maybe a foot away from the wall. It felt like earth, though it might of been just some spilled flour or corn meal from one of the storekeeper's sacks. I let my fingers slide over it, checking out the size and feel. A minute later I found the hole.

I knew what it was right away. Some time in the past a ole gopher turtle had dug hisself into this shack from the outside an' left his sign. More'n likely it was hid behind some barrels or sacks or somethin', and got missed by them men in their hurry to move everthing out to make room for me. It would sure be a help to my tunnellin' plans, since all I'd got to do now was work on that gopher hole an' make it big enough for a man to squeeze through.

But I had me a couple subjects to ponder on before I started right in to digging. For one thing it was gettin' towards the supper hour, and if folks here meant to feed me there'd prob'ly be somebody comin' along 'most any time now. A small hole was easier to hide than a big one, so I took off my hat and tossed it kind of casual over the place, where nobody'd be liable to notice it unless they was lookin' real sharp.

Then I sat down to consider on the more serious matter: the hole itself.

See, gopher turtles dig lots of holes. A few they live in, but most they don't. And a abandoned gopher hole looks awful appealing to some other kinds of critters who'd like theirselves a ready-made homestead. Two of the commonest is rattlesnakes an' moccasins.

I'd just got to mullin' this over when there was a sound outside and I heard the bolts bein' slid back. A minute later a key rattled in the lock and the door opened. I had to blink my eyes from the sudden light, but then I saw Dan standing in the opening with a lunch bucket in one hand and a pistol in the other.

"Reckon we ain't going to let no man starve whilst he's a-waitin' for his trial and his hangin'." He set the bucket down and pushed it toward me with his foot, keepin' the pistol leveled at me the whole time.

"Hope you don't mind me stayin' here while you eat," Dan went on, settin' himself down on a log just outside the door. He glanced at me kind of sharp. "That's a dirt floor in there, and I'd as soon make sure I get all of them u-tensils back right after you're done."

"No trouble." I grinned at him. My voice was coming back a mite, though it still weren't much above a whisper. "Nice to have some company for a change." When I pulled the bucket towards me and took off the lid I saw that it was rice an' black-eyed peas, with a little bit of hog meat throwed in. It smelled right good.

"Hoppin' John and hog jowl," I said, taking a bite. "Means good luck all year-round."

Dan looked at me. "I wouldn't be countin' on that too much if I was in your shoes," he said grimly. "You'll be doin' right good to make it as far as a trial, the way talk is around the settlement."

I took another bite. "Those boys still plannin' on a necktie social, are they?" After a moment I met his eyes. "What would be your part in that affair, if it was to come about?"

"Reckon I'll try and uphold the law." The store-keeper paused, then went on. "Sheriff Deal's still down-country somewheres, and there ain't nobody else who'd even say a word to keep 'em off of you. So I expect it's up to me."

I took another bite, not looking at him. "You s'pose I'm worth it?"

Dan spat on the ground. "Hell, no, you ain't worth it! You ain't worth it a bit! If it was just you I'd let you swing. I ain't doin' this for you, I'm doin' it for the law. It's the law that's worth it!"

"Uh huh." I kept on eatin', still avoidin' his eyes. "Well, I'm grateful for the thought anyhow. 'Cause you got you a innocent man here. And maybe, if there was a trial, I might even find some way to prove it." The storekeeper looked at me hard, but he didn't say anything.

"Trouble of it is," I went on, "I don't imagine you got yourself much more of a chance than I got in this deal. Except you got a choice." I handed the lunch bucket back. "You might consider on that some. I wouldn't think the less of you for it."

Dan took the bucket and got up from his log. "Damn it, Barkley . . ."

My head jerked up. "How'd you know my name? I don't recall tellin' it to you, or to anybody else this side of the river."

The other man shrugged. "Them fellers who brought the evidence against you, I reckon. Seems like they mentioned your name right off soon as they got here."

I met his eyes. "What fellers?" I asked slowly.

"Why that mercantile man from over across the river, Mr. Tinsley. And a big red-haired fellow with a bandage on his head, and Riley Caton. All three seen you up by the McClanahan place the night of the killin's, an' the redhead says you shot at him for just askin' what you was doing in the area." He studied me for a moment.

"Riley's word maybe don't mean too much sometimes, an' I don't recollect seein' that redhead before, though he says he's a neighbor of the McClanahans. But Mr. Tinsley now, he's a respected gent in these parts. Everbody knows him, and whatever he says is gospel. If he seen you, that's good enough for me. And it's good enough for anybody else in this Suwannee country too!"

Dan the storekeeper looked like he was getting right tired of explaining things to me all of a sudden. He was reaching to close the door when I asked him one last question.

"Them gents who say they seen me over by the McClanahan place that night of the killin's? Are they still about?"

"You bet they're still here. They're down to my store right now, standin' the whole town to drinks."

He was swinging the door shut as I called out, "Thought you didn't sell the stuff!"

"I don't." One bolt fell in place. "Didn't say folks couldn't drink it if it was brought in by somebody else." I heard the second bolt drop. "An' I just may be wantin' a taste myself about now!"

The key turned in the padlock and I was alone.

That little conversation sure give me some things to think on. But I'd the idea I wasn't going to have near as much time for thinkin' about 'em as I'd like to. Them boys out in the woods this afternoon had all been sober as judges when they'd first let theirselves be talked out of a lynching. Tonight would be a different story. Tinsley an' the Catons would see to that.

Weren't no doubt about what they meant to do, gettin' the whole town fired up with all their talk of "evidence," an' the corn liquor they'd brought with 'em. Weren't no doubt that Tinsley was in this all the way up to his starched collar neither, though I'd no idea what he hoped to gain by it. It was pretty clear they all had it in mind for me not to see another sunrise. And I reckoned they just might have the hosses to do it.

I'd prob'ly got two, three hours till they was all good an' liquored up, maybe a mite longer if they waited till the womenfolks had gone to bed. Dan might slow 'em down another hair with talk an' threats if he was of the mind, but if he decided to make a fight of it I didn't figure he'd last ten minutes. And for his sake, I sort of hoped he wouldn't try.

Well, I knew what I had to do. I had to tunnel out of here right quick, or at least try. And I knew what I had to do about the chance of a snake in that hole too, though I didn't care to think about it even a little bit. The idea'd come to me during my conversation with Dan, and it was a long shot if ever there was one. But it was the only idea I'd been able to come up with, and there weren't no time to think of something else.

I took myself a deep breath, or deep as I could manage with my ribs like they was. And then I sat down on the floor and started pullin' off my boots and my jeans.

'Course if there wasn't no snake in that hole I'd of got myself all indecent for no reason, and I might feel pretty foolish about it in the morning. But that wouldn't be nothin' to how I'd feel if I stuck a hand down in there an' come up with fang marks from my wrist to my elbow. I was going to play it as safe as I could. Which weren't none too safe at all, whenever I let myself think about it.

First I wrapped up my swollen right hand in the jeans material, taking as many folds around it as I could manage yet still leavin' a big ball at the front which I held onto tight with my fingertips. I mean it hurt more than a little to do that, but there weren't no way I could let go if I meant for my plan to work and for me to keep breathin'.

Next I took a boot in my other hand and crawled over to that hole. Shovin' my hat aside, I stuck the boot toe down as far as she would go. That was to test the waters, like.

And she come up right salty!

I heard the buzz of rattles an' something struck my boot once, and then again before I finally managed to pull her out. Without pausing I shoved my right hand down into the hole as soon as the boot cleared. When I felt the rattler strike at the ball of material I yanked her out and grabbed aholt of that critter right behind the head.

Or where I thought it was in the dark. And that night I reckon I was just plumb luckier than any man has a right to be. Pullin' the head loose from the fabric, I got hold of the tail with my bum hand, lettin' out a yelp of pain in spite of myself whenever I got my bruised fingers to clamp down on it. Then I cracked that snake like a whip, over an' over, smashin' its head into a bloody pulp against the logs while I was about it.

When I was certain sure it was dead, I threw the body up against the door and knelt down on the ground, gaspin' for breath and lettin' the sweat pour off my face and arms. You can just believe that this weren't no sweat from the heat nor the hard work neither.

But I knew I wasn't finished yet. Where there's one rattler there's liable to be more, and I'd got to go through with this all over again, and as many times as it took until I could be reasonable sure that that hole was empty.

I'll tell you, the second time was a whole heap harder than the first.

Only I was lucky again. First that these was rattlers and not moccasins, so's I could hear it if there was more inside there. And second that after I'd shoved my hand with the ball of fabric in a half-dozen more times, I was pretty sure that fellow I'd killed was all by his lonesome.

Still, it weren't with no great pleasure that I started diggin' at that hole to make it wide enough for me to crawl through. If it hadn't of been for the sweat gettin' into the rope burns on my neck to remind me of what I'd be facin' if I didn't get out, I don't know whether I could of managed it or not.

I was makin' pretty good headway with my hands and the toe of a boot for a while there, until the pain in my side and my bruised hand started comin' back to gnaw on me. It seemed like at first the pure-dee fear of settlin' with that big ole rattler had made me plumb forget about all my hurts for a little bit.

But now that I was maybe halfway under the wall my side started pullin' something fierce and I was having to stop more and more often to catch my breath. I'd already quit using my hurt hand for anything more than shovin' dirt aside some minutes earlier.

I'd no idea of the time, nor how long I'd been diggin' by now. Might of been an hour. Might of been a couple. Wasn't no way to tell in that dark, quiet place with nothin' but my thoughts to keep me company.

After a few more minutes I decided I had to take a break, if only a little one. I backed out of the hole I was makin' and sat back against the wall next to what was startin' to become a fair-sized pile of dirt. One thing was sure. If ole Dan come along right then and looked into this little room, he weren't going to have no trouble a-tall seeing what it was I was up to.

I was feelin' plumb nigh used up by now, and I'd as soon slept for about a week if I could have managed it. But after resting only a few minutes I could feel my side startin' to stiffen up and I knew I'd better get back to my diggin' right quick whilst I was still able. No sooner had I rolled over again onto my knees than I heard loud voices from over near the general store.

I couldn't make out what they was saying, but I reckoned I didn't need to about then. There was likely only one thought in everbody's mind in this town at the moment, and that was stretching my neck. I started back to digging with a fury born of pure desperation, throwin' dirt past me into that room like a ole hound dog rootin' after a hare.

A little while later I heard folks movin' around out in front of the storehouse. Then the storekeeper's voice rang out from somewheres near the door:

"Y'all stay back there! I ain't a-foolin'. This ole scatter-gun may not stop everbody, but it'll sure make a awful big hole in the first couple who try."

There was some angry mutterin' from what I figured to be a right sizable crowd of men, and then I heard a voice that sounded a lot like that Ira who'd held the rifle on me back where them vigilantes first took me.

"Dan, don't be a damned fool! You know he's guilty as sin. We just aim to save the law some trouble, an' make sure he don't escape out of here while he's waitin' for a trial."

I was still diggin' like a madman, not pausing to listen but just hearin' all this whilst I kept burrowing deeper and deeper into that hole, pushin' dirt behind me with both arms. The next voice I could make out clear was of that dude merchant Mr. Tinsley.

"Now Mr. Jenkins, I fully appreciate your respect for the law. But there's no sense getting yourself hurt or killed over scum like you've got inside there. These men mean to have him out, and I don't believe they're in a mood at the moment to let you stand in their way." He paused. "Why don't you just hand that shotgun to me and go on back to your wife and family?"

There was a long minute while nobody said anything, and I knew Dan was thinking it over. I wished him no harm, and sort of hoped he'd wind up doing what Tinsley asked. But I was also hopin' he'd take just a few minutes longer about makin' up his mind. It might give me time enough to break through to the outside and get shut of this place.

All of a sudden I heard Riley Caton's voice ring out, clear and sharp in the night air.

"Jenkins!"

A split second later there was the boom of a Colt .44, followed by a surprised grunt from Dan. After that it was real quiet for a long moment.

I felt my fingers clutchin' air as they broke through the ground outside the shack.

As I struggled to widen the opening, I heard Riley saying real calm-like, "We needed in the storehouse, and he was in the way. What did you want me to do, let three or four of us get killed over one man's stubbornness? Now get that key off of him and let's get Barkley out here so's we can put a rope around his neck!"

I was through and pullin' myself out into the open when I heard the bolts behind me shoved aside and the key start rattlin' in the lock. By the time a surprised shout rang out behind me I was twenty yards away and runnin' hell-for-leather towards the river.

14 🌿

A BULLET CUT THE AIR over my head as I reached the steep bank, and the boom of a shotgun showered me with leaves and twigs when I stepped off and slid down it. Without slowing down, I leaped to the edge and dove into the black water.

It was right chilly from all the springs upstream, and that seemed to help me forget about my hurts and sore muscles a mite whilst I was pullin' for the far shore. 'Course all them gents with their rifles an' shotguns comin' along right behind me didn't serve to slow me down too much neither.

I was in midstream where the current was startin' to take hold before somebody finally got a glimpse of me in the moonlight. After a couple shots sprayed water in

the vicinity, I ducked down underneath and swam along
with the river for as long as I could hold out, comin' up
maybe fifty or sixty yards further along to the east. Then
I struck out again for the north shore.

I was almost into the deep shadows of the trees
linin' that side of the river before they spotted me again.
A couple rifle shots struck the water an' the leaves
overhead, but not too close. And then I was scrambling
up the bank into the cover of the woods.

When I reached the top I paused a minute to catch
my breath and take a look behind me. I saw three or four
riders was startin' to swim their horses across the river
to where they thought I might be. But they didn't guess
too good, and I figured I had a bit of time to try and get
myself lost before they come up on the place I'd made
it ashore.

There was a cabin or two back to the west of me,
across the river from Troy, so I started making my way
downstream in the other direction. I hadn't gone much
over a mile, stayin' pretty close to the water so's not to
lose my bearings in the dark, when I come up on a deep
hole with a spring at the bottom leadin' into the Suwannee. It was runnin' clear and cold, and I was right grateful
to lay down on the bank and drink my fill. When I was
finished I sat up and took a few minutes to look over the
ground hereabouts.

I still had most of the night ahead of me, but I just
weren't in no shape to keep on moving all of that time. My
ribs was hurtin' bad, and I figured I might of pulled

something loose either with all that diggin', or with swimmin' the river, or both. I just had to hope they hadn't cut into nothing so I was bleedin' inside. And I had to find me a place to rest awful soon in any case, or else I was going to pass out where I was from pure hurt and exhaustion.

I knew a lot of these little springs an' sink-holes had lime rock caves hid back up in the sides of 'em, but after gettin' up to check around a mite I couldn't find nothin' nearby which fit that description. After a bit I started downriver again, and when I'd gone maybe another hundred yards I come up on a big old oak tree that had fallen over on its side into the water.

The roots was still in the ground in places, but there was a good-sized hole underneath where a man could get back up against the bank an' be sheltered from the weather, as well as pretty much out of sight of the river an' the woods around. It looked like the best hidin' place I was going to find without travelin' a whole heap further, and I decided this was where I'd make my stand.

I didn't have no weapons, but I'd picked up a good stout branch along the way to help me with the walking. I poked that into the opening a couple times to make sure there wasn't no other critters in there who'd had the same idea as me, and then I got down on my knees and crawled inside.

After doing the best job I could of retying the cloth strips tighter around my body, I made shift to pull in a little brush and leaves with me so's to provide some more cover and a bit of warmth against the night air. I'd left that storehouse in nothing but my underdrawers, and it was apt to get right chilly before morning.

When I'd settled myself as comfortable as I could, I pulled some more of them leaves over me and curled up like a pack rat in its nest. I was asleep in less than a minute.

Sometime in the middle of the night a couple drops of water spattered against my face and I woke up to see that it was raining a reg'lar Biblical flood outside. That was the first good news I'd had since I rode into New Troy. I was snug an' dry enough in my hidin' place here, but more'n likely them lookin' for me was gettin' theirselves plumb soaked to the skin. And at the same time ever single trace of my passing was bein' washed into the ground. I reckon I smiled just a little bit to myself before dropping off to sleep again.

❖   ❖   ❖

When I woke up the next time, the sun was already high in the sky. I laid there for several minutes, just listening to the forest sounds and watchin' out into the little patch of daylight that I could see from underneath them tree roots. After I was fairly sure there weren't nothin' round an' about that needed to concern me, I rolled over and tried to sit up.

I say "tried to," because I wasn't exactly able to manage it my very first go-round. My ribs had tightened up considerable during the night, and it seemed like ever other muscle in my body had decided to go stiff an' cold on me too. From all the night's exertions and then

179

sleeping on the hard ground, I reckon.

After a couple tries I made it up into a sittin' position, and then I just stayed where I was for several more minutes, kind of taking stock.

Weren't no question that I was in some awful sorry shape right about then, what with bein' afoot and half naked, and without no weapons at a time when the whole country was out lookin' to stretch my hide. But it come to me that things would of been a whole sight worse if I hadn't got out of that storehouse when I did. And after reflecting on that for a little bit, I reckoned any time a man like me wakes up to see the sunlight once more he'd ought to count himself lucky, and just make do from there.

Which is just what I needed to be thinkin' about at the moment. Mostly what I needed was a gun and a horse. Some clothes an' boots wouldn't be a bad idea too, if I could manage it. I reckoned the three, four days of good solid sleep without no interruptions that I was wishin' for would just prob'ly have to wait for another time.

Yet the more I thought about it, the more it seemed I wasn't likely going to get just exactly what I wanted around here in the broad daylight. I was going to have to wait for nightfall and then try to kind of appropriate those things on the sly.

Well, maybe "steal" is what some folks would of said. But it weren't in my mind to keep anything I took for longer than I needed to use it, and it appeared as how I didn't have no other choice in the matter anyways. I hadn't no money to buy, even assuming somebody in these parts would be willin' to sell to me. And there surely wasn't no sense askin' for the loan of a outfit neither. Fact was, it'd be in my best interests not to be noticed a-tall whilst I went about gettin' myself fixed up.

'Course there was one other possibility. But I wanted to give that a good bit more considerin' before deciding whether or not to try it on for size.

After a bit I crawled up to where I could peek out of my hidin' place at the river an' the woods around. I wanted a drink powerful bad, but I didn't dare go movin' about no more'n I had to for fear of leaving my sign in the clay of that riverbank for everbody to see. I'd no doubt there was still a heap of folks lookin' for me 'cross the country, and my best chance of not bein' found after that rain last night was to make myself stay put where I was.

When I'd studied my surroundings a mite longer without seein' anybody or anything out of the ordinary, I plucked some leaves from the bottom layer of a sweet gum bush growin' close by and put 'em in my mouth to help stave off the thirst. Then I crawled back out of sight and settled in to sleep till nightfall.

❖ ❖ ❖

I woke feeling some better than I had the time before, though my joints an' muscles still acted like they needed a good gob of bear grease to stop all the creakin' and complainin' when I finally went to get myself up.

But I reckoned I was in fair enough shape, considering everthing I'd been through lately.

It was comin' on towards dusk, and I made myself stay hid back underneath them tree roots until it was full-out dark before even givin' a thought to movin' into the open. I used the time for considerin' and plannin', working out in my mind just exactly how I meant to go about gettin' myself fixed up with the outfit I needed.

Reckon I'd made a decision by then, though I had to admit it was a right risky proposition. But it had the advantage of gettin' straight at the matter, without no pussy-footing around nor having to take from anybody else what they couldn't afford to lose neither.

At last I moved to the opening, and after a real careful look around I crawled outside onto the hard-packed clay of the river bank. Bringing my staff along with me to use for support, the first thing I did was backtrack to that little spring I'd found the night before and take myself a good long drink. Then I looked and listened all around for a minute or two, and laid down to take another. I mean I was some thirsty, what with all the hurts I'd had an' the exertions of the past few days.

When I'd finally drunk my fill, I eased back down the bank a couple hundred yards till I was around a bend in the river, and then I started swimming for the far shore. I took my time, trying to move quiet and not aggravate my ribs any more'n I had to. When I felt my feet touch bottom at last, I climbed out of the water and up the steep bluffs into the forest. It was maybe a mile to New

Troy now, and I was going to have to move stealthy as a Injun from here on out to get to where I was headed without being discovered.

Bein' barefooted helped some, though I weren't too cheerful about all the unfriendly plants that I knew growed in the woods hereabouts. I did find me a sandspur or two along the way, but my feet was pretty hard from wearin' boots without socks for so long, and I managed to bite my tongue an' keep my thoughts to myself whenever I had to bend over and pull one of 'em loose from my toes or my heel.

Once I'd got next to the clearing where most of the town stood, I knelt down beside a big live oak tree and studied the houses in the moonlight for a right long spell. Everthing seemed quiet and still as the grave. Folks was in the habit of goin' to bed with the sun hereabouts anyway, and I reckoned maybe they'd had enough excitement the night before to make 'em value their rest some extra this evening.

The only light I could see was in a rear window of the general store, which was a problem since that was just exactly the place I'd had in mind to visit to try an' get my own goods back. I couldn't guess why it was there, since I knew there weren't no living quarters in that building. And besides, from the sounds I'd heard just before making my escape last night, I wasn't too sure ole Dan would be around any longer to be keepin' lookout at his store.

It had sounded to me like Riley Caton shot him

183

down in cold blood whilst he was standing off that mob. Which didn't surprise me none since I'd figured Riley for that type, but still I hated to think about a man gettin' killed just on account of tryin' to stand between me and a rope.

Well, there the light was, and that was where I needed to go. So after watchin' and listening a while longer without no sign of anyone bein' up and about, I decided I was in this thing too far to go away now without at least having myself a look-see. I got up, and then movin' as slow and careful as I was able, made my way around the outside of the clearing until I was opposite the place where the store stood.

I still hadn't seen no sign that anybody was inside there. But why else would a person waste the oil an' wick, to say nothing of the risk of fire, unless they'd some powerful good reason for wantin' that light?

After a bit I plucked up my nerve and crossed the open space behind the store to a dark corner of the building that was out of sight from most of the town. When I'd listened again and still heard nothing, I eased my way along the wall until I was right underneath that lighted window.

Like most windows hereabouts there wasn't no glass or screen, and the shutters was wide open to the night air. Standing up real careful an' staying well off to one side, I held my breath and peeked in.

What I saw was ole Dan stretched out on a sort of a make-shift pallet at the back of the store. I couldn't tell if he was alive or dead right off, though there was a mosquito net over him which kind of suggested he might still be alive. An' then I heard him moan and stir in his sleep, so I knew that he'd made it at least this far. But still he looked like he'd been hit awful hard, and like he was in some considerable pain.

I couldn't see nobody near him, and when I'd moved over to the other side of the window and looked in from that direction I was right sure there weren't nobody else inside that little store. More'n likely there'd be a person watchin' through the night though, and I guessed whoever it was had just stepped outside for a bit and would be coming back before too long.

I could see my rifle an' my gun belt layin' right up on top of the counter in plain view, and my hat along with 'em. After considering for about half a second, I decided what the hell and took the chance. With a quick glance over my shoulder, I hoisted myself up and through that window.

No doubt it was a plumb fool thing to do, and my ribs let me know about that even before I dropped to the floor inside. But once I'd seen them guns, I knew I wanted 'em real bad. With that Colt an' Winchester in my hands I reckoned I'd be able to face this whole blamed town if need be.

When I'd put my hat on my head and checked the loads in both weapons, I belted the Dragoon around my waist over my long Johns. Then with the rifle in the crook of one arm, I started lookin' over the shelves to see what

I might find in the way of a pair of pants an' boots that would fit me. Somehow or another, my own clothes didn't seem to of been brought inside with them other things.

"If you can't find what you want, why don't you just ask?"

I whipped around fast, all set to start smokin' if I seen any guns in sight. But the girl who'd spoke was alone. She was just standin' there in the doorway watching me with a kind of amused smile on her face. Couldn't of been more'n maybe sixteen or seventeen, with what I'd have to call a right pert manner about her.

"I reckon you'll be Mr. Barkley," she said, still looking at me in a way that made me feel mighty uncomfortable. "And if you aren't a sight! Here . . ." She took a pair of jeans from one of the shelves and tossed 'em to me. I caught 'em with my left hand. ". . . you'd best put those on before somebody sees you and starts spreadin' it around that the circus has come to New Troy!"

Then she moved closer and started rummaging around on another shelf. "I think we've got a hickory shirt here somewheres that might be big enough. Your boots are underneath the counter. I reckon we don't carry anything like that in these parts. Just brogans." She found the shirt and held it out to me.

Well, I couldn't think of nothing to say right then, so I just went ahead and took it. When she turned around and walked over to lift up the mosquito netting an' check on ole Dan, I figured I might as well do like she said and get dressed. I stepped behind the counter to pull on the pants.

After looking down at that gent on the pallet for a minute or two, the girl turned back to me. She wasn't smiling no more, and there was tears in her eyes.

"It was Riley Caton who done this," she said softly. "My pa never hurt anybody in his life, and Riley just shot him down like a dog!" She wiped a sleeve across her face with a rough motion.

"Riley's been after me for a year now," she went on, "always lookin' me over real bold and tellin' me what he'd like to do at every chance. But I never told pa about it. I knew he'd just get himself killed tryin' to face up to Riley." Her eyes was startin' to get shiny again. "And now this happened anyway!"

She looked at me real hard. "If Riley Caton wants you dead, Mr. Barkley, then I want you alive. I want you alive so you can kill Riley Caton on sight!" She paused. "And I swear if you don't do it pretty soon, I'm going to take up pa's old shotgun and go kill him myself!"

Well, there didn't seem to be awful much I could say to that, but still I figured I'd got to say something. If for no other reason than I didn't want this young girl goin' out to look for Riley Caton and maybe gettin' herself kilt, or worse.

"Ma'am," I said, layin' my gun belt on the counter and stepping out from behind it, "I reckon Riley an' me ain't on the best of terms, though it was him chose me for a enemy instead of the other way around. And I reckon it could come down to a shootin' sooner or later. But in spite of what some folks around here seem to think, I ain't no cold-blooded killer. I won't go seekin' him out just for the sake of puttin' lead into him, and I don't think you should do it neither." I nodded toward the pallet behind her.

"Your pa appears to be a man what believes awful strong in the law. Strong enough to get hisself shot over it last night, when he could have made his life a heap simpler by just lettin' them men have their way with me. Maybe he's right. Maybe if we let the law take its course, everthing will work out for the best an' those who need punishing will get what's comin' to 'em without us having to take a hand, except by testifyin' and doing whatever other things is legal an' proper."

I'll admit I weren't too sure right then how much stock I put in that myself, having always so far been more the kind to spit trouble in the eye an' come up shootin'. But it sounded good, and I reckoned it might even be somethin' I'd ought to think on, onct I could spare the time.

At least for the moment it seemed to be makin' that girl consider a mite, which was what I said it for. I could see her eyes was still plenty angry. But after she'd looked over at her pa, an' then back at me, she finally kind of shrugged and shook her head.

"Oh, I know you're right, Mr. Barkley. And I know that's what pa would say too." She ran her sleeve across her eyes again. "But the Bible says, 'Thou shalt not suffer evil to live.' And there's something real evil about Riley, him and all that Caton bunch. If the law's going to do what's needed, it had just better be about doin' it awful soon!"

"Yes, ma'am." I was finished buttoning up the shirt, and I shoved it down inside my new jeans. "I reckon you're right about that. And I reckon I mean to try and help it out too, if I can locate my old roan horse now." I belted on the Dragoon and tied the thong behind my knee.

"I'll be wantin' to ride up-country to find Miz Eileen McClanahan tonight. She and her boy can testify to the fact that it wasn't me who killed her kinfolks, but Riley and some of them others. Maybe when folks hear what they've got to say, the law can finally start to work like it's supposed to."

15 🌿

I SAT DOWN IN A CHAIR to pull my boots on, and then I looked across the room at her.

"Your pa spoke like he thought Sheriff Deal was a fair man. When he gets back, why don't you just tell him about the way Riley's been acting towards you? I can't see that it would hurt none, and it might be a help." I stood up to stamp my feet into the boots.

"You can repeat what I said about the McClanahan killin's too, if you're of the mind. Not that I'd expect him or anybody else to believe me without proof. But you can tell him anyway."

The girl nodded. "I'll do that, Mr. Barkley. I surely will." She lifted the netting to look in on her pa one more time. Then she stood up and said, "You wait right here and I'll go bring your horse around for you. He's in the stable at our place, and I reckon I can get there and back a whole lot safer than you could."

"Yes, ma'am." I hesitated. "I reckon you can. But maybe I'd ought to go along with you anyways. That's a right mean animal there sometimes, and he don't take too kindly to strangers messin' with him."

"Pshaw!" She crossed the room to the door. "I was there when they brought him in. After I'd fed him a couple carrots and talked to him a mite, he let me rub him down and stable him just gentle as you please!" She stopped and flashed me a grin before stepping outside. "And my name ain't 'ma'am,' Mr. Barkley. It's Jenny. Jenny Jenkins!"

After she was gone, I picked up a few items of canned goods I might need, some tobacco an' matches, and a couple boxes of .44 ammunition which would fit both my pistol and my Winchester. I laid 'em up on the counter and looked underneath for a sack to carry them supplies in. I found a pencil and a piece of paper under there too.

As I loaded up the sack I glanced over towards the pallet where Dan was laying, makin' sure he was still sleepin' peaceful and not wantin' for anything. Then I wrote out a I.O.U. for all that I'd took including the clothes. I wanted him to know he'd been right about me the first time, and I meant to pay him back for ever bit of it just soon as I was able.

'Bout the time I'd finished doin' that, I heard Jenny

outside the window speakin' to ole roan in a whisper. A minute later she come through the door and closed it behind her.

"I didn't see nobody out there," she said, "and I expect they'll all be to bed by this time. But I thought you might want to leave again by the window anyway, just in case."

I smiled at her. "Now I call that right thoughtful." When I picked up the sack I left my I.O.U. on the counter where they'd find it in the mornin', and then walked across the room. Jenny took the lamp and set it behind a box so the window'd be in deep shadow. Just before stepping outside I looked back and touched my hat.

"I thank you kindly, Miss Jenny Jenkins, for what you've done to help me, and here's hopin' we'll all meet again in better times." Then I bowed real courtly like I seen Tom Bristoe do onct, and she blushed. I threw a leg out the window, took a careful look around, and dropped down into the saddle.

Wantin' to be sure not to make no more noise than necessary until we was out of sight of the settlement, I started the roan off at a easy walk. He weren't too pleased about that, archin' his neck and turnin' round to look at me as if to say why don't we just go ahead an' get shut of this place. But I kept a tight rein on him all the same, until we'd gone maybe three-quarters of a mile, and then I finally let him have his head.

When he did line out along that sand road up the west bank of the Suwannee, it was all I could do to keep from givin' out a whoop myself.

I let ole roan run awhile to settle his spirits down a mite. Then I found us a place to swim the river. As we climbed out dripping onto the far bank, I shook the water out of my boots and promised myself that just one time before I left this country we was goin' to ride a ferry across here somewheres. If only so's we could both find out what it was like to stay dry the whole way over.

It didn't take us much more'n a hour longer after that to reach the McClanahan place, even with bein' careful to pass by houses and settlements at a distance and keep awful quiet whilst we was about it. When we got close to the homestead, rather than just ride down there all a-prancin' and a-jinglin', I walked the roan up through a little piece of woods maybe a quarter mile from the house and drew rein under some trees so's to give myself a chance to study the situation over a mite.

It was only a habit of caution I had, which didn't cost nothin' but a little time and had turned out right valuable ever now an' again in my travels. I took a good while lookin' that place over, lettin' my eyes roam from the outbuildings to the house an' back again, but not seeing anything to be particular concerned about. It was all pretty much the way I remembered it from the last time I was here.

Of course there weren't no lights showin', in the house or anywheres else. But that was normal enough. Folks didn't generally leave lamps burnin' in the middle of the night unless there was sickness or a traveler was expected.

And there wasn't no reason for anybody to think I'd be comin' along tonight, more than any other time.

Still, there was somethin' about the place that I couldn't quite put my finger on. Something which held me back a bit from just ridin' on down there like I normally might have.

After studying things for a while longer, I climbed down from the saddle and slid my Winchester out of the boot. Then with the rifle cradled in the crook of my right arm, I took hold of the reins in my left hand and started leading the roan towards the house at a slow walk.

When we'd come up next to the front steps without seein' or hearin' anything out of the ordinary, I tied the reins to a post and stepped up onto the porch. That's when I saw for the first time that the door was standing wide open.

I knocked against the door jamb and called out softly. "Hello. This is Tate Barkley. Anybody to home?" When there wasn't no answer I cocked the Winchester. The sound was real loud against the silence of that open door.

"Hello," I called again. "This is Tate. Speak out if you can hear me."

There still wasn't no answer.

After a few seconds more of listenin' and hearing nothing, I stepped inside. The floor creaked a little under my feet, and then she was silent as the grave. I moved over to one side of the open doorway and struck a match.

Everthing looked just the same as when I'd left it a

couple days ago. Nothing was moved or missing, all neat and tidy like I remembered. The cook-stove was cold, and seemed to have been that way for some time. But the dishes was clean and in their places, like somebody'd straightened up for company which hadn't never come.

I went over the whole house from top to bottom, lighting a couple more matches along the way, and didn't have no more clue as to what had happened than I'd had before. Except that now I knew for sure I was alone.

The house was empty. It was just like Eileen, her kids and the folks who was with 'em, had all up an' disappeared into thin air.

When I was sure there wasn't nobody nor nothin' more worth seeing inside, I went out and made the rounds of the other buildings, looking into each to see if I couldn't find some kind of a sign as to where everbody'd got to. But I didn't notice nothing unusual until I come to the stable.

Eileen's mare was there, acting like it hadn't been fed or cared for proper in a couple days, which was just about how long it'd been since the funeral. I knew she was right fond of that mare, and she wouldn't never have left it alone like this a-purpose unless she'd had to take off out of here real sudden-like, an' maybe against her will.

That was something to ponder, though it weren't hardly enough for me to go doing any serious figurin' from right now. And I hadn't found nothing else which would even help me to make a guess about what had gone on here. That rain the night before would have washed out any sign on the ground, even if it'd been light enough for me to look for it.

I forked a little hay down for the mare, and after bringin' ole roan inside to have a bite too, I took one more good look all over the house and the grounds without findin' nothing I hadn't seen before. Then when I got back to the stable I threw Eileen's side-saddle up on the mare rather than leave it behind, and rigged a lead rope to the bridle. Finally, before hittin' the road again, I led both horses to water and let 'em have theirselves a drink.

I'd in mind to ride over towards Luraville and the Curry place first for a look-see, since Eileen had suggested that's where she'd go in case trouble showed itself here. But I reckoned if I didn't find her then, I'd need to make my way on down to that house of hers by the Gulf, where I knew she'd come to sooner or later if ever she was able.

The one thing certain was that I couldn't be stoppin' along the way to ask no local folks after her whereabouts. I hadn't forgot that welcome I'd had at New Troy, and I didn't expect much better anywheres in this Big Bend country after Tinsley and them others'd spoke their piece. It struck me about then that I weren't apt to come across lookin' too innocent neither, when they started asking theirselves about how come it was I happened to be leadin' this riderless horse with a side-saddle on it.

Well then, I reckoned I'd just have to stay out of

sight and do my investigatin' on the sly. Which suited me fine, because I figured I'd had about all the run-ins with Catons an' lynch mobs that I needed for the time being. If I didn't talk to another human for a day or so longer it wouldn't hardly hurt my feelings a bit.

'Cept Eileen and her kids, of course. I'd of give a heap to see them right now, just to know they was doin' okay, and was safe from harm.

With that in mind I didn't waste around none after the horses was took care of, but climbed right up onto the roan and started west at a steady trot. In a couple hours we was at the turn-off Mama Curry had described, maybe a half mile from her and the Reverend's homestead.

I tied the horses back up in the woods where they wasn't likely to be noticed by casual passers-by, and then made my way closer on foot. Once I'd got to where I could look over the house, it appeared ever bit as dark and deserted as the McClanahans' place had earlier. I couldn't see no sign a-tall that folks was to home there, no lights, no horses in view, nor any sounds of stirrin' about neither after I'd stood and listened for a while.

Weren't no way to be sure, of course, short of going down there and knocking on the door. And it wasn't just in my mind to do that under the circumstances. I'd never met Mama Curry's husband, but a man who'd travel through this Florida wilderness alone was likely a man to be reckoned with, minister or not. And even without all Tinsley and them had been sayin' about me, folks in these parts didn't take too kindly to strangers showin' up at their houses in the middle of the night without no prior warning.

When I'd watched and listened a bit longer, I decided the best thing for now was to just let sleeping dogs lie. I sort of doubted Eileen or anybody else was in that house tonight, but if it happened they was, I figured they'd prob'ly be as safe there as anywheres else at the moment. Safer than me more'n likely, unless I found me a good spot to hole up before daylight come.

I turned and headed back towards where I'd left the horses, always mindful of how careful I needed to move hereabouts till things could get straightened out a mite. Weren't no tellin' who-all was out there beatin' the bushes for a popular fellow like me, from Caton gunmen to honest citizens still wantin' to hang the man who'd murdered Ev an' Mae McClanahan.

After mounting up I rode west for another couple miles till I come to a little spring where I could water the horses and myself a bit. By that time I figured it must of been no more'n a hour or two left till dawn, an' I needed to find me a hiding place right soon.

We wasn't very far from the river at this point, where she come down from the north just before turning back east again. And there was considerable fog an' mist rising from the ground all through them woods. What with that and the darkness, you couldn't see a dozen feet in any direction from that little hollow where we was taking our rest break.

But when I got up and gathered the reins to leave, I

didn't have no trouble hearin' the clink of harness and the creak of saddle leather from a party of riders comin' my way. They was in amongst the trees and scrub to eastward, and seemed to be headin' right towards that spring.

I started easin' back in the other direction as quick and quiet as I was able, walking and leadin' the horses up the low bank into the woods away from the water. I'd a idea this might be a well-known stoppin' place for travelers, and I also had me a thought or two about what these folks was prob'ly doing out at this time of the night. It didn't give me no comfortable feeling a-tall.

Sure enough, 'bout the time I was maybe twenty, thirty yards off I heard 'em dismounting and startin' to water their horses. A minute later I could make out a couple men talkin' in low voices.

"You reckon that Barkley come this way, Tom? Was it me, I'd been a good thirty mile off by now, an' moving fast. Maybe twict that distance if he's found a horse."

"Uh-huh. Maybe. But remember we found his tracks on this side of the river yestiddy morning. And ole Isaac Wall seen somebody on that road down by the Curry place not more'n a hour ago, headin' thisaway."

"Yeah, but Isaac was drunk and you know it. He might-a seen the Queen of Egypt floatin' up the river on her barge if we'd thought to ask him about it." There was a little pause before the second man spoke again.

"We'll find him, anyways. If not tonight or tomorrow then the next day, or the next week or the next month.

You know we ain't never goin' to quit lookin' for him after what he's done hereabouts."

"I hear that," the other man agreed. "First Ev and Mae, and now Eileen McClanahan and her kids too. Hangin' ain't near bad enough for the kind of man who'd do something like that!"

I reckon my heart stopped beatin' for a second there when I heard what he'd said. But then the man's next words give me something else to think about.

"Y'know Tom, didn't it ever strike you kind of funny that Mr. Tinsley wouldn't stay with them folks after leavin' the funeral with 'em and all? I mean, sure he said they'd asked him to go on ahead and pick up some things for the guests at his store. But I'd of thought he or somebody'd want to ride along with 'em anyways, just to keep a eye out for trouble."

"I reckon he offered," the second man said. "But you know that Eileen. If she'd got her mind set on him leavin' 'em alone, it wouldn't do no more good than talkin' to a fence post to try and convince her of something different."

They paused in their conversation and it come to me all of a sudden that I'd best be makin' some tracks away from this place if I hoped to see another sunrise. For a moment there I'd got so busy listening to what them boys was sayin' that I'd plumb forgot about my most important job right now. Which was stayin' alive.

I reckon I meant to live long enough to kill me a couple more Catons anyhow. And a certain storekeeper along with 'em, if what I suspected was true.

I could feel one of my ole rages startin' to build up in me then, all the way down to my bones. There'd been times when I might of tried to fight it off, for a anger like that could make me right dangerous to be around. But just now, thinking 'bout Eileen and them two kids, I went on ahead an' let her come.

Still, I didn't have no fight with these riders, and the best move was to make myself scarce for the moment so's I'd have the chance later on to do whatever needed doin'. I started easin' back in amongst the trees again, hopin' to get farther out of earshot before steppin' into the leather. As I did that I caught one more snatch of conversation which did help to raise my spirits just a bit.

". . . We'll know more for sure when they find that buggy she was drivin'," the man called Tom said. "And the bodies. Then at least we might have a idea . . ."

"Hey!" This was a third man's voice, one I hadn't heard before. It sounded like he was standing over by the pool where that spring first bubbled up out of the ground. "Y'all come here an' take a look at this!"

I reckoned I had me a pretty good idea what it was he wanted 'em to see. There was soft clay all around that pool, and only the mist and their own numbers had kept 'em from finding some sign of my visit before now. I hit the saddle and touched spurs to ole roan before the echo of his shout even died away.

In another minute we was over the bank and into the Suwannee, almost before I had a chance to think about it. Somehow I managed to keep a hold on the mare's lead rope, and then we was swimming hard for the far shore.

I heard some more shouts behind me, but there weren't no shootin' till we was already across and ridin' in amongst the trees on the other side. Them gents was workin' their guns out of anger an' frustration more than bein' able to see anything, for the fog was right thick there over the water. None of their bullets even come close to where I was.

I mean I didn't sit around waitin' for 'em though. Ole roan was ready to run, and I let him. Eileen's mare managed to keep up well enough without no rider on her, so we flat made some tracks.

16

In less than a hour we was startin' to come in amongst the brakes of the San Pedro swamp. There was a bit of color showin' in the eastern sky by then, but the mist was still plenty heavy along the ground wherever water was standin', so I didn't have much fear that we'd be spotted real soon.

I'd no way of knowin' if that posse was comin' along behind us or not, but I figured ole roan could outrun almost any animal alive once he made up his mind to do it. And this time I helped him out a mite with the deciding. I expected we was at least a mile or so ahead of any pursuers by now an' maybe more, if they was back there at all.

That was a-plenty for what I had in mind, which was

to lose myself in amongst these thickets of water locust, buckeye and scrub palmetto until even a ole coon dog would of had to look hard to find me.

After I was real sure there weren't nobody following after me, then I reckoned I'd make my way on down towards the coast to where Eileen's house was. It was the only place in this whole country where I might expect anything like a friendly welcome, and I'd a mind to see old Joseph again anyhow just to let him know all that had went on these last couple days. He might have some ideas of his own about what we'd ought to do about it.

And besides that, if I was to be right honest with myself, I had some little hope left that I might run into Eileen and her kids down there sooner or later. Them last words I'd heard back by the spring suggested to me they still might be alive. And no matter how slim the chances, I'd a lot rather hold onto that thought than the other one which kept trying to push itself into my mind.

❖   ❖   ❖

I kept movin' all through the day, restin' the horses whenever they needed it but not payin' too much mind to how tired I felt my ownself. I'd a powerful urge to be finished with this trip so's I could tell my story to Joseph an' start makin' some plans for what to do next. One thing I'd decided was that I was gettin' right weary of bein' the one hunted after, and maybe I'd like to start doing a little huntin' of my own before too long.

But the travelin' was mighty slow in that swamp land, and when it come up to a hour or so before nightfall I was still maybe eight, ten miles from where I wanted to be. At last I made up my mind that there weren't no sense tryin' to keep on through the darkness an' maybe get myself lost or swallowed up by quicksand or somethin'. So I found me a little parcel of dry land and set about makin' camp.

I hadn't seen nobody else the whole day through and I decided I'd go ahead and chance a fire, at least for the time it took to fix a bite of supper. The weather was plenty warm, but a fire at twilight always seemed to cheer a body somehow. And I reckoned I could use a mite of cheering just about then.

I picked up a couple lighter knots and some other pieces of dead wood that was layin' around, and before long I had me a hatful of fire going with bacon sizzlin' on green palmetto skewers and coffee boilin' in a little pot on the coals. It felt right homey, considerin' some of the places I'd spent the night here lately. The horses was croppin' grass under the trees a few yards off, and they seemed pleased enough with the accommodations too.

After a bit I started pullin' strips of bacon off the skewers and popping 'em in my mouth as they got ready, and I was thinking about givin' the coffee a try when all of a sudden I seen ole roan's head go up. His nostrils was flared out like he'd just heard or smelled somethin' that didn't quite agree with him.

In another second I'd slipped the thong off my six-shooter and eased back into the shadow of a scrub oak with my Winchester in both hands. Then I heard a voice from out in the bushes some thirty yards away.

"Hello the fire! How's for a cup of coffee?"

Well, I'd little enough coffee made and I wasn't lookin' for no new acquaintances anyhow, so I thought about just telling 'em to take the wide way around and leave me be. But that weren't the way things was done in the wilderness, and I hadn't much practice at it.

"How many of you are there?"

"Just us two. Me an' my brother been travelin' through this mis'able swamp all day and we could sure use the refreshment. We're both of us friendly."

I thought for another couple seconds, and then I decided what the hell. If they was huntin' me they wouldn't likely be fool enough to announce it to the whole world first. It was near dark now, and from where I was sittin' I figured if need be I could get a shot or two off before they seen me good. And two shots ought to be just about enough.

"All right, come on in. But come easy with your hands where I can see 'em. I ain't in no real trustin' mood right now, so if you boys want some of this coffee you'll just have to humor me."

They done like I said, and when they walked into the light they was leadin' a couple of ponies that looked plumb played out. Them gents didn't act like they was doin' a whole lot better than their horses neither. Both was sweat-soaked with their shirt-tails hangin' out, and they had a look around the eyes that suggested to me they wasn't too accustomed to traveling swamp and low hammock lands for long stretches at a time.

Their pistols was well enough cared for though, and it appeared like they'd seen a mite of use. I noticed one man had a rifle in a saddle boot on his horse, whilst the other kept a shotgun wrapped up in his bedroll where I could just make out the stock in the firelight.

I waited till they'd tied their horses to some scrub back away from the fire and was comin' towards me, before steppin' out in the open my ownself. Kept my rifle in my hands when I did it, covering 'em both without appearing to pay too much mind to it.

"Take a seat," I said, indicatin' the log I'd pulled over to use for a bench, "and help yourselves. You'll find a cup in that sack beside you but I only got the one, so we'll have to share."

"We're mighty grateful, mister." The tall skinny one took off his hat and mopped his brow whilst his brother fished out the cup and started pouring. "It was pure-dee luck we come up on your camp a-tall. If this ain't the most hopeless wilderness God ever put on the face of the earth, then I don't know what is. We ain't seen a proper trail or a road the livelong day, just swamp an' scrub an' snakes an' more swamp from one end to the other."

"Some of us like it," I said, smiling just a little bit as I hunkered down acrost from him. "Tends to keep the outside excursionists down to a minimum."

"I reckon that's so," the tall man agreed, taking the cup from his brother and scalding his mouth on a swallow of coffee. "But I won't miss it none, once we've finally seen the last of it." He took another sip and handed me the cup.

I held it in my left hand and studied 'em both before draining what was left of the coffee and passing it back. "Just ridin' through?" I asked, as casual as I could manage.

The short man spoke up for the first time. "Ridin' out is more like it," he said sourly. He glanced at his brother before starting to refill the cup. "And not a minute too soon for my taste neither!"

The tall man looked hard at the other one. Then he shrugged and turned to me. "Fellow back there offered us a job," he said shortly. "But we didn't take to it."

I nodded. "It happens." We watched the fire for a minute before I decided to speak again. "You know," I said, "I been needin' to rustle up a spot of work myself. You reckon that fellow would still be hirin'?"

Neither one of 'em said nothin' for a long moment. Then the short one shook his head. "You don't want that job, mister. You don't want no part of it a-tall." He paused, and I'd a feeling that his brother would a lot rather he stopped right there before saying another word. But after Shorty had swallowed some more coffee, he went on.

"We don't know nothin' about you, and you don't know nothin' about us. That's just fine by me and I'd as soon keep it thataway. But I'll give you some free advice anyhow. If you ever in your life run across a kid known as Riley Caton, you keep on ridin'. Don't make friends with him, don't make enemies with him, and for sure don't you turn your back on him for even a second." The short man shook his head.

"There's something ain't right inside that boy, something all twisted up and evil like a big old water moccasin. Nobody who'd call hisself a man ought to have any part of workin' for him. That's my opinion anyhow, and you can take it for whatever it's worth."

Well, that wasn't so much news to me as Shorty there thought it was, knowin' Riley like I did. But there was one thing he'd said just now which did raise a question or two in my mind. It might have some bearing on how I went about things from here on out. So I decided I'd better try and find out what I could while these gents was still in a talkin' mood.

I noticed Shorty'd been lookin' kind of wistful time to time over towards them couple pieces of bacon I hadn't ate yet, so I invited 'em both to help theirselves an' then went about cuttin' up what was left of the little bit I'd brought with me and put it over the fire too. Them gents set to makin' a fresh pot of coffee, and I got out a big can of peaches from Dan's store and opened it up as well.

My mam always taught us boys that no matter how little you had, the Christian thing to do was to share it with them who had less. And it turned out these gents hadn't brought nothing a-tall with 'em out of that Caton camp but only their bedrolls, guns and ammunition.

Not that I'd been so good ever time about practicin'

what Mam had preached. But right now I reckoned I had me a double reason to share and share alike. I wanted these two to stick around for a little while longer at least, so's I could try and find out what else they might be willing to let on to about the Catons' doings.

Whilst they was partakin' of that bacon and peaches, I just sat back an' watched 'em awhile. Then I said kind of offhand-like, "You know I'm grateful for your advice about that Riley Caton, and I sure enough mean to take it. But the funny thing which strikes me now is that I've heard the name before. Not Riley, but Caton. Seems to me a fellow told me a few weeks back that it was Big Bill Caton who was running things in these parts. They never mentioned no Riley a-tall."

"That may have been true at one time," Shorty said, puttin' a last piece of bacon in his mouth. "But it sure ain't no more. Seems like Big Bill's got his mind fixed on other things. We never even seen him in the couple days we was there, and they say he don't hardly come round to the camp no more. He started lettin' Riley ramrod the men, and it looks to me like that kid just plumb took over." He swallowed some more coffee and passed the cup to his brother.

"We wasn't there long enough to say for sure, but I got a feelin' Bill Caton don't even know what-all's goin' on back there. He might not like it much if he did. Riley does the hirin', he gives the orders, and the men either follow him or they ride out and look for greener pastures — if they're still able."

"Didn't I hear somethin' about he'd got two, three brothers with him?" I asked. "Bill Caton, I mean. Seems like somebody said there was a right smart clan of them Catons at one time."

The shorter man shook his head. "Wouldn't know much about that. I did hear Riley's step-dad was a older brother of Big Bill's, but he's been dead for several years. And I seen another brother pointed out to me when he come into camp a couple days ago — Joe I think the name was. But he had some words with Riley about this last business they was all fixin' to ride out on, same job we quit over. After that conversation Joe left out of there right quick, and he didn't seem too pleased when he went." Shorty shrugged.

"If there was other brothers I never seen 'em, though there could be some I s'pose. Might be with Big Bill, wherever he keeps hisself."

Well, after we'd talked for a little while longer I could see there weren't much else these two could tell me about the Catons that I didn't already know. They hadn't stuck around long enough to learn no more. And for that I respected 'em a sight better than I maybe would have otherwise.

Since they was wantin' to be on their way that very night, and since I was pleased enough to see 'em do it, I showed 'em a trail they could follow pretty good in the moonlight which ought to bring 'em out near Perry along about daybreak. We parted friendly, and then just to be on the safe side, I moved my camp a mile or so to the

south of where I'd had my fire before finally beddin'
down for the night.

❖   ❖   ❖

I got a early start the next day, and by mid-morning
I'd come out of them trees along the coast to where I
could see the McClanahan place a half mile away, lookin'
ever bit as pretty as I remembered her. The sky was a
real deep blue, with only little puffs of white cloud here
an' there, so that the waters of the Gulf and that little
creek beside the house was shimmerin' all silver and gold
in the sunlight.

It was the kind of a morning to make a man right
glad he was alive, and I felt some more cheerful than I
had in a couple weeks as I rode through them salt
marshes and up to the driftwood fence in front of Eileen's
house. I noticed ole Joseph seemed to have some visitors
at the moment, for there was a two-masted schooner
layin' off in the Gulf, ridin' easy an' still on them bright
waters with her sails all furled. I expected it was prob'ly
some of them sailors they'd said put in for a visit ever
now an' again.

All it needed now to make that sunshiny day complete was for the lady and her kids to be there ahead of
me, safe an' sound an' sassy as ever. Then I reckoned I'd
face a hundred Catons without worryin' too much about
the outcome.

But I could tell from the expression on the old
Negro's face when he stepped out on the porch to meet
me, that that last wish weren't going to come off just like

I hoped it would. He seemed pleased enough to see me all right, but still there was disappointment in his eyes, and more than a little worry at the sight of me ridin' in there alone with Eileen's riderless horse like I was.

When I climbed down from the saddle he come off the steps and walked up to the gate to where I stood. His blue eyes searched mine for a moment, and then he said, "You're welcome back, Mr. Barkley. But I was surely hopin' to see you comin' along with the missus and her young-uns about now." He paused, watching me. "It's trouble, then?"

I nodded, finding it right hard to put into words what I feared the most. Joseph seemed to have a idea of it though, and his face got pretty grim. "All right," he said. "You come on up to the house an' have somethin' to refresh yo'self. And then you can tell us all about it."

As I tied the roan and followed him into the yard three men come out on the porch, two of which I'd never seen before.

"Tate Barkley," Joseph said, stopping on the steps to make the introductions, "this here's Ben Chapin an' Portugee Williams, cap'n and mate of the schooner *Mary Nell* out of Key West. They was up to Apalachicola on some business, and put in here for a visit before settin' sail for home. I reckon you remember Wilt Brady."

We shook hands all around, and I took me a good long look at them two seafarin' men whilst I was about it. They was a couple of sure enough hard cases if ever I seen one. That Cap'n Chapin was a inch taller and maybe forty pounds bigger'n me, and from his handshake I reckoned there weren't too much of it was fat neither. The one called Portugee was a deal smaller, but real tough an' stringy like old rawhide. He'd a knife scar runnin' down from his right eye all the way to his jawbone, and a hard reckless manner about him that made me sort of wonder what the other feller must of looked like whenever that fight was over.

"We was both right friendly with Cap'n Jim McClanahan," Chapin explained as we went inside to the kitchen table. "Time was. Portugee here sailed under him a bit in his younger days, and I rode out a squall or two with him myself, on land an' sea." He hooked a chair around with his leg and sat down on it so that his big hairy arms rested over the bent wood back. "Knowed his missus' people too. They was Conchs the same as us."

Joseph brought some mugs and set 'em on the table together with the coffee pot from the stove. Then he walked over to a high cabinet and got down a wicker-wrapped jug which he put on the table as well. It was a gallon of good Jamaica rum, of a kind I'd only seen a time or two, and I couldn't help wonderin' if Eileen knew he kept it there. But after considerin' for a moment, I reckoned prob'ly she did.

Chapin looked at me right hard as he reached out a hand to pour coffee in his cup. "Awful fine folks, the Cap'n and his wife," he said. "Wouldn't want nothin' harmful to ever happen to that lady now her man's been lost." He uncorked the jug and added a good-sized dash of rum, mixing it in with a spoon. "That's mostly the reason we put in here ever now and again, just to check up on things such as that."

It was a mite early in the morning for me to be drinkin' as a rule. But this time I took hold of that jug an' sloshed a good two fingers into my cup before filling it up with coffee. And then I drank her down without coming up for air onct.

The story I'd got to tell was goin' to be hard enough to say without havin' to explain to these men how I'd happened to let Eileen McClanahan get herself into a fix where she might of been kidnapped or killed, or worse. And I surely weren't too anxious to speak my piece just about then. But they'd a need to know, and I reckoned I had it to do.

The tellin' wouldn't of been near so hard, maybe, if it wasn't for the fact that I blamed myself entirely for just about everthing bad which come to pass since we left out of here for that Suwannee country.

I laid it all out for 'em just like it happened, though, without wastin' no words but without holding nothin' back neither. By the time I got through talkin' it was close to noon, and that jug of rum was some lighter than it'd been before I started. I reckon maybe we was into our third pot of coffee along about then too.

When I finally finished up, nobody said a awful lot for several long minutes. Then Ben Chapin looked across the table at me and shook his head.

"That's right hard news you brung us, lad. Right

hard. I put some considerable stock by that lady who lives on this place, and if any harm's come to her there'll be a man or two kissin' the gunner's daughter before this is over with. You got my promise on it."

He took a swallow of coffee and met my eyes. "But I reckon you done all that you could do, considerin'. So I don't blame you for what's happened." Then he paused, studying his empty cup. "There's some others will need to answer for it, though. And that right soon."

After a while he glanced over at his mate, who hadn't said nothing since I'd finished my story. "What you thinkin' about, Portugee?"

17 🌿

THE LITTLE SCAR-FACED MAN had seemed kind of lost in his thoughts. Now he looked up at me and asked, "You mentioned a youngster name of Riley — Caton, was it?" I nodded. "Said he wouldn't rest till all the McClanahans hereabouts was dead?"

"Uh-huh. Accordin' to Jamie that's what he said."

"I mind me a pup sayin' something just like that a few years back. Weren't more'n twelve or thirteen at the time, an' the last name wasn't Caton neither. But still, I wonder . . ."

He poured himself a mite of rum and drank it down, then looked across the table at the rest of us.

"It was back in '68 or '69, I reckon. We'd weathered a right heavy blow comin' into Apalachee Bay, and the swells was still runnin' pretty strong. Cap'n McClanahan was makin' for the St. Marks channel when we seen another schooner fetch up on a oyster bar just off the end of South Cape.

"We put smart about to offer help, but it was slow goin' against them heavy seas. By the time we got close enough to tell what was what, that ship was breakin' to pieces and there was only one boat in the water, a dinghy of maybe eighteen feet. On board her was the ship's master, who Cap'n McClanahan knew slightly, together with five or six of his crew.

"There was more'n a dozen other souls in the water round about that boat yellin' for help and wantin' to come aboard, and several of 'em was women passengers. But the master and his men weren't having none of it. They was makin' straight for shore just as quick as they was able. And we seen a couple pushin' them swimmers off with oars and marlin-spikes whenever any of 'em got too close.

"That there was about as low a thing as I ever recall seein', and I reckon everbody on our vessel felt the same way. But Cap'n McClanahan was the first one to do something about it. He turned the wheel over to the mate with orders to run us up as close to that boat as we could without fetching aground, and then he picked up a ten-gauge long-barreled shotgun we kept handy for sharks and stepped to the rail.

"Soon as we was close enough he ordered them men in the boat to come about. When they didn't do it fast enough, he throwed down on 'em with that shotgun.

"'I said come about!' he shouted, 'or by the heavens I'll clear your decks in the next two seconds!'

"Well, both vessels was pitchin' something fierce, but we kept that old shotgun loaded up with slugs and pistol balls and I reckon none of them men aboard the dinghy was willing to chance it. They shipped oars, and I didn't blame 'em a bit. I ain't never seen the Cap'n so mad as he was right then. He meant to do just what he'd said, and I think he would a little more rather have done it than not.

"Whilst them men was trying to hold theirselves into the swells with only just the rudder, Cap'n McClanahan kept that shotgun trained on 'em and called out again from the rail:

"'Captain Bohlen, you and your men have had your turn in the boat. Now you can take your turn in the water. All of you but the steersman have until I count three to get yourselves overboard. When I reach three I will fire. One . . .'

"Well, they done it. And the upshot of it was that with a couple volunteers goin' in the water from our ship to help, an' all other hands standing to, we got almost all them passengers safe to shore. And we brung the steersman along in irons too, to stand a Admiralty inquest.

"But it turned out that Captain Bohlen never did make it to land, and neither did none of them others who left the boat. I can't say any of us shed no tears about it though, not after what they'd been doin' or tryin' to do."

Portugee stopped talkin' to pour himself another spot of rum an' coffee, and the rest of us did the same — only I decided to skip the rum this time around. I reckon the little scar-faced gent's story was interesting enough, but I was having a mite of trouble seeing what it all had to do with Riley Caton. I was about to put some words to that thought when Portugee took a swallow and started speakin' again.

"It was a day or so later when we first seen the kid. He was maybe twelve or thirteen like I said, and he was standin' on the dock at St. Marks beside this hard-faced woman in black that I took to be his ma. The Cap'n an' me was just come from ordering some supplies, and when we got ready to step down into our boat and head back to the ship that kid come and stood in our way. He looked the Cap'n up and down for a long moment before he finally spoke.

"'You're Captain McClanahan, ain't you?'

"'I am,' the Cap'n answered, civil as always. 'Do you have business with me?'

"'Not yet,' the kid said, real mysterious-like. 'Not just yet.' Then after a minute he asked, 'You got any family, Cap'n McClanahan? A wife, maybe, an' some young-uns?'

"The Cap'n allowed as how he did, but that he couldn't see where it was any of this young gent's business. At that the kid smiled, all twisted an' odd. And he said, 'I might have some business with them too, in a few years.'"

"He stepped aside to let us pass after that, but stood watchin' us the whole time we was gettin' into the boat and I was castin' off the lines. As I took hold of the oars to turn us about he looked down at the Cap'n and said, real quiet-like, 'I had a father, once.'"

"That was all, and then he was gone. We never seen him or the woman in St. Marks again. But after askin' around a bit we did finally manage to learn who they was. A sailor on the beach told us the woman was Marie Bohlen, widow of that captain we'd made to jump in the water off South Cape a few days earlier. An' the kid was his son. Name of Riley Bohlen."

Portugee paused and looked across the table at me.

"That was all of six years ago, and I never heard another word about it from then until now. But you got to figure that Riley kid would be eighteen or nineteen years old by this time. And maybe he meant what he said."

After he'd finished we all sat quiet for several minutes, each thinkin' his own thoughts. Then Ben Chapin sat up straight and beat his big fist on the table, makin' the cups rattle an' the coffee slosh about. And doing a fair job of gettin' everbody's attention whilst he was about it.

"If that's the same Riley as the one Barkley here mentioned, I reckon he's a sure enough mad dog what needs killin'." He poured himself a bit of rum and drank it down straight, shaking his head a mite when the liquor hit his gullet. "And if he ain't the same one, I'd say he still needs killin'. For all the mischief he's done here an' about."

The sea captain's eyes narrowed, and he seemed to consider for a minute. "You say there's thirty or forty of them men that rides for him in this country?"

"I reckon maybe. But it's kind of hard to tell just at the moment." I picked up my cup and refilled it with coffee. "A month ago they was said to be that many, an' maybe more. But since then a couple things has happened which could of made a little dent in their numbers." I looked at him over the cup.

"First, they done lost some several men in shootin' scrapes that I can testify to. And second, it appears to me after talkin' to them gents back in the swamp, a few of the others might of just decided to pack up their belongings and go seekin' after greener pastures by now."

I shrugged. "'Course that's only a guess too, since I hear Riley's still tryin' to take on more hard cases wherever he can find 'em."

Chapin nodded. And then he smiled real fierce-like. "That ain't so many," he said, "however you want to cut it. I got me a half-dozen solid men aboard the *Mary Nell* to add to us five for starters. But you give me a week and I'll have a hundred more along this coast, ever one of 'em lookin' for a chance to meet up with them as'd bring harm to the family of Cap'n Jim McClanahan."

He picked up a spoon from the table without seeming to think about it, and as he spoke again he bent that iron spoon around his thumb with his fingers. Just like it weren't nothin' but a green willow branch.

"I reckon if we've a mind to," the big man said, "we can clean out this en-tire country of bilge rats such as these, an' wash her down to the scuppers with their blood whilst we're about it."

Well, it was plain enough to me that he meant what he said, and that he hadn't too many doubts about bringin' it off the way he said neither. I glanced over at Portugee, and I swear that little gent was grinnin' from ear to ear at the prospect!

That's when I got the idea these coasters here weren't no kind of men to be gettin' yourself crosswise of, no time. Me, I was just as thankful as I could be that they was on my side in this fight, and not the other way around.

But there was still a deal of plannin' and discussin' needed to be done, for no amount of hard-case men was liable to do us much good if they was to go barging into that swamp without a thought to what they might run into once they got there. Them thickets between here an' the Suwannee was some of the roughest country on earth, and it was just naturally laid out so's to encourage traps an' ambushes.

So whilst Joseph an' Wilt Brady got up to start puttin' us together a bite of dinner, we all talked things over and shared whatever we knew about the Catons, the country, and how we could do the best job of takin' the war to them.

We didn't none of us make too much mention of

Eileen an' the kids, and I reckon the others felt the same way about that situation as I did. I kept hopin' and prayin' deep down inside me that somehow they'd managed to get away from whatever fix they was in, an' would turn up any time now alive and kickin', and feisty as ever. I knowed the other possibility was there too, an' maybe it was the stronger one. But I couldn't find it in myself to put words to it. When the time come, if it come, I'd have to face it. In the meantime I couldn't see how talkin' about it was going to do nobody much good, least of all me.

After discussin' it from ever angle, what we finally settled on was to hit them Catons where they lived, first shot out of the box. That meant attackin' their main camp up in the woods with everthing we could muster. We figured if we could manage to clean up their base like that and hold it, there wouldn't be no place right handy for the rest of them boys to run to once things started gettin' hot for 'em elsewhere.

And we meant to see that it did get hot for 'em, an' stayed hot, until there weren't a Caton rider left above ground this side of Georgia that we knowed about.

First thing we'd got to do though, was find out where their camp was exactly. I'd only a rough idea from the little bit of talk I'd heard here an' there, and nobody else seemed to know much more. But then it turned out old Joseph had him some friends who traveled this country a good bit on the sly. And they'd gone ahead to describe the layout to him several months before.

Joseph said it was at this great big sinkhole some fifteen, sixteen mile south of Troy and a mite west, which folks called the Tar Bucket. Happened I'd been there a time or two myself as a youngun, though I'd clean forgot about it until he mentioned it. The old Negro went on to say that it used to be a hideout for a bunch of deserters an' renegades during the war, and afterwards the Catons just sort of took it over for their own use.

Near as I could recall, that sink sat right square in the middle of the deepest thicket and swampland you ever seen this side of the Okeefenokee. It sure weren't going to be much fun gettin' in there and gettin' out again with our hides in one piece. But if we wanted a chance to cut the legs out from under that Caton crowd on the first try, it was just exactly what we'd got to do.

Once dinner was ready, we all set to it with a will, postponing the rest of our plannin' till after we'd took care of more pressing needs. It was near two o'clock by that time and I was some hungry, having skipped breakfast earlier so's I could get on the trail and make it here the sooner.

The afternoon was comin' on right hot, and when we'd finished eatin' we decided to go out on the porch on the Gulf side to take advantage of the sea breeze whilst we continued our conversation. As we come through the door I seen the *Mary Nell* sittin' at anchor a hundred yards off the mouth of the creek, as trim a craft as you'd ever hope to find anywhere. What with the deep blue of the sky, an' the water all glassy in the sun with that two-masted ship ridin' tall in the midst of it, it made a right pretty picture.

Wilt Brady sat down next to me on the steps leadin' to the beach and took out the makin's to roll hisself a smoke. After he'd lit it he pushed his hat back on his head and stared out across the water for several long minutes.

"There's one thing I keep puzzlin' over," he said at last. "An' that's this Texas Ranger you say you met up the country there. 'Pears to me he kind of left you in the lurch. An' Eileen too, when it's all said an' done. I'd be right curious to know why he didn't never show up again after ridin' off to Live Oak like he did."

Well, I'd wondered about that myself a time or two. But I didn't have no good answers, and I said as much to Brady. Might be he'd run into a pack of Catons and got hisself hurt or killed some way, or it might of been something else happened to keep him from gettin' back when he said he would — though I couldn't imagine what.

"Leastways," I said finally, "I don't expect it were anything he done a-purpose. Tom Bristoe's too good a man to take off in the midst of trouble like that without . . ."

All of a sudden there was a shout from aboard the schooner, and we looked up to see a sailor pointin' to something out of sight to us behind the house. We all jumped up an' started around that way right quick, grabbin' iron when we did it.

Brady an' me took the shortest route, through them

pilings underneath the house, whilst Joseph and the others went back inside so's they could watch out the windows. I reckon I was about the first one to make it to a place where I could see the road. And as I knelt down behind one of them thick posts and squinted my eyes up against the afternoon sun I caught my breath, and then I let it out again in a long, slow sigh.

What I seen was that black buggy of Mama Curry's, with the gelding out in front archin' its neck and high-steppin' along like it was leadin' some Easter parade. At the reins was Eileen McClanahan, and sittin' tall on the seat beside her was Jamie and his little sister Mary.

I reckon it was a minute or two before I could say or do much of anything. Then I stood up an' let out a big Texas whoop, before finally holsterin' my Colt and stepping out front to meet 'em.

Joseph was already comin' down the 'steps, and while he opened the gate and took hold of the gelding I went up beside the buggy to help Eileen an' her kids down to the ground. After I'd got Jamie and his sister out, I took hold of their mom and lifted her up, holdin' her maybe just a mite higher and a hair longer than I needed to, before finally bringin' her back to earth.

I expect she noticed it, but she didn't say nothin' afterwards except, "Thank you very much, Mr. Barkley." She was smilin' at me when she said it.

After a minute she turned and untied her bonnet, then took it off and stood looking at the house for a long moment.

"It's good to be home," she said finally. "Whatever may happen now, it is very good to be home!"

I followed her up the steps and stood by whilst she greeted the other gents waitin' on the porch. Then we all went inside and took seats in her parlor, which was some roomier than the kitchen. She didn't say too much else until after Joseph had got back from the stable and there was coffee bein' passed around. Then she looked across at Ben Chapin.

"I'm glad to see you here, Ben," she said seriously, "and your crew with you. I'm afraid I may have need of your help." Eileen paused to glance at the rest of us. "I expect this place to be attacked very soon, by a large body of Caton men. They will come tonight perhaps, or tomorrow at the latest."

As it turned out, Eileen an' the kids had run almost smack-dab into that bunch of Caton riders on their way here. They'd managed to avoid 'em last night in the dark, but didn't have no way of guessin' just how close behind that crowd might be followin' after. Eileen figured, rightly it seemed to me, that there weren't no other reason for them to be ridin' this way unless they meant to come here an' burn her place to the ground, prob'ly expecting to kill anybody who got in their way whilst they was about it.

It wasn't really so much of a surprise after all, but it sure did put a crimp in our ideas about bringing it to them before they could come after us. And we'd got to be about makin' us some fresh plans awful quick, or else we was going to find ourselves on the short end of a right lively shootin' disagreement.

Come to think of it, we was already on the short end of this deal if Eileen's guess at their numbers was anywhere near right. She said she figured they was maybe twenty-five or thirty riders out there in the woods, and I didn't have no reason to doubt her opinion in the least.

We'd only got us a bare dozen here all told, and that was countin' Eileen. 'Course if the rest of Ben Chapin's crew was anything like him an' that Portugee, I reckoned them boys might still add up to quite a few. And old Joseph weren't nobody to take lightly neither. Since I expected to do my share, I figured we'd at least let them Catons know they'd had 'em a battle before it was over an' done with.

But all the same it weren't exactly the kind of odds I'd care to bet more'n a nickel or two on, if I was a gamblin' man.

18 🌿

WHEN EILEEN HAD GOT THROUGH tellin' us what-all she could, Cap'n Chapin sent word for four of his crew to come ashore, leavin' two on board the *Mary Nell* who'd take turns keepin' watch from the mast.

A short while later them sailors drew up to the dock and I helped 'em unload their boat. They'd brought with 'em a box of brand-new Winchester rifles, together with maybe six, seven hundred rounds of ammunition. Soon as I seen what they was I glanced over at the Cap'n, but he just grinned.

"Cuban trade," he said. "Good deal easier to ship than horses or beef, and a sight more profitable too."

Ben Chapin just naturally seemed to be the one to take charge of the preparations, bein' a man that givin' orders come easy to. And it appeared he'd had hisself more than a little experience with fightin', on land as well as on the water.

Eileen's house was the main place we wanted to protect o' course, and it turned out to be right well suited for the job. Sittin' up high off the ground like it done, the windows allowed for a good view an' a clear field of fire in ever direction out over them salt marshes. What's more, with that creek to the west of us an' the Gulf on the south, we'd only got to worry about attack from the east an' the north mostly. I'd a feelin' Cap'n McClanahan give some careful thought to all of that before he ever started in to buildin'.

Whilst Wilt an' Joseph an' Eileen went about movin' furniture and things inside the house to provide some cover against bullets that might come through the walls, the rest of us set to work makin' a sort of a barricade between and amongst the pilings underneath, usin' the two boats, some barrels an' driftwood we found, and whatever else was near to hand.

Ben Chapin thought it might be a good idea to have a couple men waitin' inside the stable too, ready to fire at them attackers from the rear when they got up close to the house. So we filled up some feed sacks with sand an' put together a sort of a rifle pit inside there to lie behind, back a ways from the open door but with a good view of the yard. And as a kind of a afterthought, I kicked a board loose from the wall on the Gulf side before leavin'. Just in case them men needed a way out should things get a mite too warm for 'em in there.

Time we'd done all that the sun was disappearin' behind the trees and it was goin' to be dark right soon. But Chapin had him one more idea, which involved a stand of cabbage palms he'd seen some sixty, seventy yards off from the house. He sent me an' a couple others over there to pick up all the dead fans we could find. There was a plenty lyin' on the ground, and we made several trips bringin' 'em back inside the yard.

When he started us to puttin' 'em up by the road and places so's they overlapped a bit, I'd a pretty good idea what he had in mind. If you was to set fire to one of them palm fans it would make a strong bright light for some several minutes before it burnt down to the stalk, and us natives had been usin' 'em for night travel ever since. Layin' against each other the way we set 'em, when you lit one the others would all catch sooner or later. And with luck we'd have us ring of fire around that homestead which could give us a powerful edge with our shootin' at least once during the night.

Eileen had supper ready just about the time we got done, and everbody took turns comin' up to the house and eatin'. First was the two sailors posted out to the stable, since they'd got the most distance to cover and we'd no idea when that Caton attack might come. I waited amongst the pilings underneath with Portugee and the other two men until they was finished, puttin' the time to good use cleanin' and checkin' my weapons. Chapin, Wilt, Eileen and Joseph would all be stayin' up above during the fight, with the kids bedded down in the middle hallway where they'd be about as safe as anyplace.

When it come time for us four to start tradin' off upstairs, I was some surprised to see a piece of the wood planking over my head move to one side and a rope ladder drop down, not six feet from where I was kneeling. All the time I'd stayed here on an' off, I'd never once noticed that trap in the floor.

'Course I hadn't had no reason to look for it earlier, and I reckon Eileen had kept it covered over by some kind of a rug or something anyways. But now it give me just one more example of the thoughtful way her husband had designed and built this place from the git-go. It took a canny man, and one who'd seen a fight or two, to leave hisself a extra way out apart from the obvious.

I let the other gents eat before me, not feelin' especial hungry anyhow and welcoming the little bit of time it give me to be alone with my thoughts. Seemed like a awful lot had been happening the last three, four days, and I felt the need to let some of it kind of settle in before I'd be ready to face what lay ahead of me tonight. Man can't afford to have too much else on his mind when he'd ought to be thinkin' about staying alive in Apache country — or Caton country, which struck me right then as bein' close to the same thing.

Normally I ain't much given to ponderin' the motives of men an' like that. But here lately it had got so complicated in this Florida country that I was finding it right hard from day to day, just keepin' track of who was a enemy and who wasn't. I needed to try and sort it out in my mind a mite, if only so's I could put it aside then and pay closer attention to the matter at hand.

When the trouble first started a month or so ago, I'd no doubt that Bill Caton was the one I'd got to worry about most. Just from knowin' him and his family, and from the word I'd got that he was big boss over all them thievin' renegades.

Well, I reckoned he was still a outlaw and a right dangerous man, one who'd kill you soon as look at you if he thought it would make him a dollar or do him any other kind of good. But all the same, it seemed pretty clear now that most of my troubles an' those of Eileen McClanahan hadn't had nothing to do with Big Bill at all. If anything, it sounded to me like Bill might be startin' to lose his grip a little bit. Maybe because of all them thoughts he was havin' about running for office and makin' hisself "respectable."

It appeared to me that Riley was the one callin' the dance now, at least as far as the gang was concerned. And in a lot of ways that was a whole heap worse. Bill was in it for the profit and power, so most of the time you could make a pretty good guess about what he was liable to do, and why. Riley was a different story. Weren't no telling what might be runnin' through his twisted brain, or what he might be apt to do at any particular minute.

Now that merchant Mr. Tinsley was a puzzle, and

one I couldn't rightly figure a-tall. He didn't seem near the type to be trailin' along with Riley Caton, but it sure appeared like he was doin' it. I guessed that he'd something in mind for hisself though, and he'd just decided Riley was a handy way of gettin' to it. I'd a feeling Mr. Tinsley was the kind of a gent who figured he was just a notch above everbody else in the thinkin' department, and he believed makin' fools of men like Riley an' Big Bill Caton wouldn't be no problem at all for a bright little feller like him.

If he thought that, I'd a piece of important news for Mr. Tinsley: He weren't nothin' but a plain damn fool, and he'd be awful lucky if he lived long enough to find it out.

When Portugee and the others come down the ladder, I went on up an' had a bite to eat, sharin' the table with Eileen and Ben Chapin who had just finished their own supper and was still settin' over coffee. We talked about this an' that, but it seemed like none of us could think of a whole lot to say right then. Our minds was fixed on the night ahead, and I expect we was all prob'ly wishin' it was over and done with, one way or the other.

Eileen walked back towards the trap door with me, and just before I got set to climb down she put a hand up on my arm.

"Be careful tonight, Mr. Barkley." I turned to face her. "Do what you must do, but please don't take any foolish chances." She smiled just a little bit. "I'd like to have you join us for breakfast."

For a long moment I stared down into her eyes, thinkin' all sorts of things I hadn't no business thinkin', especially right now. Finally I just nodded. "Yes, ma'am," I said, takin' her hand from my sleeve and holding it a second before I let it go. "You take care of yourself too."

Then I turned real quick and went down the ladder before either one of us could have a chance to say somethin' foolish.

It was good an' dark by now, bein' pretty close to the new moon and the little piece of that not yet up in the sky. When I looked out towards the Gulf I could see a few whitecaps from the breeze that come after nightfall, and if I studied the horizon real close I could make out the dark outline of the *Mary Nell* against the stars. There was two men still aboard her, but they didn't have no lights burning a-tall.

The crickets an' frogs was havin' theirselves a reg'lar shivaree out there in the marsh some distance off, but right here by the house it was all still and quiet like the grave. Ever now an' again I could hear Portugee or one of the other sailors stir around a mite, tryin' to find a more comfortable position. And once somebody swore softly as a sand crab crawled acrost his leg. But for the most part we all sat tight, and we didn't talk.

I'd been back from supper maybe two hours before I heard the faint rattle an' creak of harness from the direction of the woods, near where the road come out onto the salt flats. I listened a minute, and when I was sure of what I'd heard I glanced over at Portugee who was closest to me. I could barely see him nod in the dark.

Scrunching down a little lower behind the barrel where I'd been keepin' myself, I lifted my Winchester to take a bead on the road at a place where I thought them boys might appear. A little sliver of a moon was up by now, and between it an' the light from the stars I expected I could make out men movin' in the open pretty good.

But when the first rider showed himself I held my fire, and so did everbody else on our side. We watched him ride up to a corner of the garden fence maybe a hundred yards off and stand in his stirrups before callin' out:

"Hello the house!"

None of us answered.

"I said hello the house! If there's anybody inside there you'd best get yourselves out an' away from it real quick! We mean to burn the place, and the only chance you're going to get to leave it is this one right here!" He paused a moment, but still there wasn't no answer from us.

"All right then," he said finally, "you've had your chance. Soon as I count up to thirty we're comin', and if you're still inside you'll just burn along with everthing else!" He turned his mount real sharp around and rode back off towards the woods.

It occurred to me then that most likely them Catons didn't have no idea how many of us was around the house at this moment. Could be they figured it was only old Joseph, or maybe one or two others dependin' on whether they expected Eileen or me to of made it back. But unless they'd been scoutin' us during the day, they wouldn't know nothing about Cap'n Ben Chapin and his crew, much less them dozen Winchesters they'd brought along with 'em.

I had me a idea some of them men out there was fixin' to have theirselves a real uncomfortable surprise.

'Bout that time I seen a dozen riders break from the woods, comin' straight towards us at a gallop. Half of 'em carried lighter knot flambeaus in their hands; the others had their guns out and was shootin' up a storm. 'Course they couldn't see nothin' to shoot at 'cept the house and the windows, but they was sure making some lead fly around those places.

We let 'em come until they was maybe thirty yards away, waitin' on Cap'n Chapin to fire the first shot like we'd agreed. Then we all cut down on 'em to onct, takin' aim at them gents with the torches right off.

Well, we emptied four, five saddles on that first volley, an' the rest turned tail just as quick as they could get their horses pointed in the other direction. I figured prob'ly a couple of them might of took some hits too, but they all managed to stay in the saddle till they'd got back into the woods at least.

Whilst them riders was runnin' away from that killin' fire of ours, there was a bunch of other shootin' started up from the trees an' scrub all around us to help cover their retreat. I reckoned Eileen hadn't missed her guess at them Caton numbers by too much, 'cept maybe to underestimate 'em just a hair. It looked to me like there was more'n two dozen rifles firin' at us now, from all around in a half circle runnin' north to west.

Not that I was spendin' so much time with my head poked up over that barricade as to make a real good count, you understand.

Still, they was a right fair distance away and anything they hit was liable to be a heap more luck than marksmanship. It was the same way with us, for we was shootin' at their muzzle flashes and matching 'em almost bullet for bullet. Some of them sailors of Chapin's was usin' two Winchesters apiece, and we all had us enough ammunition to last from now until then.

After while it sort of settled down to reg'lar firing, maybe one or two shots a minute, and neither side was doin' much damage that I could tell. One of them sailors underneath the house with me had took on some lead during that first attack, and though he was still breathin' he was right hard hit and out of the fight. I'd got me a fresh hole in my hat, but apart from that I didn't know of no other casualties on our side.

'Course I couldn't be entirely sure about them folks up above us or in the stable, neither. But at least there was still shootin' coming from both places.

When the battle had been goin' on for a hour or more like that, I happened to look over towards Eileen's garden plot across the road an' seen some rustlin' in amongst the corn an' beanstalks, which didn't exactly appear to be the wind. I was just about to turn an' say something to Portugee about it when a half-dozen men rose up and charged the house on foot.

I dropped the first one with my Winchester and sent another stumblin' back through the bean rows with a piece of lead in him. But then I felt somethin' like a red hot iron laid acrost my left arm an' shoulder, and I fell back, droppin' my rifle. When I come up again with my pistol in my hand Portugee and them others was shootin', and a moment later there was a double blast from Eileen's shotgun up above which pretty much wrote a end to this latest Caton try.

Three bodies was sprawled out in the sandy road, and the rest had crawled off into the swamp to lick their wounds. I threw a couple shots after 'em with my Dragoon just out of hurt an' meanness, but near as I could tell I didn't hit nothin' but leaves an' air.

With Portugee's help I managed to patch myself up some then, using strips of cloth from my new shirt an' cussin' all the while we was doing it. I'd been creased twice by the same bullet, once in the lower arm where I'd been holding the Winchester, and then again in the shoulder. It wasn't nothin' serious after we'd got the bleeding stopped, but it sure enough hurt like the blazes. Portugee give me a drink of rum out of a tin flask he carried, and that seemed to help a bit anyways.

It got awful quiet then for a real long spell. Ever onct in awhile somebody out in the woods would throw a little lead in on us, and we'd answer 'em back. But for the most part it seemed like them Caton boys was takin' theirselves a bit of a rest now, and prob'ly discussin' the situation a mite too. Maybe they'd had enough and was ready to pull out, but I doubted it. More likely they was trying to regroup theirselves and plan for some kind of all-out attack later on.

After a time I heard that trap open up overhead, and Eileen come down the ladder with her arms full of lint and other medical fixin's. She didn't say nothing, but just went right over to that sailor who'd been hit and started in to workin' on his wound. I'd a thought to say somethin' about her not exposing herself to the added danger down here, but I kept it to myself.

In the first place, I already knew by this time there weren't no point in arguing with that lady once she'd got her mind made up about somethin'. And in the second place, that boy were hit hard and I feared he might not make it through till morning. I couldn't think of no better way to die, if a man had to do it a-tall, than with all that womanly softness close by and them warm butternut eyes lookin' down into his.

Once she'd fixed up the sailor's wound and made him comfortable as she could, Eileen got up and come over next to me. When she seen my torn shirt and the rough bandages we'd made out of it, she looked up at my eyes and shook her head. Then she went to work puttin' on fresh dressings, along with some kind of grease she'd brought with her that seemed to ease the fire a bit.

Neither one of us had a whole lot to say whilst she

was doing that. But at last when she was finished, she looked out towards the dark forest. Then she asked, "Do you think they will come again?"

"Pretty near sure of it."

"It will be bad, won't it?"

"Bad enough, I reckon." I never did see the point in lyin' to a woman about somethin' like that, and especially not this one. Most women I'd knowed could stand the rough times 'bout as good as a man anyway, if they had a idea what to expect.

"There's still more'n twenty of 'em," I said, "near's I can figure. An' not half that many of us. Besides," I went on, "them Catons strike me as right determined men."

"Wilt Brady was shot in the shoulder and leg," she said quietly. "He'll be all right I think, but not very much help in what's to come."

I nodded. Weren't no reason to say nothin' more, since Eileen could count at least as good as me. Seven of us were left here on the shore, an' two aboard ship who didn't seem to be doin' us a awful lot of good right now. Maybe three times that many Catons.

Eileen sat next to me for a little while longer, then she went back to kneel beside the sailor.

Along about three or four in the morning, he died.

19

I MADE EILEEN GO BACK up into the house pretty soon after that, puttin' the ladder in and closin' the trap behind her. I was looking for the attack to come any time now. It weren't no more'n a hour or two till dawn and I couldn't feature them Catons charging across no open salt flats in full daylight if they could help it.

Sure enough, after only a little bit of waitin' the moon went behind a cloud and them riflemen out there in the grass an' scrub started shootin' real often and regular. They'd managed to get theirselves up a mite closer to where we was in the dark, and most of 'em was no further than a couple hundred yards away now. Close enough to do some damage if they seen any targets to shoot at.

"Get ready," I said as we began raisin' up off an' on

to answer their fire. "I expect the next thing you'll hear is riders comin'!" Me, I got out some matches and started easin' myself over towards the nearest of them palm fans that we'd put up earlier. If we was ever goin' to use the light from 'em, I reckoned now would be the time for it.

I'd a bit of coal oil in a tin can that I'd kept handy, and a torch made out of some rags tied to a stick. When I'd soaked them rags real good, I propped my Winchester up against a piling and crawled out from underneath a corner of the house on my belly, holdin' the torch in one hand and them matches in the other.

I hadn't hardly got into position good when I heard a bunch of horsemen coming, hell for leather. I lit the torch right quick and raised it up over my head, touching as many fans as I could reach before throwing it onto another batch nearby. Then I flat made some tracks back under that house. Bullets was spittin' sand all around me and thunkin' into the pilings and timbers overhead whilst I dove across the barricade. When I lit on my hurt arm an' shoulder I let out one big yelp of pain before rollin' over and startin' to get up.

By the time I'd finally got a hand on my rifle and took a look around, she was burnin' bright as day out in front of the house and them riders was some perturbed. Everbody was firing now, and I saw three saddles emptied before I could get off a shot. A couple Catons was spurrin' away from the fight, but the rest was droppin' down to the ground, meaning to try and get up closer on foot, I reckoned. I was drawin' a bead on the nearest one when I heard a shout from Portugee:

"Behind us! The creek!"

I whipped around real sharp an' seen this raft comin' out from the other side, with a half-dozen men on her and three, four pine logs piled up at the front for cover. Quick as I could work the lever, I emptied my Winchester at 'em. But aside from making them boys hug the deck a mite closer, the only damage I could see that I done was to throw up a good-sized shower of bark an' splinters into the air.

I hauled out my Dragoon, but held my fire. Portugee and the other sailor was shootin' at 'em too now, but without a bit more effect than me. In another couple minutes that raft full of Catons was going to be almost amongst us, and it looked like there weren't a thing we could do to stop her.

And then I seen one of the prettiest sights I reckon has come to my eyes in a good long while.

There was a great big ole roar from the *Mary Nell* out in the Gulf, and a tongue of fire an' sparks spit from her afterdeck. A second later them boys on the raft was soaked to the skin from the cannon ball's near miss.

I mean they was as surprised as me when that happened, and it sort of discombobulated their thinkin' a mite. One of 'em stood up to swear, and Portugee nailed him through the brisket. A couple others dropped their poles in the water, an' the rest didn't seem to be near so interested in gettin' across that creek as they had been a minute earlier.

The second shot from the cannon took 'em right square amidships with a exploding shell, and it was all she wrote. That raft come apart in great big pieces, and the men on board with 'em. I reckon a couple made it into the water and swum ashore, but they was goin' the other way from us when they did.

We all let out a cheer when that shell hit, and for a second there I guess we wasn't paying too close attention to anything else nearby. It weren't till I turned an' blinked to clear the spots away from my eyes that I seen the form of a man next to our barricade takin' aim at Portugee Williams' back. The Dragoon bucked twice in my hand almost of its own accord, and I watched him slump to the ground. Then I seen another man comin' over the barricade.

When I shot into him I called out a warning, for there was others comin' acrost too by that time. Then a huge blow at the back of my skull staggered me and I realized I'd just gone stone blind.

I remembered the instant of awful fear at seein' nothing but blackness before my eyes, and the desperate way my hand reached out to try and get back the pistol I'd dropped. But them was the last things I remembered for a long spell.

❖　　　　　❖　　　　　❖

When I finally opened my eyes again it was daylight, and I was layin' on my side in that same bed in the same room where I'd been brought the last time I'd got myself shot up in a fight with the Catons. I could even see my pants on the same chair across the room, with my boots on the floor beside it.

For a minute or two there I couldn't help wonderin' if maybe I'd just dreamed all them things I thought had happened during the past couple weeks. But then I realized it was my head was bandaged this time instead of my side. And behind my ears was a throbbing and a aching so bad that I just knew some big old blacksmith had been usin' my noggin to bend horseshoes around. I mean I was some afeared to turn over, lest my head kept right on rollin' off onto the floor.

When the truth finally struck me though, I reckoned I could put up with the pain for a bit longer if need be. I was that happy to be able to see again.

I hadn't been layin' there awake but a little while when the door opened and Eileen come in. With her was old Joseph wearin' a bandage around one hand, and behind them was Tom Bristoe and a gent I hadn't never seen before.

Bristoe looked down and shook his head. "Beats me how some folks ever manage to get anything done, spendin' half their lives in bed like that." He glanced at Eileen and grinned. "You ask me, ma'am, this man ain't so much hurtin' as he just likes having pretty ladies takin' care of him at ever chance."

I raised myself up on a elbow, grittin' my teeth against the pain, and met his eyes. "You come on over here Bristoe, and let me bend this bedpost around your skull just a little bit. Then we'll see how much you like it!" But after I'd said that I had to grin too.

"Sorry to take so long in gettin' back to you, son," the Ranger said, more serious. "I'm afraid it was all a reg'lar mix-up from the word go."

Eileen was fixin' some pillows for me to lay back against, and when she'd got me situated a mite she stood up an' looked across at him and the others. "He came when needed," she said, "and in the nick of time too. If the posse hadn't arrived when it did . . ."

"Posse?" I'd a feeling I might be missin' out on a part of the story here.

"Oh, forgive me. This is Sheriff Deal." The gent I hadn't met took a step forward and hooked his thumbs in his trousers so that I could finally see the star behind his coat. "He and Mr. Bristoe rode here with some men from New Troy, and they arrived this morning just as the outlaws were making their final attack."

"We was huntin' Catons from the start," Deal said in answer to the question I imagine was on my face. "Not you. I reckon we've got all that straightened out finally. After talkin' to Dan an' Jenny Jenkins, and this Ranger here, it was pretty clear to me what must of happened. And then when I heard Miz McClanahan's story and that of her boy this mornin'. . . . Well, it appears like somebody made a right serious mistake up-country there a couple days ago."

I reckoned they had, and I'd some pretty strong feelings about it too. But there was something else I wanted to know right then, which struck me as a tad more important.

"You say old Dan was still alive when you saw him. You expect he's going to make it?"

"That's a tough old bird there. And he's gettin' some awful good care from that wife and daughter of his. Yes, I reckon he'll make it."

"I'm glad to hear it. Dan Jenkins is a fine man."

"Yes he is. And the rest of them folks up to Troy ain't so bad as you might think neither, from your only experience with 'em."

Deal paused, meetin' my eyes. "You know, I got some of them boys with me now. And I'd just as soon there weren't no trouble when you see 'em. Ira Johnson and the others wanted me to tell you that they're awful sorry over what happened, and that they just hope you can be a big enough man to forgive and forget."

Well I had to think about that for a minute or two. "I'll forgive," I said at last. "But I ain't so sure about the forgettin' part. Maybe it'd be a good idea if them gents didn't forget none too soon neither, about what almost happened. Not just to me, but to Dan Jenkins as well."

The Sheriff nodded. "You're right, and I'll tell 'em so." He started to leave the room, then turned back. "In the meantime, it may do you a little bit of good to know that between you folks here and our comin' along in time to round up strays, that Caton gang is just about wiped out. We took a good dozen prisoners, an' most of them hurt. The rest prob'ly won't stop running till they're clear to California."

"How 'bout Riley?" I asked, havin' a idea I knew the answer.

"He weren't among the bodies," Joseph said, "nor one of them as was took prisoner neither." He nodded toward the open window where I could hear men an' horses movin' about. "I heard a couple-a them say this was all Riley's play, though. Seems Big Bill weren't along on this ex-pedition, nor any of his brothers. An' they might not have even knowed nothin' about it."

Deal shrugged. "Well, I reckon they'll all be leavin' the country now anyway," he said. "Ain't hardly nothing left for 'em here except a rope."

Joseph an' me shared a look just before he followed the sheriff out the door, and I expect we both had us a few doubts. About Riley anyway, an' Big Bill too for that matter. But maybe now weren't just exactly the time to bring it up.

I looked over at Bristoe. "All right, *hombre*," I said. "'Pears to me you got a little explainin' to do. What happened up there in that Big Bend country to keep you from showin' yourself until just this mornin'?"

The Ranger took a step toward the bed. "It's kind of a long story," he said. "But I guess the short of it is that I just got myself sidetracked a little bit.

"On my way into Live Oak I got word that feller from Texas I been huntin' was seen ridin' through the area only a couple hours before. I made me a quick decision, found this big farm kid alongside the road, and wrote out a note for him to deliver to the sheriff in town. Then I lit out after

that gent before the trail could have a chance to get cold."
He paused and looked kind of sheepish.

"Reckon maybe I was in such a big hurry that I didn't
notice how that kid seemed to be a mite slow on the
uptake whenever I spoke to him. Turns out he was a
feeble-minded youngster who'd never even been to town
by hisself before. I heard later that when he'd got halfway
there he just plumb forgot why it was he was a-coming,
so he turned around and went home." Bristoe shrugged
and shook his head.

"By the time I'd finally made it into Live Oak myself
after losing my man's trail at the river, the sheriff had
done gone off on a fishing trip and wasn't nobody
around who knew where he'd went. I spent a couple
hours searchin' without no luck, then give it up and
headed back to the McClanahan house. But when I got
there that place was plumb deserted. Wasn't nothing I
could do but camp out till mornin', and then start makin'
inquiries around the neighborhood."

The Ranger run a hand through his hair before
continuing. "You never seen such a mixed-up bunch of
stories as I got when I started askin' folks about you, and
about this lady here and her kids. Some said they was
dead. Some said you was. At least two groups of men
was out tryin' to find you and make you that way if you
wasn't. It weren't until I come into Troy the next day and
met up with that Jenkins gal an' her dad that I felt I was
finally beginnin' to get the straight of it."

Bristoe grinned. "You know, that's a right spirited

filly there. And not much inclined to keep her opinions to herself. She told me right off how she figured it was Riley an' that Tinsley was behind all the troubles. Then when Sheriff Deal come along she told us both again, without mincing no words neither time. Soon as Deal got a chance to talk to the father, he was inclined to agree. That's when we gathered up a posse and started down thisaway."

"Well," I said after a minute, "that's quite a story. But when you come down to it, I reckon it's turned out pretty much like the feller says: All's well that's ended well. At least for the moment."

Then I had a thought. "Say, where you reckon Tinsley is now? I'd still like to have me a word or two in private with that gent over the things he was sayin' about me up to Troy."

Bristoe shook his head. "I ain't seen him. His place was locked up tighter'n a drum when I rode by it a couple days ago, an' nobody I talked to seems to of heard nothing from him since the McClanahans' funeral."

"I shouldn't wonder about that," Eileen said coldly. "It was Mr. Tinsley who led us into the Catons' hands as we were driving back from the service." We all looked at her, and she went on to explain.

"He'd been talking all morning about my brother-in-law's property and something to do with railroad right-of-way, though I was in no mood just then to pay him much mind. But on the way home he asked me straight out if I would sell the homestead to him." She shrugged.

"Naturally, I told him I would want more time to think about any transaction like that, and would certainly consult an attorney before making a decision.

"My reply seemed to make him angry, and he was silent for a while. Then as we came to a little-used trail through the woods he brought the subject up again and told me there was something I must see which could change my mind. When we'd followed him off the road for a short distance he suddenly spoke and three men came out from the trees.

"They meant to take us prisoner. And it was only Jamie's — James' — quick thinking which saved us."

She smiled then, and there was more than a touch of pride in her voice as she went on.

"He picked up my shotgun from the floor of the buggy quick as a wink, and pointed it right at those four men. Then he told them that if they put one hand on a gun or moved an inch from where they were before we got turned around and away from there, he'd let them have both barrels right in their faces. I believe he meant it, and I'm sure those men thought so too. They all sat very, very still until we were well out of sight."

We talked a little while longer, 'bout Eileen's escape from the Catons and how they'd made their way down here takin' a roundabout route through the swamp an' all. But after while my eyelids started gettin' droopy and I couldn't pay so close attention to what she was sayin' as I wanted to. That's when everbody decided it might be time to leave me be for a bit an' let me catch up on some sleep.

❖   ❖   ❖

When I woke up it was full dark outside. But there was a lantern burning low on a table by the bed. And sittin' in a chair right next to it was Eileen McClanahan.

She 'peared to be readin' a book when my eyes first opened. But I laid real still for a while without saying nothin', and I got the feeling maybe she wasn't payin' too awful close attention to them words on the page after all. Ever few seconds it seemed like she'd glance up towards the bed where I was, and then she'd have to find her place in that book all over again.

When she finally seen me lookin' at her, I almost thought she blushed for a second there. But then she took her time markin' her place in the book real careful, before finally closing it and settin' it up on the table by the lamp.

"Are you feeling better?" she asked, soundin' a bit more like a old maid school marm I'd knowed once than the soft, appealing woman I saw sittin' beside me. She was got up for bed now, with a robe wrapped around her and that red-gold hair fallin' all down over it past her shoulders. In the yellow glow from that lantern, I guess she looked more fetchin' right then than I'd ever seen her. And that was saying something, too.

"Yes, ma'am," I answered after a second. "My head feels a heap better, though it's still some sore yet. But I reckon I'll be able to stir around a mite come morning."

"There's no need for you to try doing too much too soon," she said. "I believe we are quite safe here for the time being. And later on there will be others to do what is needed as well."

"Yes, ma'am." I'd a few ideas of my own about what needed doin' when, and who ought to do it. But she looked so warm an' lovely at that moment that I just couldn't bring myself to argue about it.

"There's some broth warming on the stove," she went on, getting up from her chair. "Would you like me to bring you a bowl?"

I grinned. "Reckon that might do for starters. But if you got a whole steer out there somewheres, I expect I could do a little damage to it too, hoofs and all!"

Eileen moved around the bed and began fixin' the pillows for me to sit up. "Let's just try the broth for tonight," she said, leaning over me to adjust the covers. "You're still weak from your wounds, and it might not be a good idea to put solid food into your stomach just yet. In the morning, if you feel up to it . . ."

A wisp of her gold hair fell across my cheek whilst she was reaching out to help me up on the pillows.

And I kissed her.

Since she didn't fight it near as much as I'd expected that first time, I wrapped my good arm around her and kissed her again.

She pulled back a little bit after that one, and sat on the edge of the bed looking into my eyes for a long moment. At last she spoke.

"Mr. Barkley," she said, sounding like she might be a little bit out of breath still. "I don't think . . ."

"Uh huh." I nodded. "I reckon I didn't think neither. I just finally give in to what I been wantin' to do ever since the first time I seen you." She kept lookin' at me for a while, and then she nodded too.

"I know."

That was all she said. But when I went to kiss her a third time, we both took it slow and made it count. After that I held her next to me for a long while without neither one of us saying anything a-tall.

20 🌾

I WAS UP AND ABOUT the next day like I said I'd be, but I surely wasn't feeling none too spry about it. That bullet crease at the back of my head had cut clean through to the bone, and it was still plenty sore even though the throbbing had eased up a mite by now. The hurts in my shoulder and arm had stiffened up some during the night too, and ever now and again I could still feel a little tug from my busted ribs as well.

I mean I was movin' some slower than usual when I finally rolled out of bed around eight o'clock in the morning.

Eileen had already been up two, three hours by then, cookin' breakfast with Joseph for that whole crowd, includin' the ship's crew, the posse, and their prisoners too. Everbody had stayed over after the fight it seemed like, campin' out around the house rather than make that long ride back to Troy with night a-coming on.

When I'd got myself to stirrin' and had a good hot cup of coffee in my fist, I went outside and spoke to some of them posse members, takin' Joseph with me to explain about that Caton hideout up in the swamp an' all. Maybe Sheriff Deal was right about them outlaws all leavin' the country, but we couldn't be real sure about it whilst there was still that Tar Bucket place for 'em to hole up at.

If it turned out to be deserted, I reckoned we'd all rest a sight easier for havin' seen it ourselves. And if it weren't empty then we'd still got us some cleanin' out left to do. Either way it was in my mind to have done with it now, once and for good. There weren't no sense leavin' no loose ends hangin' about that might come back to haunt us later on.

It happened that most of the men I spoke to seen it pretty much the way I did. They'd about had their fill of Catons an' their like, and they wanted a end to this business right soon now. After I'd finished makin' the rounds there was a dozen or so willing to ride along, countin' Tom Bristoe, the sheriff, and a good number of his posse.

The others had families or businesses they'd got to get back to, and would just go on ahead an' take the prisoners up to Troy so's they could hold 'em there for the judge. At least that's what they said they was goin' to do, and I think they meant it this time.

When I'd got myself a bite to eat, I went out and started saddlin' up the roan. It was a good long ways to the Tar Bucket from here, and I meant to be on the road before the sun had a chance to get itself too high in the sky.

I got to confess I was strugglin' a mite with that big Texas saddle because of the shape I was in at the moment. So it didn't hurt my feelings a-tall when Jamie showed up out there to the stable and give me a hand hoistin' her onto ole roan's back. The boy didn't say nothing whilst I tightened the cinch and shoved my Winchester down in the boot. Just stood there watchin' me with a real serious expression on his face.

"You leaving, Mr. Barkley?" he asked finally, when I turned around to look at him.

I nodded. "Reckon we still got us a job to do up-country so's to make it safe for you and all those other folks hereabouts. Job like that won't stand much wastin' around. Me an' these men got to be about it now whilst the time is right." I paused. "You understand?"

"Uh huh." The kid didn't say nothing else for a long moment. Then he asked, "You comin' back?"

"Had it in mind," I said, pickin' up my bedroll an' saddle bags and startin' to tie 'em behind the saddle. I looked across the roan at him. "You know any reason why I shouldn't?"

"Nope. Just askin'." Jamie hesitated, and then he said kind of quiet-like, "I want you to." After a moment he added, "And I reckon Ma wants you to, too."

"I'm glad to hear that," I said, gathering the reins to lead the roan out in the yard. "'Cause I like visitin' here myself." When we'd walked a few steps into the sunlight I looked down at the kid beside me and asked, "Your ma tell you that her ownself, did she?"

"Nope." Jamie grinned up at me. "Just a feelin' us men gets about their womenfolks ever now an' again."

I smiled back at him. But then I couldn't help recallin' how Eileen had acted this mornin' when I'd mentioned my plan to her. She hadn't been too pleased with the idea, and had been right definite in makin' her opinion known to me. Seems it weren't in her mind for me to go ridin' off nowhere until my hurts was better, and even then she'd the feelin' we'd ought to discuss it some first.

Of course once she seen my mind was made up and all her talk weren't likely to change it enough to notice, she did ease off a mite. But then she kept to herself and stayed so quiet that I couldn't tell whether she wanted me to come back or just keep on ridin', after I'd finished up with that business at the Tar Bucket.

I put a hand on Jamie's shoulder and thanked him for his help before climbing up into the saddle. Then just as I was startin' to turn the roan's head to go join the other men waitin' out by the road, Eileen and Joseph come out on the porch, together with Cap'n Ben Chapin and Portugee Williams.

The old Negro waved and wished me luck, whilst the

two seamen come down the steps to shake hands and say so long. They meant to stay one more night just in case. But then they'd be settin' sail first thing in the morning, having already stayed over here a sight longer than they'd planned on. I understood their thinkin', for to a ship's captain and crew ever hour ashore is money lost.

Eileen hesitated a bit, then come down herself and walked over to where I was. She looked at me and reached up to take my hand, holding it for a long moment whilst our eyes met.

"Take care, Mr. Barkley," she said at last. "And come back to see us when you're finished with what you have to do."

"Yes, ma'am," I said. "I mean to do that."

Eileen held my hand for another second, then let it go and turned away. She crossed the yard and went up the steps into the house without looking back.

❖   ❖   ❖

It was gettin' on late in the afternoon when we finally come up through the swamp near that Caton hideout, everone riding real easy an' quiet with our Winchesters acrost our saddle-bows. The trees was almost thick as a reg'lar wall beside the trail there, and I reckon we was each more than a little wary of a ambush.

Bristoe and me was ridin' maybe a dozen yards ahead of the others when we caught our first whiff of smoke. It was faint right there at the start, but we both exchanged a look soon as we smelled it. In another few minutes it had made itself right distinct.

Seemed to be more of it in the air than you'd expect from just a single campfire, or even a couple of 'em. But less than a forest fire, maybe. Leastways one of any size. Weren't much chance of that anyhow, with the weather as wet as it'd been lately. But it was something you always had to think about.

The men with us was smellin' the smoke too by now, and for a while we rode ahead even more slow and cautious than before. Then we come up on the edge of that big old sinkhole and we all drew rein.

I eased myself down from the saddle and started forward real careful, movin' from tree to tree and using ever bit of cover I could find. Bristoe come along after, some ten yards behind me and well off to one side, whilst the rest of the posse dismounted and spread out in a semicircle along the edge of the sink.

I'd gone maybe fifty yards when I caught sight of a good-sized clearing, with smoke rising up to the sky from several places in the midst of it. As I eased closer through the trees I seen they was a bunch of log and palmetto shacks all around that clearing, and a number of these was either on fire or smoldering in rough squares where they'd already been burnt to the ground.

I crouched down behind a little stand of palmettos and watched for a few minutes, but didn't see no people moving about till a thatched roof right acrost from me suddenly burst into flames and a man come out from the doorway with a torch in his hand.

It was Bill Caton. He was still wearing his store-bought suit. But it was some muddy and wrinkled now, and seemed to of been tore in a couple places too, where he might of been ridin' kind of careless through the scrub. He had a Colt belted round his waist which he hadn't had on when I'd last met him, and a second pistol was stuck down into his pants in front.

A minute later another man come out of the shack next door, who I recognized as Bill's brother Joe. Seemed like he'd just set fire to that place too. And then the both of 'em met in the middle of the clearing to exchange a couple words that I wasn't close enough to hear.

I glanced to right and left, but couldn't see no sign of anybody else in that clearing a-tall. Bristoe was kneeling beside a tree a little ways to my right with his Colt in his fist, and I could hear the others of our party startin' to move in behind us. So I stood up from my hiding place and throwed down on them two Catons with my Winchester.

"Hold her up right there, boys," I called. "I got me some friends along this time, and it 'pears to me like you're pretty fair boxed as well as outnumbered. You just stay where you are and let your hands rest easy until we come in."

I could tell Big Bill weren't too pleased when he heard my voice. But he didn't seem so awful surprised about it neither. His eyes found me as I stepped forward, and he just nodded. Then he lowered the torch in his hand real slow and let it drop onto a patch of sandy ground in front of him. The rest of the posse walked into the clearing, and he looked up and managed a lopsided grin when he seen Sheriff Deal amongst 'em.

"Howdy, Sheriff. Didn't expect to see you down this way quite so soon." He jerked his head back towards the burning buildings. "'Nother couple weeks with some good rains, and you'd of thought this place'd been de-serted for years. Few months longer and you might even of had yourself a time findin' it a-tall."

"Uh huh." Ned Deal nodded. "I reckon it's a good thing we come along when we did then, ain't it?" He turned to a couple members of his posse. "Mort, Frank, you go on and take a look around inside them shacks that are still standing. See what you can find that might do for evidence."

"Evidence?" Big Bill was doing his dangdest to look surprised and innocent right then, and I reckon he almost managed it. "What kind of evidence?"

Deal shrugged. "Smugglin', bootleggin', 'shine, theft. Murder, maybe. I ain't too particular." He looked Caton in the eye. "Whatever I can use to lock you up, or least to run you out of the country. We mean to have a end to your doin's hereabouts Bill, onct and for all."

Bill Caton took off his hat and shook his head sadly. "Ned," he said, "Ned, I'm real sorry you feel that way. I always did try to cooperate with the law whenever I was able." He smiled then, a kind of a sly crooked smile. "And you know, you just ain't going to find nothin' a-tall like what you're huntin' for round here. Not a-tall." He met the sheriff's look. "You can take my word on that, Ned.

And you know my word's always been good." Caton glanced at me.

"Barkley here must of told you it was that crazy kid nephew of mine who done all the killin' and raidin' in these parts. That's what I've heerd anyways." He paused. "And it seems to me you ain't got no witnesses that could testify to nothin' else."

I looked at the sheriff and he looked at me. Bill Caton had us, and he knew it. Eileen, Jamie, Tom Bristoe, Dan and Jenny Jenkins an' all the rest could say plenty about Riley and some of the others. But we didn't have nothin' on Big Bill hisself except our suspicions and what everbody thought of as common knowledge. It weren't likely there was even none of his gang members left around who could testify. And that's assumin' they'd be willing to in the first place.

"What about Mr. Tinsley?" I asked after a moment, lookin' over at the sheriff. "He might know something if we can find him. And he don't strike me as the type who'd stand up awful good under some real serious questioning."

Big Bill put his hat back on and shook his head. "I'm afraid I got some more bad news for you boys. It seems like Mr. Tinsley ain't going to be able to testify to nothing no more, 'least not before the likes of us. I heard he got hisself into a little altercation with a cattle buyer on the road to Newnansville a couple days ago. Fellow by the name of J. H. Swain." Caton shrugged and glanced at me and the sheriff.

"'Pears this Swain is some kind of hell on wheels with a six-gun. Somethin' Tinsley said happened to strike him wrong and the next thing you know Tinsley's layin' on the ground with a hole between his eyes. Swain said he was reachin' for the gun in his belt at the time, and he had two friends for witnesses. Looked pretty much like a case of self-defense, and the way I heard it nobody felt too inclined to argue." Caton shrugged.

"Of course Tinsley didn't have no say in the matter. Alls he got was six feet of ground and a marker sayin' he come out second-best."

"Swain, you say?" This was Tom Bristoe, who hadn't spoke hardly two words since we'd got to the Tar Bucket. When I glanced over at him he had a funny look on his face. "J. H. Swain?"

"That was the name I heard." Caton nodded towards his brother. "Joe here was told the story by a couple teamsters who said they seen the whole thing."

"They say which way he was headed?" The Ranger turned to face Joe.

"North an' west, maybe." Joe shrugged. "Seems like they said he was comin' from Gainesville, ridin' towards the panhandle. But I could be wrong. Didn't pay too much mind to that part of it, tell you the truth."

Bristoe nodded, then holstered his six-gun. "Well," he said, reachin' up to give his hat brim a tug. That sounds like it might be the man I come here to see." He held out a hand to me. "See you around sometime, Barkley." I took his hand. "You take it easy, hear?"

When we'd shook hands he turned his back, and walked off towards the place where he'd left his horse without another word. I watched after him until he disappeared in amongst the trees, thinkin' that he'd been a right good friend for a Ranger, and I sort of hoped we did run into one another again sometime.

As I turned back to the others I seen the man named Mort comin' across the clearing from where he and Frank had been searchin' the cabins. The first words he spoke to the sheriff didn't do nothing but confirm what I'd already suspected, knowin' Big Bill's love for careful planning like I did.

"There ain't nothin' in this camp what looks like evidence to us," he said. "Not even no clothes nor personal belongin's left behind to speak of." He pointed to one of the trees at the far edge of the clearing, where his partner was standing over something on the ground. "But what we did find, you'd best come and take a look at right now."

Well, we all trooped over there takin' Big Bill an' Joe with us so's to keep a eye on 'em, and looked down at the crumpled figure layin' at Frank's feet.

It was Riley's half brother Bay. He'd been shot bad through the gut, and it didn't take no surgeon to see that he weren't going to be with us for a whole lot longer.

I knelt down on one side of him, and the sheriff on the other. Bay's eyes was wild with pain. I'd seen a few men hit the way he was, in the war and afterwards, so I'd a idea what he was feelin'. But it weren't something

I cared to dwell on if I could avoid it.

I glanced over at Big Bill, but he shook his head. "Not me, Tate. We didn't even know he was here. Must of been somebody done that to him last night, or early this morning before we got here."

Bay's lips was moving, and I bent close to hear him. "Two . . . days. Been here . . . like this . . . two days."

"Who done it, Bay?" Sheriff Deal was askin'. "Who was it shot you an' left you here to die?"

The man on the ground worked his lips, but for a minute he couldn't seem to get no sound to come. Then he said real faint, "Riley. It was Riley . . ."

Mort had gone back to the horses to get a canteen, and he come up to us about then an' give Bay a little swallow, and then another. The hurt man choked a bit, but he nodded gratefully. And when he spoke again his voice was a mite stronger than before.

"Told Riley I wouldn't go along . . . with no attack on that woman's house . . . had enough." Bay reached for the canteen and took another drink. "He smiled an' said okay. Then he shot me . . . Shot me an' walked away . . . 'thout another word."

Well, all I could do was just shake my head. I reckon I'd knowed for some time Riley Caton was a cold-blooded killer, and at least half crazy along with it. But a man who'd shoot his own brother down, gut-shoot him a-purpose like that . . .

I reckon them other men standin' round felt about the same way I did, 'cause nobody said nothing then for a long time. Finally I took out the makin's and rolled a cigarette, lighting it and holdin' the end up to Bay's lips so's he could take a puff.

Ned Deal stood up, then took off his hat and throwed it on the ground. "I swear I'll see that Riley hang if it's the last thing I do! First the McClanahans, an' now this. If he ain't left the country en-tire . . ."

"He ain't left." Bay's voice was almost normal when he said that. Then he added more quietly, "He come back this mornin'."

21 ✺

"THIS MORNIN'?" I wasn't too sure I'd heard him right.

"He was wild. Crazier than ever I seen him. Cussin', throwin' things around, shootin' up the empty camp. Swearin' what he'd do to anybody who'd had a hand in all that happened . . ."

"Wonder he didn't finish you off whilst he was about it," one of the men piped up. Then he fell silent, embarrassed at realizing what he'd said.

But Bay just grinned a sort of sickly grin and looked over at the man. "He would of. Had it in mind, I think. Only trouble was . . . I asked him to." We stared at him. "When Riley come up to stand over me I asked him to finish me . . . put me out of my pain. That's when he laughed an' got up on his horse to ride away."

Bay shook his head, then fell to coughing. They was deep, body-shudderin' coughs that lasted several minutes. When he finally come up for air his eyes was real bright and I could see a trickle of blood runnin' down his chin.

"Barkley," he said, grabbin' hold of my sleeve with his fingers, "Barkley, you care anything about that woman and her younguns you'll go back to 'em and you'll stay with 'em. From now until doomsday. Or till Riley's dead and in the ground one. He's crazy, I tell you. Just plumb don't-care crazy. An' he means to . . ." The fingers on my arm got tighter and Bay tried to raise hisself up off the ground. ". . . means to . . ."

He stared into my face for a long moment, his lips workin' but not making no sound. When his fingers finally relaxed I laid him back down on the ground as gentle as I could, and reached out to close his eyes.

After Sheriff Deal had detailed a couple men to tend to the buryin', the rest of us walked over towards the middle of the clearing together. I was thinkin' some real serious thoughts about Bay's last words right then, for I'd no reason a-tall to doubt his warning nor what he figured Riley meant to do to Eileen and her kids. I might of expected as much myself, and Bay had knowed his brother a heap longer'n me. I reckoned I'd just better be ridin' south again soon as I was able, and not stop to gather no daisies along the way.

What with them thoughts runnin' through my brain,

I was only half listenin' to the conversation between Deal and Big Bill Caton that was going on. But still I heard the tail end of it pretty clear.

"Bill," the sheriff was saying, "I expect you're right as rain about us not having no evidence to use against you in a court of law. I suppose from a legal standpoint we'd just have to let it go at that and turn you loose." Bill Caton smiled and started to say something, but the sheriff wasn't finished talking.

"But Bill," Deal went on, "you know all the same you been mighty troublesome to folks in this country. We've sort of looked the other way because you're a home boy an' all, and I blame myself for that as much as anyone. But if it hadn't been for you and your gang I reckon Riley wouldn't of had his chance to do all the things he done, murderin' honest people and all. And that's just something we can't have no more of."

He stopped and looked Caton in the eye.

"So I reckon what I'm saying, Bill, is that we'd all be obliged if you and Joe was to ride out of here tonight and not come back. Ever."

Big Bill stared hard at the sheriff. Then he took off his hat and swore. "I'll have you know my family was runnin' this country before you was knee high to a toad frog, boy. If you think you're going to run me out of it now . . ."

"I ain't telling you what you got to do," Deal said calmly. "You know I'm swore to uphold the law, and the law says you're free to live wherever you've a mind to."

He studied his boots for a long moment.

"But I do got to advise you, Bill, that there's men in this country who're still pretty riled up about all that's happened, and they might be wantin' to take things into their own hands if you're still here tomorrow. Few of 'em could be a little disappointed about missin' out on that hangin' a couple days ago anyhow. You just got to realize that I can't be responsible for what they'd do whenever I'm not around." He looked at the Catons.

"And I ain't going to be around for a while now, Bill. I got me a farm to tend to, an' a wife what ain't seen me for a heap longer'n both of us would like. And I'm going back an' spend some time with 'em. Don't see how I'd be able to help you out much if you was to get yourself into some sort of a fix in the meantime."

Bill Caton looked into the sheriff's eyes, and then he looked around at the other men standing near him. One of 'em was that Ira fellow I'd had my own run-in with, and I reckoned I already knew the hard sort of man he was. Bill must of seen something like it in the rest of 'em too, because after a minute he just shrugged and grinned.

"I reckon when you put it thataway, Sheriff, a little change in scenery could be what the doctor ordered after all. I hear there's some fine open country out in them western lands, all kinds of opportunity for a enterprising man. We'll just ride out thataway and have us a look."

Ned Deal nodded. "You do that, Bill. I think it'd be the best thing for all of us."

I didn't plan on waitin' round to see the Catons ride out. I was already itchin' to be in the saddle and on my way back to Eileen's place by then, so I said my good-byes to Deal an' the rest of 'em, and started back towards the woods where I'd tied ole roan.

Nobody offered to ride with me, and I couldn't blame 'em none. They all had families of their own to look after, and as long as Riley Caton was in the neighborhood it weren't just Eileen an' hers who might be in danger, but anybody that crazy kid happened to run crosswise of in the meantime.

Just as I was leavin' the clearing I heard Big Bill's voice callin' after me: "Luck to you, Tate! Maybe we'll meet again in better times!"

I turned back. "Maybe," I said. "Luck, anyway!" I lifted a hand, then went on up through the trees. I figured I could afford to wish Bill Caton luck at least, though the meetin' weren't nothing I could bring myself to hope for anytime soon.

❖   ❖   ❖

I put the roan to makin' tracks just as quick as I hit the saddle. It had been a long day for both of us, but Bay's words back there just kept naggin' at my mind and wouldn't let me rest. I knew he was right, that Riley was killin' crazy, and that the kid wouldn't stop tryin' until either all the McClanahans was dead or he was. I reckon it was something I'd always known, somewhere down inside of me.

'Course it weren't like Eileen an' the kids was all

alone and unprotected right now. Cap'n Ben and his crew would be stayin' with 'em till morning at least. And even after that, ole Joseph weren't no man I'd care to take lightly when it come to settlin' accounts with bullets an' gunsmoke. Nor Eileen an' her shotgun neither, for that matter.

But still there was somethin' driving me on, call it a feelin' or a premonition or whatever you want. I just couldn't get it out of my head that Riley Caton was out there somewheres, an' that there weren't nothin' a-tall inside that twisted mind of his except killin' some folks I'd growed mighty attached to.

Ole roan was showin' his mustang breeding now, chewin' up the miles underneath his hoofs like it was the first time we'd hit the trail in a month of easy livin'. Never mind that we'd already rode most of a day to reach that Tar Bucket. He seemed to feel the same way I did about the need to get back where we'd left from without wastin' around. And I reckoned if I could manage to stay in the saddle, he'd manage to get me there just as soon as it could be done.

Still, it was comin' on to daylight before we finally reached them salt flats around Eileen McClanahan's homestead, with the sky all gray and threatening like there was a storm a-brewing somewheres close by. When I pulled up at the edge of the trees to look things over an' give ole roan a blow, the sun was risin' gold and crimson amongst a wall of clouds to my left, and I could smell rain on the fresh breeze that was blowin' in from the Gulf.

The roan tossed his head and snorted, knowing the scent of heavy weather at least as good as me. But I held him steady and we rested a couple minutes longer, watchin' over the house and the coastline roundabout.

Before long I seen the *Mary Nell* puttin' out to sea, moving steady off into deeper water with half her sails set. Like any good sailor, Cap'n Ben Chapin knew that if a blow was on its way the safest place he could find would be as far from shore as they could get to before it hit.

Everthing about the house and outbuildings looked real quiet an' peaceful in the morning air. I couldn't see nobody stirrin', but of course if the sailors had left then the rest of 'em would be up an' about by now. I loosened the thong on my Dragoon Colt just in case, but I seen no reason to expect nothin' down there but a "Howdy" and some of Eileen McClanahan's good biscuits.

When I clucked to the roan we started off down the road at a walk. But a couple big drops of rain began fallin' before we'd got halfway there, and tired as he was that mustang picked up his feet into a shamblin' trot so's to make it into the shelter of the stable before the sky opened up on us for sure. We'd almost reached the gate when I seen Joseph come out on the porch to greet us.

He seemed a bit surprised that we'd got back so soon, but he smiled real broad and lifted up his arm to wave. Then he turned to say somethin' over his shoulder, and that's when I seen the flash of a six-gun through one of them open windows of the house.

The bullet caught Joseph under the left arm and spun him round, throwin' him up against the railing as he clawed for the pistol at his belt. A second shot took him in the side and he pitched forward onto the porch, still clutchin' at his Colt but with fingers that seemed numb and useless all of a sudden.

My Dragoon was already in my fist when the second shot rang out, but there weren't nothin' inside there that I could see to aim at. Whoever done the shooting had been standin' back to one side of the window and well out of sight of the road. A minute later there was a big rumble of thunder, and I heard Riley Caton's voice shoutin' over it from what would of been Eileen's kitchen.

"Drop the gun, Barkley! Then get down easy and come on in the yard here where I can see you." He paused, but I didn't move. "I got the woman and her younguns with me!" I noticed the kid's voice was gettin' a mite shrill now. "I swear I'll shoot 'em all dead in another minute if you ain't just where I told you to be!"

Still I sat tight, not budging a hair but workin' my mind in a frenzy to think of what to do next. I knowed Riley meant to kill everone inside there anyway, if he hadn't already. What I needed was something that might change the situation enough just to give us a tiny bit of a chance.

After a second I called out: "So you say! How do I know they're in there, or that they ain't already dead?" I was stallin' for time, talking just to keep off the shootin'. Then it come to me to use the only kind of logic which might make some sort of sense to that crazy kid. "I ain't about to get myself killed," I shouted, "over no bunch of corpses!"

There was a long pause whilst I held my breath and gritted my teeth. Then the door of the house was flung aside, and Eileen appeared in the opening with little Mary. When they stepped out onto the porch I seen Riley in back, holding Jamie in front of him like a shield with the barrel of his cocked .44 pressed hard up against the boy's head.

"All right!" the kid yelled. "Now do you believe me?" He purely looked a sight just then, ragged an' unshaven, with his hat missin' so that his hair stuck out all over his head like some wild man from the South Seas. And the fire burnin' in that young man's eyes didn't leave me with no doubt that our time was just nearly up.

"You got ten seconds, Barkley. And then I start shootin'! One . . . Two . . ."

There was a huge clap of thunder, and Jamie moved all of a sudden, like a greased pig in Caton's arms. First he ducked down under the gun at his head, and then he stomped down hard as he could on top of the kid's foot. That give me the instant I needed, and I drilled Riley through the shoulder just as Eileen threw herself down on the porch to cover her daughter's body with her own.

Riley staggered when he took the bullet, but he weren't finished yet by a long ways. His gun blossomed flame and I felt the shock in my side as I fired into him a second time. Then he disappeared through the door-way, throwing another wild shot behind him as he ran.

I was off the roan an' through the gate before the smoke begun to clear, and in another second I was up them stairs makin' a dash for the front door. A bullet grazed my cheek as I went through it, and I fired at the flash and heard the kid grunt before I hit the floor and rolled over a couple times behind some furniture in the parlor.

When I come up I could make out the sounds of scufflin' and scrapin' out towards the back door, and I forced myself to my feet again an' started thataway on the run. I stepped out on the back porch and seen Riley stumblin' off acrost the sand, with the rain pouring down all around him, soakin' his bloody shirt through to the skin.

He was hit hard, but he was game. When he looked back and seen me, he fired a shot which struck the post I was leanin' against and knocked splinters into my face. Then he turned around to run again, but his legs give out and he pitched forward on his face. As I started down the steps the kid rolled over and begun clawin' at the cartridges in his belt, trying to reload his empty six-shooter.

I walked over to where he lay and looked down, my Dragoon still ready in my fist. Riley Caton was watching me, and when I come close he sort of shrugged and just smiled that lopsided grin of his.

"Out of bullets," he said, needlessly. "So I reckon

the fight's over for now, ain't it?" He looked up into my eyes and almost sneered. "You ain't the type to shoot a unarmed man. Are you, Barkley?"

"I reckon not," I said, leveling the Dragoon at his head. "If you was a man."

And then I finished him with a hole right over the bridge of his nose.

The rain was comin' down in regular torrents when I turned to start back towards the house, and somehow it appeared like the closer I got the more up-hill that beach become. I couldn't recall no slope like that from crossin' it before, but this time it seemed like I was purely hard-pressed just to keep puttin' one foot before the other.

Finally I missed a step and went down on my knees. Next thing I knew I was layin' on my back looking up into Eileen McClanahan's face.

"Ain't we . . ." I said weakly, ". . . already done this sometime before?" I tried to grin then, but everthing sort of faded out into blackness instead.

22 🌿

THAT HURT IN MY SIDE weren't near so bad as last time, the way it turned out. Seemed like Riley's bullet had struck the thick leather of my gun belt first before plowin' into me, and alls I got out of it was a nasty crease along the bottom of my rib cage when it spun away. But that on top of my other hurts and another night without sleep had been enough to plumb take the wind out of my sails for a time there.

I guess I didn't argue too much when Eileen put me to bed and made me stay there, feedin' me and tendin' to my needs an' all. It was right pleasant to have somebody do for me like that for a change, and I wasn't too proud at the moment to take advantage of it.

She put me in one room and got old Joseph into the

next, and before you knew it that house was organized like a reg'lar hospital. With Jamie an' his sister acting the part of nurse and orderly, Eileen McClanahan just naturally took on the job of cook, chief surgeon, and all-'round medical authority.

Old Joseph had been hit powerful hard, but he was about as tough a gent as I ever met, especially considerin' his age an' all. I reckon it was a right near thing for the first day or so. But after the fever broke and he started takin' nourishment, he seemed to get stronger ever time I seen him. Weren't too long before it began to look like he was going to pull through in good shape.

Me, I was up and stirrin' a bit the next day. But it took three, four days longer before I finally got to feelin' something like my old self again. I used the time for catchin' up on my sleep, and sittin' out by the Gulf listening to the water lap up on the shore an' the sea birds call out to one another whilst they went about their fishin' and other tasks.

Sometimes Eileen would come out and set with me of a evening, and we'd watch the sun go down an' talk of this and that. She was a right feeling woman as it turned out, as well as a thinkin' one. And it was pretty clear that she'd had to keep most of them feelin's locked up inside of her for a real long spell.

Seemed like what she talked about most often was her husband Cap'n McClanahan, and how they'd met and come to live here by the Gulf an' all. Me, I just listened, knowin' she hadn't had nobody to tell them thoughts to since her man was lost, and feelin' privileged that it was me she chose to share 'em with at last.

Her husband must of been a powerful fine man, and I wished I'd had the chance to know him. But it made me feel a mite uncomfortable too, hearin' a woman talk about such private things with a gent she'd only met a short time ago. And then I reckon I couldn't help comparing myself to the Cap'n a little bit, an' feelin' like I hadn't accomplished near as much as I'd ought to have in my own thirty-one years.

❖   ❖   ❖

When I'd been layin' around that homestead a week or more, takin' life easy and growing fat and sassy on Eileen's biscuits an' gravy, I found myself lookin' out more and more often across them salt flats towards the trees in the distance. I even started ridin' over thataway onct in a while of a morning, without no particular place to go but just wantin' to feel ole roan's back between my legs again.

Finally there come a time after one of them rides, when I led the roan back to the stable an' stopped inside the door for a long minute. Then I turned and looked at him.

"Well, boy," I said. "Reckon we got it to do, don't we?"

When I come up to the house I went to Joseph's room first off. We'd got to talking some whilst he was laid up, and I knowed he'd been a wanderin' man hisself, so he'd prob'ly understand. Maybe he'd even be able to give me some idea of how I might explain it to Eileen an' her son Jamie.

The old man's eyes was closed when I first stepped into the room, but soon as I got near the bed they opened up and he studied me for a minute or two. At last he spoke.

"You leavin' now. Ain't you?"

"I reckon."

"Knowed it was comin', soon or late. Knowed it even before you did, I 'spect." He paused and studied me for a while longer. "You done told the missus yet?"

"Nope. Honest truth is, I ain't so awful sure how I'd ought to go about doin' that."

"Just tell her. She was a sea cap'n's wife. She'll understand." He hesitated. "And the boy will too I reckon, given time. He got his daddy's blood inside him powerful strong."

I stood there another minute without speaking. Then I said, "You heal up now an' take care of yourself, hear? And you keep on takin' care of that lady, too." I smiled. "I just might be comin' back sometime to check up on the kind of job you been doin'."

Joseph smiled too. "You welcome to do that, Mistah Barkley. Anytime a-tall." He held out a hand. "You keep well yourself."

When we'd shook hands I stepped out into the hall, knowing I'd got to see Eileen next but still not havin' no idea of what it was I was going to say when I did. I could hear the sounds of her stirrin' round out in the kitchen though, and I reckoned I'd just as well go on back there and get it done.

She was bent over the table workin' at something

when I come in, and I stood in the doorway for several seconds watchin' her without saying nothing. At last she turned around and met my eyes.

"I've got your saddlebags packed with food for several days," she said, "together with a few other things that you might need. There's some fried chicken and biscuits on top, and you'd best eat those first."

When she seen the look on my face, she shrugged and kind of half-smiled. "I've noticed the way your eyes keep staring off into the distance, Mr. Barkley. And I guess I've known what that look meant all along. When you rode out this morning . . . Well, somehow I knew it would be today."

She reached in the pocket of her apron and pressed something into my palm.

"There's a gold double eagle. You can consider it a loan if you like, until you've found work and can pay us back. It's little enough for all your help in any case. If I didn't need to save something for Jamie's and Mary's education . . ."

"Ma'am," I said. "Eileen . . . I can't . . ."

"Take it," she said, putting her hands behind her when I tried to give the coin back. "And don't argue. You'll need it I expect, before you finally get to wherever it is you're going."

"Yes, ma'am." I pocketed the shiny bit of gold, knowing I'd already done lost that argument the minute she first handed it to me.

"Well," I said, picking up my saddlebags. "I reckon

I got to be going."

"Yes." She hesitated. "Take care of yourself, Mr. Barkley."

"I'll do it. You too, ma'am." I turned to the door.

And then I stopped, turned back around, and kissed her. Long and hard. After that we held onto each other for a time, with neither one of us talkin' or movin' from the spot where we stood.

When we finally come out onto the porch, first thing I seen was Jamie standin' by the gate, holding ole roan's reins and reachin' up to pat him on the neck. I glanced at Eileen.

"It's startin' to look like a fellow can't get hisself set to go no place around here," I said, "without everbody in the whole blame neighborhood knowin' what his plans are before he does!"

She just smiled whilst I went down the steps and walked over to say my good-byes to the kid. After we'd shook hands like a couple men, I climbed up in the leather and waved to 'em both.

"Be seein' you," I said, not realizin' till that moment how much hope a fellow might put into them three words.

"Any time, Mr. Barkley." Eileen's voice followed me out the gate. "Feel free to come calling whenever you're in the neighborhood!"

And I'd a mind to do it, too.

Trouble of it was, I hadn't no idea how long it might be till that "whenever" came.

THE END

Historical Notes

Blind tiger: A drinking establishment existing in "dry" counties without benefit of (official) legal or social sanction. Most of them were every bit as rough as that described in the story. Nobody went there for the "atmosphere."

Conchs: A term used to describe natives of the Florida Keys, many of whose families first arrived in the 1700s. A tough, independent breed, accustomed to taking their living from the sea and coping with anything Mother Nature and those from elsewhere might throw at them.

Coweta raid: For many years prior to its becoming a U.S. Territory, Florida's liberal Spanish rule had made it a haven for escaped slaves and displaced Indians from the north. One of the largest colonies of black freemen and Red Stick Creeks (who farmed their lands with the aid of their own black slaves) was on the southeastern shore of Tampa Bay. When the impending transfer of the territory from Spain was announced in 1821, several wealthy Americans saw in this an opportunity to "clean up" a pocket of potential resistance and line their own pockets as well. They employed Indian leaders Charles Miller and William Weatherford to organize a band of 200 Coweta Creek warriors and invade still-Spanish Florida, with the goal of wiping out the Negro settlements and taking their occupants captive for resale in the U.S. The expedition was highly successful, not only destroying hundreds of homes and bringing 300 new slaves back to their northern masters, but even finding time to make a brief side trip to plunder the Cuban fishing ranchos at Charlotte Harbor.

Double-pen log cabin: The most common type of dwelling in 19th-century Florida — the original "Cracker house." Hand-hewn logs were laid out to make two separate structures some eight feet apart, with the floors raised well above the ground. Between and around these "pens" (each of which was a separate sleeping room) a broad covered porch or "dog trot" was built, where most household activities took place if the weather permitted. A detached kitchen (to reduce the risk of fire) was constructed behind the house, in which meals were also eaten during inclement weather. Screens and window glass were virtually unknown; smudge pots and mosquito netting were the only defense early pioneers had against the ever-present insects.

Dragoon Colt: Officially known in Samuel Colt's catalog as the Old Model Holster Pistol. Some 14 inches long with a 7 1/2-inch barrel, it weighed four pounds two ounces and its .44-caliber bullet packed quite a wallop. Tate's was more than 10 years old at the time of this story, but nobody threw away a good weapon that could still do the job.

Fort Buckeye: A "settler fort" during the Seminole Wars, located some 15 miles west-southwest of present-day Mayo.

"Haints": Ghosts or "haunts." Anybody who has spent a night alone in the Florida wilderness will understand why even a hard-headed gent like Tate Barkley might have a few doubts about whether or not such things exist.

Hammock: The original Indian word means "shaded area." There are two kinds of hammocks in Florida: *high hammocks*, which rise a few feet above surrounding lowlands and make fertile farming country; and *low hammocks*, which lie along creeks or the flood plains of rivers. These last are magical spots characterized by sweet bay, cypress, fallen leaves, and the deep silence of the Florida wilderness. Neither should be confused with the northern malapropism "hummock."

Hopping John and hog jowl: On New Year's Day, Southerners traditionally eat black-eyed peas and hog jowl (pronounced "jole") as an omen of plenty throughout the year — after all, how much "higher on the hog" could you get? (Tate's reference in the story is clearly tongue-in-cheek though, given the circumstances.) If you mix rice with black-eyed peas and a little pot-liquor, you have made "hopping John."

Lafayette County: Established in 1856, at the time of the story it included all of present-day Dixie County.

Lighter knot: The pitch-filled knot of a pine tree. Brick-hard and highly flammable, these were often used by natives to start and maintain bright, hot fires. A "lighter-knot flambeau" is made by shaving one end of a lighter knot so that it can be easily lit by a match, and then holding it up at the other end for use as a torch.

The Natchez Trace: A trail connecting Nashville, Tennessee, with the Mississippi River at Natchez from earliest times. In antebellum days every mile of it was packed with danger. Indians, highwaymen, and all manner of misfits and low-lifes frequented the Trace, grateful for the many hiding places and ambush spots it afforded. Joseph never says what his "apprenticeship" there consisted of, but for a black man at that time and in that place, it probably didn't have anything to do with upholding the law.

New Troy: An early settlement on the south bank of the Suwannee River, several miles northwest of present-day Branford. It was the county seat of Lafayette County from the 1860s until 1893. Nothing remains of the town now but pine forest and a few Cherokee bean plants.

"Painter": Cracker term for the Florida panther.

Piney woods rooter: Florida's special breed of wild boar, said to be descended from stock brought into the country by Hernando de Soto in 1521. If this is true, it must have changed considerably over the centuries. Weighing up to several hundred pounds, with a massive head and shoulders, four tusks that might reach six inches in length, and a perpetually foul disposition, it was long known to be one of the most dangerous creatures in this dangerous land. It killed and ate rattlesnakes regularly, and was even reported to have fought alligators upon occasion.

San Pedro swamp: A vast area of lowlands occupying most of present-day Taylor and Lafayette counties. Much wetter in the old days, at a time when painters and piney-woods rooters outnumbered marinas and condominiums in the state.

Side-saddles: Real ladies rode side-saddle in the 1870s, even in the American West. Eileen does slightly understate the difficulty of riding one without a stirrup, however. To continue on after hers was broken, she would probably have had to "cheat" and ride astraddle — or else walk. But then she's a very determined woman . . .

Sinkholes: Caused when the land's surface caves in after water has sufficiently dissolved the underlying lime rock. They range from a few feet in diameter to hundreds of feet across, and can be found almost anywhere in north and central Florida. One of the largest is the Devil's Millhopper near Gainesville, now a state park and wildlife preserve.

J. H. Swain: An alias used by John Wesley Hardin during his three-year sojourn in Florida.

On May 26, 1874, Hardin and several friends killed the sheriff of Comanche County, Texas, in a saloon shoot-out. A $4,000 reward was offered for Hardin's capture dead or alive, and he fled to Florida by steamboat with his wife and young daughter.

For the next three years, using the alias "J. H. Swain," Wesley Hardin operated logging, cattle and saloon businesses in North Florida and Alabama while still being pursued by the Texas Rangers. During his stay in Florida Hardin's wife gave birth to a son in 1875, and a second daughter in 1877.

Hardin was finally captured on August 23, 1877 aboard a train near Pensacola, by Ranger Lieutenant John Armstrong. Armstrong pistol-whipped the famous gunfighter into submission after Hardin's weapon got caught up in his suspenders when he tried to draw. The outlaw's young companion Jim Mann was not so lucky. He was shot and killed by Armstrong after a brief exchange of gunfire.

John Armstrong used the reward money from Hardin's capture to retire from the Texas Rangers and establish a 50,000-acre ranch in Willacy County, Texas, where he lived a largely peaceful existence for another thirty-six years.

The "Tar Bucket": Still known to hunters in Lafayette and Dixie counties, this large sink in the rough country south of Mayo was the hideout for a good-sized party of Southern deserters and Union sympathizers during the War Between the States. Calling themselves the "Independent Union Rangers" and commanded by a man named W. Strickland, they burned homes and ravaged the countryside from Madison to Lake City and points in between. At one time they even had their own government and constitution. Big Deserters' Hammock and Little Deserters' Hammock are within a few miles of the "Tar Bucket."

Other Books by Lee Gramling

Ghosts of the Green Swamp

Ninety-Mile Prairie

Thunder on the St. Johns

Trail from St. Augustine

Trouble in the Everglades

War Clouds Over West Florida